THE SINNER

THE ASSASSINS GUILD, BOOK #4

C.J. ARCHER

"What nourishes me, destroys me."
— Christopher Marlowe

CHAPTER 1

Sussex, spring 1599

Catherine, Lady Slade, wasn't surprised by her husband's death, despite his youthful age. After all, Stephen was fond of over-indulging, both at the table and in bed, although not always *their* marital bed. What did surprise her was the manner in which he died. She expected a cuckolded husband to eventually take offence or mayhap a pheasant bone to choke him. Yet he'd been struck through the eye by an errant arrow during a hunt. It didn't make sense.

Not only were his retainers superb marksmen, but she'd been told Stephen had fallen back to fix a saddle strap that had worked loose. Someone would have had to turn around to shoot him from the front, implying a deliberate act of murder, but she knew his men loved him too much to have done that. Indeed, they'd not even seen it happen. Despite her protestations that something was amiss, the death had not been investigated.

Another thing that surprised Catherine—Cat—were the tears she shed for him at his funeral procession. They were genuine. Stephen, the second baron of Slade, hadn't been a bad husband, as husbands went. He made sure the drafty old stone house was fitted with warm tapestries and hangings, he gave her jewels on her birthday and pretty gowns to wear whenever he thought she needed one. Unfortunately, those trinkets and gowns came at a hefty cost—one her husband couldn't afford.

It was one of life's sureties that upon a man's death, his creditors will come knocking before the day was over. His brother, the heir, couldn't pay immediately, but he did manage to postpone them with promises of future repayment plus an additional sum. It had been a worrying time. It still was.

Cat was the only one who cried at Stephen's funeral. John, the new baron, was too busy insuring the two mourners he'd paid to walk behind the coffin looked suitably overwrought. Considering it was one of the coldest, wettest days of a bleak spring, they had no difficulty in giving off an air of misery. Cat had suggested twenty mourners more appropriate for the most prominent personage of the valley, but John had thought two ample, considering there was no way to pay them.

"Couldn't he have been buried with a banner of arms?" she asked John as they walked side-by-side behind the coffin, huddled beneath a canopy carried by the household servants who were now thoroughly drenched. "He deserves that at least."

"He deserves exactly what he's getting." Although he spoke quietly, Cat knew John was angry or frustrated, perhaps both. He'd hardly moved his lips. Ordinarily it was a sign that she should leave his presence, but this time she couldn't. He would have to endure her, and she him. But for how long?

John, now the third baron of Slade, was a tall, slender man with dark eyes and slick, black hair that skimmed his shoulders. That was the sum total of his virtues. His wet mouth rarely turned up in a smile and never in a laugh. He preferred silence and study to dancing, riding, hunting and, well, everything that required him to leave his desk. Although Stephen's younger brother had always lived with them, he kept to himself. That was the way Cat preferred it. Until now. Now she wished she'd gotten to know him better. After all, he held her future in his hands.

"He did run up some debts," she admitted, avoiding a muddy puddle only to brush up against old Doyle, one of the servants carrying the canopy who'd been with the family for years. He gave her a flat-lipped, sympathetic smile that she returned. "But a man ought to have a funeral befitting his status." She cast her eye over the pitiful number of mourners, the plain coffin and the tattered banner of arms leading the procession. Her father-in-law, the first baron of Slade, had been sent off with forty-eight poor men and women dressed in black to follow the coffin, several mourners, two heralds of arms, a goodly sized banner of arms and four smaller bannerolls. It had been a grand affair that suited the magnificent figure her father-in-law had been. Her husband had cut an equally impressive figure, yet his own brother wouldn't pay any more than he had to. It was a sorry sight.

"He emptied the baronial coffers and left me nothing but debt," John went on haughtily. It was as if pointing out his brother's lack of skill at managing the estate made him feel more superior. "If he wanted a grand funeral, he should have set some coin aside for it."

"Now, John, that's hardly fair. He may not have been much of a thinker—"

"He was as dull-witted as a hammer."

"He was a good man."

John merely grunted. He increased the length of his stride, whether on purpose or by accident, Cat couldn't determine. She had to hurry to keep up or be drenched by the rain, since the servants holding the canopy followed their new master and not their previous master's widow.

Widow. The word slammed into her chest with the force of a fist. She was a widow now, and a childless one at that. She was alone in the world with her own family gone, but luckily still young enough to remarry. Widows had certain rights, thankfully, and a lifelong income from her late husband's estate; but Cat didn't want to move out of Slade Hall until her cottage could be made ready. Hopefully her brother-in-law would allow her to stay until then.

"When can we speak about my future?" she asked, peering up at his stern, heavy-browed profile.

"Now."

"Now? But Slade is being buried as soon as we reach the church."

"What better time to discuss it? I'd rather talk trade than listen to the old vicar drone on."

Trade? Since when was her future a matter of commerce? Her pace slowed but John and the canopy did not. An icy drip fell off the canvas and trickled down her neck into her ruff. She shivered and hurried to catch up, stepping in a puddle that was deeper than it appeared. Water sloshed over the top of her ankle boots and thoroughly wet her hose. She wished she'd worn pattens.

"And don't call him Slade anymore," John said with an abrupt nod at the coffin winding its way ahead of them up the hill to St. Alban's church. "I am now Lord Slade and you'll address me appropriately."

"I'm going to find it difficult to adjust." She blinked back fresh tears and touched her gloved fingers to her tingling nose. "He may not have been the brightest star in the sky, but he was a good husband. A good man."

"He was a lout and a poor baron. Look what he sank to." He indicated the two pathetic mourners, the tattered banner, the small number of retainers and servants. Cat's heart lurched. She should have insisted on something grander.

"You'd better adjust to life without him, and adjust quickly," he went on. "You've got work to do."

"Pardon? What sort of work?"

"Catching your next husband."

She stumbled and put out a hand to John's—Slade's—arm to steady herself. He snatched it away almost as soon as she regained her footing. The man loathed being touched, something he'd made clear on her wedding day when she'd gone to kiss her new brother-in-law's cheek only to have him lean out of the way.

"I've not even buried my last one!" she protested.

"We don't have the luxury of time. The sooner we make it clear you're available, the better."

We?

Cat bit her lip and managed not to snap back at him. He wasn't a man to trifle with. She had often argued with Stephen, and usually won, and was no stranger to speaking her mind, but something about John's—Slade's—countenance made her hold her tongue. He was in a dark mood today, more so than usual. Perhaps his brother's death had affected him more than he let on. Her heart softened a little.

"It's a shame you're so plain and small," he went on in that tight way he had of speaking. "I hear there are a few earls on the hunt for a new wife, but you're not up to their standards. It'll have to be a baron or knight for you, at best."

Well, of all the ill-mannered things to say to a woman, that was quite possibly the rudest! She may not be the prettiest woman, or have been blessed with a comely figure, but she wasn't ugly. Just plain. It hadn't seemed to worry Stephen too much when he'd chosen her over several other women. Apparently he had admired her gentle nature and sensible manner. On the other hand, he *had* strayed from their bed. Frequently. A gentle nature and sensible manner apparently made for a good wife, but not lover.

"I have the summer cottage," she said, more in an attempt to make herself feel better than remind John that she had an asset to bring to a marriage. "Indeed, I don't have to find a new husband straight away. I can live there until I'm ready." That way she could be out of John's way and live her own peaceful life while she mourned her first husband and carefully chose her second.

He shook his head, spraying droplets of water from the ends of his oily black hair. "You can't. Your charming yet stupid husband sold it."

"He did what!"

"Don't make me repeat it, Cat. The servants are listening."

"But it was my mother's! My dowry!"

"So? He sold it to pay off some such debt. I don't know which

5

one. The paperwork looks as if it were done by a five year-old. If only he'd employed a man of business who hadn't cheated him, he wouldn't have gotten himself buried so deep."

The cottage…gone. The only link to her family, sold off as if it were an excess apple from the orchard. Why had Slade never told her he'd sold it? He'd not once indicated he was in financial difficulty. The man she had trusted to have her best interests at heart had left her vulnerable and poor. John was right, and yet he was not. Stephen was indeed foolish, and it seemed he possessed a heartless streak after all.

Cat would never cry over his death again. She would still miss him, like she missed a misplaced button or the sun on a day when she'd planned to go for a ride, but his loss was an irritation, nothing more. She wouldn't mourn him to any great degree now.

"What am I to do?" she murmured. "My widow's portion…?"

"Is worth nothing, if the estate's income is nothing," John said, speaking with cool disinterest. "You're to come with me to London and find yourself the best husband you can." He looked at her chest. Admittedly her breasts were small, but did he have to wrinkle his nose like that? "I'm afraid you'll have to call on some other womanly virtues. With no money and no connections, you'll have to use what you can. I suggest you take the first offer that comes your way."

Tears sprang to her eyes again, but she dashed them away with the back of her hand. "Why are you being so horrible?"

"I'm not being horrible, Cat, I'm being practical. I can't afford to keep you. Since Stephen made no arrangements for you and I can't send you back to your family, you're now my burden. I want you to become someone else's burden as soon as possible. Do you understand?"

She hated when he spoke to her as if she were a child. She was the same age as him! "Of course I understand," she snapped. Forget being cautious and demure, this was important. "The fact that I am Lady Slade means nothing. You would rather see me sold off like the summer cottage than cost you a single shilling. I suppose if a cruel earl wishes to wed me, it doesn't matter."

"I doubt an earl would be interested, but I follow your gist and the answer is yes. You're in no position to choose. Indeed, you should be thankful for any offers that come your way. *If* they do."

She tried to voice her indignation but all that came forth was a splutter. How could he be so cold? They were brother and sister in the eyes of the law and it was his moral duty to care for her. Did that mean nothing to him?

"Your father was too soft on you, Cat, and my brother too. It has made you a little too willful, if I am honest. It's time you learned some discipline. A hard husband will do you good."

"And if I cannot find a husband at all?" she asked weakly. "Where will I go?"

"I hear the blacksmith needs a new wife to care for his children."

"The smith! But I am Lady Slade! How dare you suggest—"

"Those sorts of airs will not do you any good as a smith's wife."

"John! Be reasonable. You cannot force me to wed anyone. It's my own choice."

"Of course it is." The sly smile he gave her sent a chill sliding down her spine. "But if I throw you out of the house, where will you go without a husband? I'd wager even the blacksmith is better than starvation."

She stopped and stared at his broad back as he began the ascent to the church. The servants all looked back at her with sorry expressions, but did not stop. She got wet, but she no longer cared. The rain was nothing. The cold was nothing. Her future was beginning to look much bleaker than she'd ever expected.

CAT WAS GIVEN an entire two months to mourn her husband, but that was only because the new Lord Slade couldn't leave the estate while it teetered on the brink of ruin. Fortunately he kept to his study day and night, and she hardly saw him. When he did emerge, usually in the late evening, he didn't so much as nod at her in greeting as he passed through the great hall where she embroidered or sewed. It was as if she didn't exist. She began to hope he'd forgotten about getting rid of her.

Everything changed in early June, when he announced they were to leave the following morning for London. Indeed, it wasn't Slade who announced it—he insisted she call him Slade now—but his liveried retainer, Mr. Hislop. Hislop had ventured into the village from parts unknown almost five years ago and had struck up a friendship with Slade, then merely John. They'd been inseparable since, and upon Stephen's death, the new baron had raised Hislop to be his second in command in all estate matters. It was quite an honor for a man who refused to divulge his past to anyone. He could have been born in a field or a gutter, for all Cat knew. Slade must have known, though. Cat couldn't imagine her shrewd, careful brother-in-law allowing just anyone to see his ledgers.

She had not liked Hislop when he lived in the village and she liked him even less since he'd moved into the house. He slunk around, his footsteps making no sound on the stone floor. Cat would think she was alone, only to turn around and find he'd snuck up behind her. He would watch her too through slitty, golden eyes. Eyes that were intriguing upon first acquaintance, but cool and detached the longer one looked at them. He wore his red-gold hair and beard short, neat, not a strand out of place. The thin scar slicing through the hair on his chin seemed out of character. His clothes were always spotless, as if his manservant spent all night cleaning them. Perhaps the poor fellow did. It would take a brave man to say no to Mr. Hislop.

Cat certainly didn't dare. She accepted his command with a demure nod of her head then went in search of her maid. They packed together, choosing only the best gowns and jewels Cat had left. Slade had sold off most of the lovely things Stephen had given her over the years. It was a shame. She finally had a use for them and they were gone. There'd been few occasions for finery at Slade Hall, with Stephen preferring hunting and drinking with his retainers to entertaining other nobles. Court, however, was different. She was expected to be a bauble among other, shinier baubles. If she wanted to attract a good husband, or simply to have a choice, she needed to present herself in the best light. Otherwise it was the blacksmith for her.

UPON ENTERING the Presence Chamber at Whitehall Palace, it became clear to Cat that she was not going to enjoy court life. She looked as glamorous as a sack of turnips next to the ladies with jewels in their hair, at their throat, on their fingers and covering much of their clothing too. Indeed, most of the lords glittered brighter than Cat with their gold earrings and rings. They must be wealthy indeed to afford such things. Even Slade had managed to find a doublet made of the finest silk with silver buttons down the front. She wondered where he'd found the coin to pay for it.

He nudged her in the back and she stumbled forward. "You have to greet Her Majesty first," he murmured as he nodded at a gentleman and lady who blinked vacantly at him. Clearly they had no idea who he was, but were curious nonetheless.

"I know that," Cat said. She tried to see through the throng of bodies, but couldn't. She was much too short. In which direction was the queen?

Slade clicked his tongue. "Follow me. And try to look..." He scanned her from top to toe, taking in the widow's hood covering her brown hair and black dress that lacked embellishments of any kind. He sighed. "Nevermind."

Cat wanted to poke her tongue out at his back as he walked off, but there were too many people watching; some surreptitiously, others openly.

The press of bodies in the Presence Chamber wasn't as beautiful up close as it was from the entrance. Indeed, there was a distinct stink in the air which an abundance of rose water dabbed on the skin couldn't hide. The combination was cloying. Cat coughed through her curtsey to the aging queen, but managed to suppress it as she rose. The queen spoke a few words and offered sympathies upon the death of Cat's husband. How remarkable that such an aged and illustrious personage remembered them. It had been some years since Cat had last been to court, and she hadn't been particularly memorable then, let alone now.

The presentation lasted only a moment before a new arrival was nudged forward by an older man, perhaps her father. Cat and Slade backed away and blended into the rest of the courtiers.

"Now what?" she asked him.

"Now we both have our own business to conduct."

She caught his arm before he walked off. His jaw hardened and his lips pinched tighter as he jerked free. "You promised to point out the eligible gentlemen," she said. "Please, Slade. Please help me." She hated to beg, but she didn't have a choice. She knew not a soul. Slade had at least some familiarity, albeit limited. As the second son of a minor baron, he'd been to court a few times in recent years. It was a few more times than Cat.

"I can spare you only a moment," he muttered under his breath. He nodded at the stairs leading to the balcony that overlooked the Presence Chamber. "Come with me."

He led the way up to the balcony where a number of lords and ladies stood in small groups. None paid Slade and Cat any attention as they found a position that gave them a good view over the audience below.

"That gentleman with the gray hair, wearing the green doublet," Slade said, indicating a fellow leaning against a pillar. "That's Sir Henry Hamilton. He's in need of a new wife and mother to his eight children."

"Eight!" Cat peered down at the portly figure. "He looks quite aged."

"He's in his fifth decade."

"That's much too old."

"The man in black and crimson beside him is the baron of Purcell. He's currently out of favor with Her Majesty, but you shouldn't let that put you off."

"Why is he out of favor?"

"He's Catholic."

"But I'm not Catholic."

"Convert. A good wife believes what her husband believes."

"My husband cannot force me to believe the same as he," she scoffed.

Slade snorted through his nose. "An attitude like that will not help you, Cat. Not here. Do you see the other young ladies?" He swept his hand in an arc to encompass the giggling girls nearby, the more accomplished ones down below, all of them richly adorned and beautiful. "They are your competition. Do you think a headstrong widow of no fortune and nothing to recommend her has a hope of securing a husband with them around?" He answered his own question with another derisive snort. "Pay attention." He turned back to the balcony and continued to point out unmarried gentlemen. It took only a moment more.

"That's all of them," he announced, turning away, impatient to be off.

"But there are so few!" Cat protested. And all of them were either aged, infirm, or both.

"That's all of the ones *here*," he said with bored indifference. "There will be others who don't come to court. If you ask about, I'm sure you'll learn who they are."

She glanced at the girls huddled together as if sharing a secret. None took any notice of Cat or Slade. "Can you introduce me to some ladies of your acquaintance then?"

He cast his eye over the audience below. "I know no ladies here."

She couldn't tell from his tone whether that troubled him or not. After all, he must also be in search of a wife, now that he'd gained the title. She was about to ask him if that were so when he moved away.

"My lord, wait!" She clutched his arm again but let go upon seeing the anger brewing in his dark eyes. "Where shall I meet you when it comes time to leave?"

"Make your own way back to the house. I don't know how late I'll be."

"My own way! But I have no escort."

"You're hardly an innocent girl in need of protection. Besides, it's not far."

Indeed it wasn't. Hislop had secured rooms for them in a house fronting Charing Cross, since the palace was full and Slade wasn't important enough to warrant accommodations within its walls. Still, a woman walking alone even that short distance at night was courting danger. Slade ought to have more care for her. She might not be legally under his protection, but he had a moral responsibility at the very least.

"I cannot believe your callousness," she hissed. Her own rage had begun to build. She had largely suppressed it since Stephen's death, not wishing to upset the man upon whose good will she relied upon, but there was only so much indignity she could endure. "Where is your gentlemanly honor? Your duty to your brother?"

But Slade wasn't looking at her. His attention was fixed on something down below in the Presence Chamber. Cat followed his gaze to a gentleman standing near the entrance, hands arrogantly on hips, a sapphire blue cape around his shoulders and a hat that wouldn't have looked out of place in a birdcage, it sported so many long feathers shooting from the crown. The hat obscured his face, but not his figure. Even from a distance, Cat could see he was leaner than most of the men there, and considerably younger. Indeed, he moved into the Presence Chamber with an assured swagger and an air of superiority that only a youth possessed, and an important one at that.

Everyone seemed to know him. Gentlemen clapped him on the shoulder as he passed, ladies curtsied low or offered up simpering smiles. One of the more brazen ones stepped into his path and thrust out her considerable chest. He made a great show of bowing over her hand before kissing it. She cast a conceited smile at those around her and glowed with satisfaction.

Slowly conversations fell silent around him as he moved through the crowd to the queen. Even the girls near Cat stopped their giggling long enough to gasp and whisper.

"Lord Oxley is here," one said, breathy.

"Look at his fine legs," said her friend, giggling into her hand.

"I hear there are other fine things about him," said another, leaning over the balcony to get a better look. "Things only a lover would know."

That set off her friends again and they collapsed into snickers that would have had their mothers scolding them for unladylike behavior.

"Who is he?" Cat asked Slade.

"The Earl of Oxley."

"And why is he such a curiosity?" The silver-gray feathers on Oxley's hat, unlike any she'd seen before, shivered with each step, far above the heads of everyone else. "Aside from his flamboyant hat, that is."

"He's a favorite of the queen, but he rarely attends court by all accounts."

"I wonder why he's here now."

"A matter of business? To look for a wife? I don't care."

"He's not married or betrothed? A man in his position?" How odd.

"He's eccentric by all accounts and hasn't chosen a bride yet. Don't get your hopes up, Cat. He can command a bride worth a hundred times more than you."

At least he hadn't mentioned Cat's plain looks again. It would seem her financial difficulty was more of an impediment in the marriage stakes.

"And a thousand times prettier."

Or perhaps not.

The earl removed his cape with a spectacular flourish that

seemed to amuse the queen. He threw the cape at her slippered feet and bowed down on one knee. Cat couldn't hear their exchange, but it was clear that he was making a gift of the cape.

"What would Her Majesty do with a gentleman's cape?" she asked.

"Do you not see the fastenings at the collar?" Slade asked. As he said it, the two large button-like fastenings flashed in the torchlight.

"Sapphires," she said on a gasp.

"Oxley is as wealthy as the queen herself. Those baubles are probably spare ones he had lying about."

Her Majesty leaned forward, her head slightly bent, listening to whatever Oxley was saying. She seemed to be hanging on his every word. Then she fell back, giggling behind her hands like a girl. Oxley bowed low once more and backed away. Cat tracked his movement to a group of overdressed dandies nearby and watched as he fell into raucous conversation with them.

"Oh do look up here," pleaded one of the girls peering down at Oxley. "I want to see that divine face."

As if he'd heard her, the earl tilted his head back and looked up. He scanned the scattering of people on the balcony, nodding at some and bowing elaborately to the group of girls which set their giggles off again. His gaze continued and slipped over Slade and Cat before flicking back again. Even from a distance Cat could see he wasn't as young as she'd first thought. He had a strong jaw and finely chiseled nose and cheeks. His skin was browner than she expected, the hair blonder. The contrast had a warm, handsome effect. Even more mesmerizing was his mouth. It was full without being womanly, and curved into a wicked bow. When first he'd skimmed over them, he'd sported an arrogant smile, but it vanished upon the second inspection. Then there were his eyes. She may not have been able to see them well, but she'd wager they were a remarkable shade of blue. A man as beautiful as the earl of Oxley simply *must* have blue eyes. Whatever color, they were staring directly at her with an intensity that warmed her belly and further south. No man of such beauty had ever looked at her like that. Like he could see into her. Like he *knew* her.

He suddenly looked away, the inspection over. It had been as brief as it had been powerful. The effects of it, however, lingered long after he moved on. Cat's heart beat strong in her chest, having momentarily stopped beneath his scrutiny. Her face heated, her limbs too. Indeed, she felt hot all over.

"He seemed to take an interest in you." Slade sounded surprised, or perhaps just disbelieving. He frowned down at Oxley, now in conversation with the gentlemen and ladies crowding around him. "Come on." He grabbed Cat's elbow.

"Where are we going?" she asked, struggling to walk casually alongside him and not draw attention to the fact he was gripping her much too hard.

"To strike while the iron is hot and before the dozens of other desperate wenches get in before you."

"My lord?"

They passed the girls who were now openly watching Cat with sneers on their painted mouths. "We're going to meet the earl of Oxley, and you are going to charm him."

Cat felt sick.

CHAPTER 2

L ord Oxley wasn't an easy man to pin down. Whenever Cat, dragged along by Slade, got close, he would spy another friend and move off in that direction. It was almost as if he were avoiding them. Of course, that couldn't be true. He didn't even know them.

They finally intercepted him in the shadowy perimeter of the Presence Chamber as he made his way toward the exit. If he were aiming to be stealthy, he failed. Bright yellow silk breeches and a hat of impressive proportions were not the most ideal disguise for blending in. Besides which, the man was tall. There were few taller than he in the audience and none whose shoulders were so broad. Surely his doublet must be bombasted to create the effect.

"Let me go, my lord," Cat said to Slade as his bony fingers dug into the flesh at her elbow. "You're hurting me."

"It's for your own good. Ah, excuse me, my lord!" he called out to their quarry ahead of them. "My Lord Oxley!" he said again when Oxley didn't stop. "I have a matter of great importance I need to discuss with you."

"That's overstating it a little," Cat muttered.

But it did the trick. Oxley stopped. He didn't turn immediately, however. There was a brief pause in which those manly shoulders hunched a little and his head lowered, as if he were resigning himself to enduring an arduous task. Perhaps he knew Slade by reputation if not in person. Cat certainly found her brother-in-law a test of endurance most of the time.

Finally Oxley turned to face them, his eyes flat, bored, and his mouth stretched into an unconvincing smile. "Who are you?" he drawled. "And what is it you want with me?"

Oh dear. They'd managed to annoy the nobleman already. Slade's plan was in danger of failing and he hadn't even presented Cat yet.

Slade bowed low. "Good evening, Lord Oxley. Forgive the intrusion, but I wanted to introduce myself. I am Lord Slade of Slade Hall, Sussex. I have been admiring your...hat, sir." He glanced up at the extraordinary piece. "It's very...tall."

Oxley seemed to change then. The boredom vanished from his eyes and the smile became genuine. He whipped off the hat and presented it to Slade with an elaborate bow. "Then you may have it, my good man."

"But my lord, it's your hat! I couldn't possibly—"

"Take it. I have another just like it at home. Indeed, I have several and I see that you're in need of good headwear." He drew Slade's brown fur hat off his head between thumb and forefinger as if he'd picked up a rat by its tail. "I can give you the name of my milliner if you like."

Slade cleared his throat and watched desperately as his hat was flung into the corner. "I am humbly grateful for your generosity, my lord."

Oxley leaned closer, conspiratorial. "A hint, Slade, if you will permit me to aid you. Her Majesty likes to see her gentlemen wearing a little color. Dung is not her favorite shade, even when dressed up with shiny buttons." He flicked the top button of Slade's doublet. As Slade looked down, Oxley tapped him on the chin and laughed. It was a child's diversionary trick, but Oxley made it seem fresh and amusing. Or perhaps that was more because Slade was trying very hard to hide his indignity at being the butt of such a simple joke.

Cat pressed her lips together to suppress her smile. She wasn't yet sure what to make of Oxley, and she planned on remaining quiet to observe him for as long as possible.

Unfortunately, Oxley had a different plan. He thrust out his hip and placed his hands at his waist, studying her. "And who is this jewel? What lovely skin! And those eyes! I am in the presence of a goddess."

Slade snorted, but quickly covered it with a cough. "This is my sister-in-law, Catherine, Lady Slade. She's in mourning for my brother, hence the drab attire."

"Drab? Not at all! Not on such a slender, leonine figure." Oxley bowed, sweeping his arm across the front of his body in an arc. "I am your servant, my lady."

Cat rolled her eyes before he straightened, and managed to give him a return smile as she curtseyed. "My lord is too generous with his praise."

"Indeed not," Oxley said. He waggled his fingers at her face. "Your eyes are quite the most interesting shade of blue."

Her eyes were a dull slate blue-gray. She had no illusions that this man saw her as anything other than a plain, smallish woman. Oxley's eyes, however, were something to behold. She'd been right. They were blue, but not the striking deep color of the sky. They were pale, almost colorless. More like a lake in winter, covered in a thin layer of ice. Lakes in wintertime could be dangerous, unpredictable places, but there was nothing dangerous about this man. He seemed as predictable and harmless as a peacock. Cat matched his smile with one of her own.

"You are quite the flatterer, my lord," Slade said. "But there's no need. Cat is not used to it and doesn't expect it. Her tastes are simple. Her thoughts even simpler."

Cat bristled. It was one thing to have Slade belittle her when it was just the two of them, but quite another in front of others. Particularly when Lord Oxley could help her get away from Slade

Hall. He may be too far above her to be a candidate for husband number two, but he seemed extremely well connected. A recommendation from him could serve her well. Time to curb the damage before Slade caused more.

"What my brother-in-law is trying to say is that our conversations rarely cover topics of interest to us both. Lord Slade prefers to read his ledgers while I prefer the wonders of Homer. Slade thinks the theater not fit for a lady, but I am of the opinion that all ladies should experience it. With an appropriate escort, of course."

She hoped she'd judged Oxley correctly. He seemed like the sort of man who enjoyed wit and cultural amusements over talk of wool bales and crop yields. The plethora of ladies who had vied for his attention ever since his arrival wouldn't be so eager if he were as boorish as Slade.

Oxley's eyes sparkled and he seemed to appraise her anew. "You've been to the theater, Lady Slade? You enjoy such pastimes?"

"I've only seen the traveling troupes in summertime near Slade Hall. I do long to visit one of the magnificent theaters in Bankside, though. I hear the new Globe is quite a sight to behold."

"It is," he said with warm enthusiasm. "If one doesn't mind the occasional drunkard lolling on the doorstep. And you must be sure not to leave your pouch in clear sight. The cutpurses at Bankside take that as an invitation."

"As they should," she said with mock seriousness. "If a person is foolish enough to flash their coin about, they ought to be relieved of it. Clearly they have too much."

He grinned. "You seem like a worldly sort of lady, unlike many here." Did she catch the hint of a sigh? The sense of *ennui* in his drollness?

She must be mistaken. He'd not seemed at all bored with the ladies as they'd crowded around him earlier. Indeed, he seemed to enjoy their attentions very much.

"It's true that I spend far too much time in the village near Slade Hall," she said.

Slade nodded soberly. "Far too much time."

She rolled her eyes and Oxley grinned. "Although I wouldn't call myself worldly," she went on. "The village is a great leveler, however, if one ventures beyond the main road. We too have drunkards lolling in doorways, and more besides."

Oxley gave her a look of horror and pressed his hand to his breast. A large oval-cut sapphire ring winked in the candlelight. "It doesn't sound like the sort of place such a poised lady as yourself should endure. Where was Lord Slade? Protecting you, I hope."

She laughed. "My late husband was too busy hunting. The current Lord Slade was too occupied."

"With his ledgers?" Oxley winked. "I'm glad to see you've survived unscathed, dear lady."

She leaned closer and whispered loudly. "Or have I?"

She wasn't sure what she was saying, or why she was saying it in that breathy voice. Something about this man with his cool eyes that weren't icy after all, and his easy humor made her feel light headed and quite brazen. When he laughed or smiled, as he seemed to do often, warmth spread through her body to her extremities. It set her alight in places she'd thought dormant. Feminine places.

"You could take her, my lord!" Slade cried.

"What?" Cat blurted out. She blinked at him, not sure whether to be horrified, ashamed or amused.

"Er, I mean, you could take Cat to the theater." Slade had a silly look of contrition on his face. It was quite out of place. How had Cat not seen him as the fool he was before? He'd always seemed so stern to her, so composed and in control, but Oxley reduced him to a bumbling idiot by his mere presence.

Unfortunately that made her a fool by association. She wanted to dig a hole and bury herself. She didn't dare look at Lord Oxley. To make it worse, her face grew so hot he must have noticed.

"I'm not available tomorrow," Oxley said smoothly. "Or I would be delighted."

"The next day then," Slade persisted. "We can stay in London a little longer."

"I'm not free, alas. Indeed, I'll be leaving the city very soon."

The silence thinned. Cat wished she could run and hide. She had not felt quite so humiliated since, well, ever. She kept her head bowed so that she didn't have to see Oxley's handsome face screwed up in distaste at the thought of taking her to the theater, thereby announcing some sort of connection between them.

"You can see all the theaters of note from this side of the river," he was saying with rather more enthusiasm than necessary. "There's no need for Lady Slade to venture over to Bankside."

"An excellent suggestion," she cut in before Slade could open his mouth and put the other foot in. "I'll do that. Thank you, my lord. It's been our great and humble pleasure to meet you, but we mustn't keep you any longer."

His eyes briefly flashed, adding warmth to their depths. But it passed so quickly that she began to wonder if she saw it at all.

He bowed to her. "It has been *my* pleasure, Lady Slade. Enjoy your stay in London. I hope your brother-in-law will find the time to take you to the theaters himself."

He gave Slade a shallower bow. "Take care of my hat, sir."

Slade said nothing as he watched Oxley retreat to the door, only to be held up before making his exit by a dark-haired lady whose tight dress barely contained her cleavage. She leaned against Oxley's arm, pressing her virtues into him where he couldn't fail to miss them. She giggled behind her fan then he said something and she tapped him lightly with it. He seemed absorbed by her attentions. Widow Slade was already forgotten.

Cat turned away, and tried to ignore the sinking sensation in her chest. She had enjoyed her conversation with Oxley. She'd wanted it to continue, but of course it could not. He was a busy noblemen with high friends. She was the widow of a poor baron and the sister-in-law of a tedious man.

That tedious man reeled on her. "You let him go! Stupid girl. You almost had him."

"Don't be ridiculous," she said, curt. "He was simply being

polite." And if anyone was responsible for Oxley's leaving, it was Slade.

"He liked you. I could tell. Not sure why, but I suppose you're witty when you want to be, and a dandy like Oxley likes wit." It was quite the compliment coming from Slade and took her by surprise.

"It's no matter. He was never going to consider me as a wife. He could have any lady in this room." Wit wouldn't be enough for a handsome, dashing earl. It was something she had accepted long ago.

Slade heaved a sigh and glanced around at the glittering women, from the giggling girls to the more mature and elegant ladies. "True. I briefly hoped he might take you on as a mistress, but I see now that it's hopeless."

"Mistress!" He would dare suggest such a crude thing to his own sister-in-law?

"As you say, you're not a contender for a wife, but I do know that Oxley has a mistress. Several, in fact, although not all at the same time." He directed a nod at the buxom woman smothering Oxley with her charms. "Of course, if *that* lady is the sort he prefers, then I'm afraid you'll never be a contender. Pity. I hear he's very generous to his mistresses. You could have had a comfortable life, even after he grew tired of you."

He walked off and Cat watched him go, not bothering to follow. She couldn't believe what she was hearing. Her, a mistress to an earl! Or to anyone, for that matter. It was such an absurd notion. She was hardly the right sort, as he pointed out. Mistresses were flirty and buxom. Cat was a mere mouse by comparison. The best hope she had was to wed a dull, moderately wealthy baron of no particular importance. It had been adequate enough when she married the first time and would be adequate for her second marriage. There was no point in aiming for something more, someone higher.

She swallowed past the lump that had risen to her throat and glanced around the room at the courtiers, with their jewels and expensive clothes, laughing and getting drunker with each cup of wine. None would take any notice of her. She could never hope to make an impression on the gentlemen when there were so many ladies to choose from. Just like she'd made no impression on Lord Oxley. He'd not even glanced back at her as he walked off.

It was silly to be disappointed by his disinterest, and no one had ever accused her of being silly before. Yet the lump in her throat remained.

* * *

HUGHE'S MIND was still on his conversation with the Slades as he made his way to the exit. That was his only excuse for not seeing Lady Crewe until her breasts squashed up against his arm.

"My dear boy," she cooed, wrapping her talons around his elbow. "Didn't you see me? I've been trying to gain your attention all evening."

He was never sure why she called him 'boy'. He may be five years younger than her, but he did outrank her husband. "My heartfelt apologies, madam." He kissed the heavy cheek she offered. It was sweaty from exertion, and he wondered if she'd chased after him. "It wounds me to know that I may have offended you. I didn't see you." He waved at the courtiers still mingling in the Presence Chamber and caught sight of Lady Slade's lithe figure before the crowd swallowed her up. She had a slender waist, a small frame and sweet face. It was her eyes, however, that had caught his attention. That and her wit, but the eyes first. As soon as he realized who had waylaid him, he'd intended to make his excuses and leave immediately, but he'd been held captive by those orbs. It wasn't just their color, although they were as blue as the sapphire on his finger, but it was...what? For once, poetic words failed him. He couldn't think clearly. He felt like he was in a mist and couldn't see a thing ahead of him.

He supposed that's what happened to a fellow when he was unexpectedly waylaid by the widow of the man he'd killed.

"Oxley?" Lady Crewe's fan tapping against his shoulder brought him back to the present. "Oxley, are you listening to me?"

"Of course, my dear lady." He had no idea what she'd been saying. Probably something about her middle son seeking a page's position in Hughe's household. It was why he'd ended his affair with Lady Crewe a year ago, after a delightful six months. Hughe had thought he'd finally found someone who agreed with him, that love was a sentiment sensible people should avoid. Little had he known that she'd planned to use their relationship to further the interests of her family. He had indeed tried to avoid her, and several others, throughout the evening. Among them were past mistresses and family members of noblemen he'd assassinated. It would seem he had overwhelmingly failed on both counts.

Lady Crewe clicked her tongue. "You were not. Your mind was still on that plain little cat." She giggled, making her breasts jiggle against his arm. "Cat, you see. Her name is Catherine and her brother-in-law calls her Cat."

"Ah! You mean Lady Slade." He managed to sound flippant when he felt anything but.

"You knew who I was talking about, you sly fox. Yes, Lady Slade. She seemed to have your entire attention. Her conversation was riveting, was it?"

"She does have a certain wit," he said, trying not to smile. Women like Lady Crewe had a way of sinking their claws into others they considered rivals and he didn't want her to get the wrong impression. Lady Slade was *not* a rival in any shape. She never would be. He had two golden rules when it came to women —avoid eligible ladies, and avoid relatives of his targets. Lady Slade was both, added to which she would make a poor choice of wife. Although imagining his mother's horror if he brought home such a bride made him smile. It would serve her right for constantly badgering him to marry.

But it would never happen.

"What are you smiling at?" Lady Crewe said, touching her closed fan to the corner of his mouth. "You're not picturing that little chit in your bed, are you? She's most certainly not your usual type."

He had a type? He thought he'd always been quite well-rounded when it came to his choice of mistresses, eligibility notwithstanding. "You think not?"

"For one thing, she's got no sense of style."

"She's in mourning."

"Black can be made to look becoming with the addition of a few jewels."

That got him thinking. Lady Slade had worn almost no jewelry. A set of earrings and a wedding ring, and both of those were simple. Still, they'd suited her. With eyes like hers, she'd not needed jewelry to draw the gaze away. Better to allow eyes of such depth and luster to be admired unhindered.

"And the cut of that gown!" Lady Crewe shook her head. "She may be in mourning, but she's not dead herself. If the rumors are to be believed and she's here looking for a new husband, then she ought to wear something that reveals more throat and..." She rubbed herself against his arm like a dog in heat. "And more."

"Perhaps she's not the sort of woman who wishes to flaunt herself so soon after her husband's death."

She snorted. "Or perhaps her womanly features aren't so womanly. Going by the flatness of her gown, I'd say I'm right."

He'd had quite enough of her waspish company. He'd not thought Lady Crewe so cruel, but then he'd never spoken to her about other women. Their conversations, when they'd had them, were always about her sons. He tried to extricate himself from her, but her talons dug into him. She'd be shredding his sleeve next.

"What was Lady Slade asking of you?" she said. "Let me guess. She offered herself up as a potential wife? No? A mistress?" Another snort. She often snorted, sometimes derisively, sometimes to show displeasure or even pleasure. For the first time, he thought the noise suited her. There was certainly something piggish about her behavior tonight.

"Neither," he said, jaw tight.

She placed her fan over her mouth, but it didn't hide the mirth in her eyes. "Do not tell me that a woman like that didn't offer herself to you! Silly creature. Doesn't she know that you could solve all her problems with just a few months of commitment? And such fun commitment too," she cooed, nuzzling into him.

He leaned away, but wasn't able to politely remove his trapped arm. If she continued on in such a gross manner, he may have to do it impolitely, and in front of onlookers too, of which there seemed to be many. He spotted Lady Slade watching from the balcony. Even from a distance, he thought he saw misery lurking in her eyes, although it hadn't been there before. What had made her so unhappy?

He came back to the conversation with Lady Crewe as if she'd suddenly hit him over the head. "What do you mean?" he asked, frowning at her. "What problems?"

"Don't you know? She's as poor as a mouse, and as plain as one too. She hasn't got a hope of securing a good second marriage. I feel a little sorry for her. She's out of her depth trying to catch the eye of every eligible gentleman here. It makes her look quite desperate."

He stared at her. "Poor? Did her husband leave her in debt?" He knew full well the previous Lord Slade hadn't been a wealthy man, but Hughe had left enough money for his widow to cover his debts and live on for an entire year. It had cost Hughe a considerable sum, but he'd done it anyway. It was the least he could do for her. That and removing the monster from her life.

The previous Lord Slade had been a murderer, liar and adulterer. According to some sources, he beat his wife. According to others, he simply neglected her. The rumors on that score hadn't been consistent. The charge of murder, however, had been true. He'd investigated himself and discovered Slade had murdered the husband of one of his mistresses. Hughe and his man, Cole, had gotten to Slade after investigating first and proving to themselves that Slade had indeed murdered the man when he'd confronted

Slade about his relations with his wife. There had been no doubt about his guilt.

But there had always been one thing that bothered Hughe. He had never discovered the person who'd hired him and brought the matter to his attention. Hughe always checked out his anonymous clients; he always discovered their reason for hiring him, just to be sure there was no ulterior motive. Thanks to his complicated network, no one was ever aware they had hired a peer of the realm to undertake an assassination.

"Quite a lot of debt," Lady Crewe went on. "I believe she's very poor and the estate is in difficulty. It's fortunate her brother-in-law is prepared to keep her or she'd be in serious trouble."

"Fortunate indeed," he muttered. He couldn't imagine how she had coped with that leather-brained fellow all these weeks. Slade Hall certainly wouldn't be filled with witty banter and amusements of the sort to entertain such a quick mind as Lady Slade's. Yet she *was* fortunate to have someone to look after her. So many widows had no one.

"The question is, for how long will he keep her?" Lady Crewe said. "I can't imagine a new wife wanting the previous lady of the house in residence, and by all accounts, Lord Slade hasn't got the softest of hearts. Driven by greed, so I've heard. It will be interesting to watch the story play out, don't you think?"

"Interesting is not the word I had in mind," he said, flatly.

"Now, about my Francis," she said, rounding on him.

"I have to go. It's been a pleasure, Lady Crewe, as always." He jerked himself free and bowed. He hurried away before she had a chance to protest. The usher opened the door for him and he finally—finally!—exited into the courtyard.

The night air was cool compared to the stuffiness inside, yet it was still a warm evening for so early in the summer. Soon the queen would leave for her annual progress around the countryside if she were well enough, but for now, she enjoyed the splendor of Whitehall along with her courtiers. Hughe had made his biannual visit to London as promised, and had met with his old friend Rafe

Fletcher and Rafe's wife. The couple had bred quite a brood and seemed in good spirits. But it was time for Hughe to go home to Oxley House. It was the base for his operations, and although his mother was there, his men were too. There was a new operation to coordinate, another dish of justice to serve. The target happened to live near the village of Sutton Grange, where his newly married friend Orlando Holt lived. It was an unfortunate location, so near people Hughe cared about, but it couldn't be helped. If the brute wasn't stopped, other girls would suffer. Hughe would send his most seasoned, level-headed man, Cole, to do the work. There was no one like Cole for getting tasks done with utmost efficiency and minimum fuss. Cole would never do something so stupid as fall in love and leave the Assassins Guild the way Orlando had. Luckily for Orlando, his wife was delightful or Hughe would never be able to forgive him.

Hughe retrieved Charger from the palace stables and after a few moments talking to the grooms, rode out of the gate. He had no man with him since he preferred to travel without an extra burden whenever possible.

Unfortunately the air wasn't cool enough to take his thoughts away from Lady Slade. The sorrow on her fine, oval face haunted him. The notion that she may be impoverished thanks to his actions ate at his gut. Where had his donation gone? He'd left it with the mayor of the village and watched him deliver it to the house himself. Cole had later asked the mayor if he'd given it to the lady and he'd assured Cole that he had. Perhaps he'd lied and given it to the brother-in-law instead.

The cur. He would have to—

"Stop! No!"

The cry drifted to him on the breeze. A woman's cry. Bloody hell, where was she?

"Stop it at once, you're hurting me!"

To the left. Hughe dug his heels into Charger's flanks and kept his ears peeled for more sounds. He swept the area and finally saw the clump of figures in the darkness dead ahead.

"Help!" the woman screamed.

Charger streamed forward and Hughe drew his sword as it became clear two men stood over a woman on the ground. Both men held knives at her throat. "Unhand her!" he shouted. "Or by God I'll cut off your limbs."

One man scampered away without a glance back. The other stood his ground. Hughe didn't want to kill anyone tonight, and not in front of a woman, but if the man didn't move soon, he was going to get a blade through his belly. Thank God he collected his wits and realized he couldn't win against a sword-wielding gentleman on horseback. Hughe let them go, not because he wanted to, but because the lady was unaccompanied and he couldn't leave her alone and at the mercy of more vagabonds.

She was indeed a lady. She wore a hooded cloak and leather shoes, although when he jumped down he saw that the soles were a little worn.

He sheathed his sword. "My lady, are you all right?" He crouched beside her and touched her shoulder. Her body shook as if she cried silently. "My lady, you're safe now. Let me help you."

She sat up and touched her hand to her temple. "I'm all right. Thank you, sir." She pushed the hood off her head and two big doe-like eyes blinked back at him. Eyes that he recognized. Eyes that were going to haunt him from this night on. "Lord Oxley! It's you."

"Lady Slade," he said, bowing. Bloody hell. It would seem he couldn't get away from this woman no matter how hard he tried.

CHAPTER 3

$\mathcal{L}$ady Slade appeared unharmed, but rattled by the experience. She shook uncontrollably. Hughe knelt beside her and took her small hand in his own. Tendrils of hair had escaped from her widow's hood and dangled around her face like springy coils. He brushed them aside. What he saw made his heart lurch. The moonlight revealed lashes damp from crying and a cut on her cheek. He wiped the trickle of blood away with the pad of his thumb and received a wobbly smile in return.

"Do you have any other injuries?" he asked, checking her over. If those men had done more damage, he'd hunt them down and gut them.

She gingerly touched her cheek. "No. I'm all right, my lord. Your arrival was fortuitous. Thank you." She blinked those big eyes at him again. "I am so very grateful."

"Any gentleman would do the same."

"No, my lord, they would not." She spoke with jaded conviction, but conviction nevertheless. He hated to admit she was right.

"Where is Lord Slade?" he asked, glancing back to the palace gate. "Why didn't he escort you?"

"He wasn't ready to leave."

Hughe frowned. "He allowed you to walk alone at night? In

London?" He shook his head. Some gentlemen didn't deserve to be known as such. "The man is a fool. Worse than that, he's negligent." He squeezed her hand and he was relieved to feel it tighten around his. "Can you stand?"

"I think so."

He helped her up and she seemed capable of standing without assistance. Nevertheless, he did not want to let her go. Not yet, just in case she suddenly weakened. "Are you sure you have no other injuries?"

"Quite sure. They had only just knocked me off my feet when you arrived." She felt her waist under her cloak and pulled out a girdle with nothing attached. "Blast! They stole my purse!"

"Was there much in it?"

"A few coins."

She was lucky that was all they took. Her earrings and ring were still in place, her ears and finger too. It was common enough for thieves to lop off body parts to retrieve the valuables attached to them.

She sighed and withdrew her hand from his to press it to her temple. "I'm sorry, my lord," she whispered, her voice trembling. "I need a moment to collect myself."

He stood and waited as she dabbed at the corner of her eyes. Should he comfort her? How did one do that? He wasn't used to weeping women. He'd tossed several ladies out of his bed when they began to cling too hard and want more than he could give. None had cried. Nor had he seen his mother cry, but that wasn't surprising. She was tougher than any battle scarred warrior. So Hughe just waited and watched and hoped Lady Slade didn't want more than his presence.

"There," she said with a toss of her head. "I'm composed now. Besides, I should be grateful."

"Grateful?"

"It's not every day a lady is rescued by a knight riding a white horse." She rubbed Charger's nose and his horse nuzzled her hand in approval.

He smiled. "Charger deserves all the credit. He's got a weak spot for damsels in distress."

She laughed. It was good to hear her laugh. She wasn't too upset by the ordeal it seemed. "I'm sure he learned that from his master." Her soft voice whispered over him like a breath of warm air. It was a voice he could listen to for an age and never grow tired of hearing.

He cleared his throat and buried those kinds of thoughts. "Do you have far to go?"

"Lord Slade rented some rooms for us in a house yonder." She nodded toward a shadowy cluster of buildings not far away. Whitehall was located outside the ancient city walls along a main thoroughfare. It was one of the queen's favorite palaces and impressive in its vastness, yet it still wasn't large enough to hold every nobleman who came to visit. It would seem Slade hadn't been allocated rooms and had needed to rent nearby instead. "It's not far."

"Far enough that you shouldn't have been walking there alone."

Her only response was to curtsy. "Thank you again, my lord. I appreciate you coming to my aid."

She walked off. He gathered up Charger's reins and fell into step alongside her. She stopped and stared at him, a question in her eyes.

He shrugged. "You're not going home alone."

"I couldn't possibly ask you to escort me. I'm sure it's an inconvenience—"

"I'm not doing it for you, I'm doing it for me. I need the company. Charger isn't much of a talker."

She laughed and even in the darkness he could see how it made her eyes twinkle. Her mouth had the most delicious curve to it when she smiled. "In that case, I shall oblige."

They set off along the road, with its unforgiving gravel surface that must have scraped her as she'd fallen. God's blood, just thinking about the small, gentle lady at the mercy of thugs made his skin crawl. What would have happened if he hadn't intervened?

Bloody Slade had a lot to answer for. Tomorrow, Hughe would let him know what he thought of him. Tonight, he would enjoy a pleasant walk.

"Does Charger often come to the aid of damsels in distress?" she teased.

"All the time. It's vastly annoying. He's forever charging off without a care in the world for me, clinging to the reins and hoping the vagabonds don't think it my fault for interrupting their sport."

"He's very brave."

"Or foolhardy."

"Oh no, definitely brave. I admire him greatly. And look, he doesn't even preen at my praise."

"Ha! He doesn't preen *now*. Be assured that when he returns to his stable mates, he'll toss his mane and bore them all with the details of how he single-hoofedly fought off ten men the size of giants."

"I don't believe that, sir. He seems like a humble character. Perhaps you're just jealous because he's such a handsome creature. I mean, look at that mane, that tail! Like falling snow."

"Jealous? Me? Ha. Clearly you have not seen my hair, madam." He touched his head to remove his hat but remembered he'd given it to Slade as a joke because he hated the blasted thing. It was hideous in the extreme and he'd worn it far too often of late. Time to get a different hideous hat made. His milliner would be pleased to see him, and collect his money.

"Your hair is very pretty too, my lord," Lady Slade said with mock admiration that had him smiling. "Although it's not nearly as blond as Charger's mane."

"Your attempted flattery comes a little too late. I bow to my horse's superior locks."

"To be fair, he doesn't have quite the conversational skills of yourself. Is he shy perhaps?"

"Only a little hoarse."

She groaned.

"Come now!" he protested. "I'm struggling to keep up with your wit. It was the best I could do on short notice."

She laughed again and he was pleased to see that she seemed to have recovered from her ordeal in remarkable spirits. He admired her fortitude. Few women of his acquaintance would be so resilient.

"I'm sure a gentleman of culture such as yourself could think of something wittier," she said.

"Alas, you must have me confused with someone else, madam. I am neither witty nor do I know anything about culture. I'm rarely in the city. My exposure to culture is limited to village fairs, gambling with friends and hunting. Indeed, those could be considered vices rather than entertainments."

Her smile vanished. Her forehead creased and she pressed her lips together.

"My lady? Have I said something to upset you?"

She shook her head. "No. Of course not. I'm sorry, I was just reminded of something."

Her husband. A gambler, hunter, liar, murderer, cur. Yet if he'd read her reaction correctly, she missed him anyway.

"Would you like to tell me what you were reminded of?" If he wanted to learn more about her circumstances, he was better off going directly to the source instead of relying on court rumors. "Or who?"

She glanced at him briefly before looking away. "My husband. He died two months ago in unusual circumstances."

"Unusual?" As far as the world knew, the last Lord Slade had died in a hunting accident. Lady Slade was supposed to believe that too. Hunting accidents were as common as leaves on the ground in autumn.

"According to the official records, Stephen died while hunting. But I have my doubts."

"Go on."

She shook her head. "No, my lord. I shouldn't have mentioned anything. What's done is done. He's gone. I refuse to dwell on the past and must focus on the future. Besides, why spoil a perfectly companionable walk with talk of murder?"

"Murder?" Bloody hell. She knew something and he needed to find out what so he could reduce the damage.

She put her hands up and shook her head but he insisted.

She relented with a sigh. "Very well. It may be nothing, understand. It's just that Stephen was a good horseman and an excellent hunter." She told Hughe how his position at the back of the group meant someone had to turn around and deliberately aim at him to hit him in the head. One of his friends, no less.

He let out a breath. It was all circumstance and conjecture. She had no real proof. "Is that all?"

She hesitated before nodding. Was she holding something back?

"He was a good man, your husband?" he asked. He might as well put to rest the thoughts troubling him ever since Lady Crewe had suggested the Slades had no money.

"Good enough. He was kind to me and to others. I didn't think I'd miss him so much, but I do."

Kind? That was not the description he'd heard. "He never hurt you?"

"No."

"Neglected you?"

"I suppose some might think so. He preferred hunting and riding to being stuck in the house, as he put it. Sometimes he and his friends would be gone for days. That arrangement suited us both. I don't call it neglectful at all."

She seemed to be speaking the truth and not trying to couch it in terms favorable to her late husband. Hughe didn't think she loved the man, but she certainly had a soft spot for him.

"Forgive me, my lady, but I can't help noticing...your husband left you poor, didn't he?"

If she thought his question impertinent, she didn't show it. She gave a slight nod. "There was no money left after his debts were paid. The estate also suffered thanks to a scoundrel of a land steward. But the new Lord Slade will set it to rights. He's got more of a head for such things. I am confident in the future of Slade Hall."

"Are you as confident about your own future?"

She shook her head.

"There is nothing for you as the widow?"

"Nothing. Does that shock you?"

"No," he lied. "It happens to the best of men from time to time. I'm sure your brother-in-law will treat you as he ought and see that you're comfortable."

She said nothing for a long time and Hughe had the sinking feeling that he'd guessed correctly. Slade wasn't in the least concerned about his widowed sister-in-law. He wouldn't care if she wed a monster or lived in a barn, as long as it wasn't at his expense.

"My lord," she said, hesitant. "The reason I'm telling you this is because I have a favor to ask."

"Ask it, my lady. I am at your service."

She bit her lip. "I feel a little foolish now that the time has come."

"Ask anyway before you lose your nerve entirely. I find it best to get these things out in the open rather than regret not speaking later."

"Wise words. Well then. My question is, do you know of any gentleman in need of a wife?"

"You being that wife?"

She nodded. "I'm not overly particular. As long as he's kind and doesn't beat his women, then I'll take a gentleman farmer in good standing. Do you know of such a man?"

"I, uh…" He scrubbed a hand through his hair, suddenly lost for words. He had a most unwelcome thought of Lady Slade in bed with a coarse man, his calloused, filthy hands groping at her silky skin.

Bloody hell! What had come over him? He didn't even know if her skin was silky. Just because he'd rescued the lady didn't mean he ought to bed her. She most certainly wasn't lover material. Far too easy to grow attached to. And besides, she didn't seem like the sort to accept the position of mistress, no matter the man or the reward.

"I'm sorry, my lord," she mumbled. "I didn't mean to put you on the spot. It was selfish of me—"

"No! Not at all. Clearly you're not used to how court works. Lords and ladies use each other all the time to get ahead. Not that you're using me!" Christ, his tongue was running away when usually he had it under complete control. "That is to say, I will gladly introduce you to any suitable gentlemen of my acquaintance. Unfortunately, I can't think of any right now."

Sir Harold Featherstone wouldn't do. He lived in the north and it was blasted cold up there. Lord Makepeace recently lost his wife, but he wouldn't suit either. The man had no sense of humor and Lady Slade clearly did. Every other eligible gentlemen in the realm was either too old, too young, too foolhardy, too cruel, infirm or too…something. Lady Slade needed someone who enjoyed life, but did not over indulge. A man who would not only be kind, but would appreciate her wit and intelligence. He ought to know how lucky he was. She was no classic beauty, but her husband must be able to see that her beauty was of a quieter, rarer sort. Unfortunately for her, no such man existed that Hughe knew.

But she had asked him to help and help he would. He may not be able to introduce her to anyone worthy, but he could see to it that she didn't have to endure a moment's more destitution thanks to him. He may have neglected his duty to her by not delivering the money himself, but he could rectify that situation. Tomorrow, he would.

"Thank you, my lord." She stopped and rounded on him, forcing him to stop too. Charger nudged his shoulder in protest. "You've been so kind to me, and after we so rudely cut off your exit tonight too."

He winced. "Was it that obvious that I was trying to escape?"

"A little. Although I'm not sure Slade realized. He's not very good at observing and understanding people."

"But you are?"

Her eyes brightened. Even in the dark he could see the heat flare in them. The desire. He ought to back away. Ought to run and flee. But he did not.

Charger nudged his shoulder again, pushing him forward. She caught him by the arms and his hand flew to her waist. So narrow. Her face was close. That mouth inches from his own. Those eyes stared back at him like deep pools filled with barely disguised passion. It took every ounce of effort to hold back. To not kiss those deliciously plump lips.

Then she leaned closer and pressed her mouth to his. Hesitant. Uncertain. And he was gone. He could not pull away. Didn't want to. He dropped Charger's reins and caught her in his arms, scooping her close, lifting her off her feet. She was light and delicate. A feather to his cloddishness.

She smelled of earth and a floral scent that he couldn't identify, but wanted to wallow in. She tasted like sweet wine and felt as hot as a furnace. He couldn't get enough of her, of her kiss. Couldn't get close enough, not even when he held her against him. She must be able to feel his cock tenting his breeches, but he didn't care. Not when she cupped his face in her hands, turning his mind to mush. This woman...she had unhinged him. He was utterly lost and he did not want to be found.

He became aware of the pounding of hooves and whoops of delight. He knew he ought to pull away, but like a small boy with a favorite toy, he could not set her aside.

"Another conquest, eh Oxley?" The rider chuckled and whooped again. "Run, dear lady. Run for your life before he breaks your heart!"

Hughe set her down on her feet and angled himself between the rider and Lady Slade so that she could not be identified. He broke the kiss, however. The mood had been shattered. Behind him, the hooves thundered away and faded into the distance. They were alone again.

He rubbed the horse's nose as he gathered his wits once more. "My apologies, my lady."

"No need to apologize, my lord." She gave him a sheepish smile with lips swollen by his kisses. "I enjoyed it."

Her good humor tore at his heart. Bloody hell. He shouldn't have done that. What had come over him? He was always so careful, always choosing the right sort of woman to kiss. Lady Slade was most certainly the wrong sort. Far too eligible, too sweet, too...everything!

"I...I don't know what came over me," he said, looking away at the row of houses nearby. He couldn't bear to see the effect his words had on her. Couldn't bear to know if he'd hurt her. "It won't happen again. You can be sure of that."

It was a long time before she answered. So long that he almost looked at her. "Of course it won't," she snapped. "Why would it?"

She was angry. Good. Anger was better than tears and pleas. He should have known a woman like her wouldn't plead. He had another way to fuel her anger further. A way that he fell back on time and again, that had almost become second nature to him. He would be Hughe, Lord Oxley, the foolish, irritating, fop.

"La!" he cried, thrusting out a hip. "I am so pleased that your sensibilities aren't injured, my dear lady. There is nothing worse than injured sensibilities, don't you find?"

"Pardon?"

He waggled his fingers in the air and touched his head. "My hat! Dear lady, you've addled my wits so much that I have left my hat somewhere! I do hope it has not met with foul play. I love that hat. Truly love it."

"You gave your hat to my brother-in-law. Don't you remember?"

He did not look at her. He didn't want to see the confusion in those intelligent, innocent eyes. He'd allowed himself to lower his guard around her, for some reason he couldn't explain. He'd let her see too much of the real Hughe. It had turned out to be a very stupid mistake.

Cat stared at her rescuer, but he did not look at her. He held his chin high, his nose higher, as he led his horse onward. What had come over him? Had that kiss truly confused him?

That was absurd. It had most certainly been a mind-blowing event, but it shouldn't have completely changed his nature. She'd seen hints of his foppishness at court, but there'd been no sign of it when he'd scared off those thugs. When he'd kissed her, well, he had certainly not been the sort of man who cared more about his hats than the woman in his arms. How odd. And humiliating. Was he putting on these airs so he could avoid talking about that kiss and what it meant?

If so, the man was a coward and not at all the gentleman she thought him to be. It was like she'd been exposed to two completely different people. One intelligent and amusing, kind and brave; the other his opposite in every way. She didn't like this one at all.

"Now, my dear lady, if we're to catch a husband for you, you must follow some simple rules."

She stumbled alongside him, hardly listening. This entire evening had been one strange event after the other, full of extreme lows and highs. She was still reeling from it all and her heart still pounded from the hunger of their kiss. Stephen had never kissed her like that. Never made her knees weak and sent her pulse thudding in her ears. Not ever.

"No more black," he declared. "I know you're in mourning, but it's time to set aside the widow's weeds and sport some color. What do you think of yellow?" He plucked at his bright yellow doublet. "It catches the eye, does it not? And it makes one easy to find in the dark, which is a benefit when there are no candles about."

She let him prattle. He quickly moved on from clothing to jewelry, hair and an account of the virtues of the gentlemen at court. "You mustn't be too fussy," he cautioned. "I know some are aged, and many are fat, but the important thing is a lack of brains.

I have it on good authority that a dull-witted husband makes the best sort."

She knew that to be true at least.

"I shall endeavor to find you the dullest, most witless husband court has to offer. It shall be a challenge, since there are so many, but at least you'll have a choice."

He continued on like that all the way to the house. She couldn't shut the door on his face fast enough. She even forgot to thank him again for saving her.

Cat undressed herself since she'd not brought a maid with her—too expensive to feed an extra mouth in the city according to Slade. She slipped under the bedcovers. Her body still hummed all over, not from the attack but from the kiss. Not even Oxley's strange change of behavior could eradicate the memory of his lips, soft and warm against hers, and the way his strong hands held her waist firmly as if he would never let her go. She'd discovered that his doublet was not bombasted, and his impressive shoulders and chest were entirely due to muscle, not padding. Oh yes. Quite impressive.

She stretched out her legs and refused to think of the Lord Oxley who'd said goodbye to her at the door and only remember the one who'd rescued and kissed her. That man was a gentleman. A woman could too easily forget her plan to wed and agree to be his mistress instead, if he offered. Forget the moral high ground. She wanted to live a little and be with a man who set her on fire with just one kiss.

Unfortunately she was positive the position of mistress wasn't vacant, otherwise he'd have kissed her again. And more.

HUGHE FOLLOWED Slade and his man for most of the morning as the baron ran some minor errands. He wasn't seen, disguised as he was as a dirty laborer in a city teeming with apprentices and laborers working on construction sites. The ragged clothing and cap was an outfit he kept for times he needed to blend in and travel light. There was no need to hide anyone in a cart this time, or inside a barrel. He didn't even carry a sword, sporting only a club strapped to his hip like most London laborers, ready to jump into a brawl at the merest incitement.

Slade and Hislop avoided the shops along Cheapside. There would be no souvenir purchases from their city visit. To Hughe's surprise, they didn't venture toward the docks either, where he expected Slade to connect with a merchant or two. It's what he would do if he found himself in need of cargo to buy low and sell high. There was always something coming in from the Orient or the Continent, or even just a relationship to forge for the future.

No, Slade drank in an alehouse then headed back to The Strand, where the grand estates occupied by the nation's wealthiest men swept from the wide thoroughfare down to the bank of the Thames. Hughe had a house there. It was ironic that he would travel so far on foot only to wind up where he'd begun that morning.

Or not quite. Slade stopped a few houses up from Hughe's London residence, at Lord Marchment's gate. Perhaps Slade wasn't as badly off as Hughe thought. Lord Marchment sat on the Privy Council. He was one of Her Majesty's intimate advisers. If anyone could drag Slade out of poverty, it was Marchment. The man had one finger in the treasury and several others in various lucrative pies.

Hughe leaned against a horse's trough positioned at the side of the road and pretended to rest. In truth, he was watching through near-closed eyes, and thinking. He did not like Slade. He was a poor brother-in-law and a sly fellow. But was it possible that *he* had been Hughe's anonymous client? Had he wanted his brother dead so he could take over his estate? Even an impoverished estate was better than none.

Surely the man wasn't that cold-hearted?

Hughe expelled a breath. Even if it had been the new Slade who hired him to eradicate the old one, the old Slade was a killer and probably a rapist too, although the latter had been difficult to prove. There was no doubt about the former charger of murder. Hughe had thoroughly investigated him, and he knew with absolute certainty that Cat's husband had murdered the villager, Crabb, when Crabb had accused Slade of forcing himself upon his wife.

Slade had never been challenged over the death, but a little prodding of the right people and connecting some very clear dots had proved to Hughe that Slade did it. He wasn't a good man, by all accounts, although it would seem he'd thoroughly duped Cat into thinking he was. Then again, she admitted to hardly ever seeing her husband during their life together. It may be the ideal type of marriage in Hughe's book, but he couldn't image it making her very happy. She needed companionship and conversation, someone to keep her warm at night and nurture her. Keep her safe.

Slade and Hislop emerged through the gate. They didn't head back into the city, but toward Whitehall and Charing Cross. Most likely they were returning to their rented rooms to dine. Since he was so close to home, Hughe returned there to change.

Some time later he made his way out, once more dressed as Lord Oxley the fop. His peacock blue doublet and crimson breeches earned him a number of sniggers and pointing fingers that he didn't acknowledge. His two servants trailed some distance behind on horseback, most likely embarrassed by the attention. They were young and not used to their master's ways yet.

Their journey was short, only to the narrow three-story house at Charing Cross where he had delivered Cat the night before. Cat. The name suited her. She was as lean as a feline, her skin as soft, her eyes as quick. He would like to murmur that name in her ear while he had her in his arms, in bed, and—

Enough, Oxley!

The neat, prim landlady led him up to the room acting as Lord Slade's study. She kept glancing warily over her shoulder at Hughe's hat. He had to admit it was an absurd piece, with peacock feathers springing from the back like tails. He couldn't wait to remove it, which he did upon seeing Slade.

The man glanced up from his desk, a look of shock on his oily features. "My lord!" He rose from his chair and gave an awkward bow over the desk. "What a pleasant surprise."

The landlady retreated as silently as she presented him.

Hughe sat, sweeping his cape around his body like a bird wing. "It is, isn't it?"

Slade sat slowly, looking past Hughe to the door. Hughe did not turn to see who stood there, although he assumed the thickly muscled Hislop was hovering nearby. He looked to be handier with a blade than the soft Slade. On the other hand, it could be Cat listening. Hughe steeled himself.

"What can I do for you, my lord?" Slade asked. He tried out a smile on Hughe, but it didn't suit him. It quickly slid away without a trace.

"I came to warn you."

"Warn me?" Slade cocked his head to the side. "What about?"

"About allowing your sister-in-law to walk home alone at night in a strange city." He leaned forward, and in the only moment of seriousness that he would allow himself, he pinned Slade with a fierce glare. "Do not do it again or I will see to it that whatever befalls her will befall you. Doubly." He leaned back. "Do you understand, or do you just like leaving your mouth open to see what you can catch?"

"I…uh…"

"It's a simple question, Slade. Do you understand?" He pushed back the edge of his cape to reveal his sword hilt for good measure.

Finally Slade's jaw clamped shut with an audible snap of back teeth. "Aye, my lord. I understand." He pressed his palms flat to the table and watched Hughe through dark, narrowed eyes. "Is there anything else, my lord?"

"There is."

"Can I get you refreshments? Wine?"

"No. I'm here on a matter of business. I wish to know how your brother died."

After a moment in which Slade stared at him, his mouth once

more flopping open, Slade told Hughe how his brother had met his end. The official version. He did not bat an eyelid, yet Hughe didn't quite believe his story. Like Cat, he guessed that Slade didn't accept that his brother met with a hunting accident. Was that because he knew otherwise?

"Do you know the woods near Slade Hall, my lord?" Slade asked.

Hughe saw no reason to lie. "I've been there, yes."

Slade's brows rose. "And yet you never visited us? My brother would have been hurt if he'd known."

"Your father might have been the baron then. I don't recall."

"How long ago was your visit?"

"Two years." Indeed, it had only been two months, but Slade wasn't to know that. If Slade did indeed hire Hughe to kill his brother, he *couldn't* know it. None of Hughe's clients ever discovered his identity. He was very careful about protecting not only his own, but that of his men.

"Then it was certainly my brother," Slade said. He had a strange look on his face, and an oddly sharp twist to his mouth as if he found something amusing. He glanced past Hughe again to the doorway. "Were you there before or after the floods that nearly drowned us that year?"

Bloody hell. Hughe knew nothing about a flood. "Before."

"I see. Then you must have visited before March of ninety-seven." Slade's smile grew thoughtful and once more his gaze flicked behind Hughe.

Hughe gave in and glanced around. There was no one there. He frowned. Had Cat appeared only to just as quickly disappear? "I suppose." He turned his attention back to Slade and caught the tail end of his sneer. He frowned harder. What the hell had just happened? Was Slade testing him? Hughe had been so distracted with the thought of seeing Cat again he'd lost the thread of the conversation. He only hoped he hadn't said anything to implicate himself.

"About your sister-in-law," he said. "Something must be done about her."

"I agree." Slade steepled his fingers and pressed them to his lips. "Do you have something in mind?"

"I do." Hughe lowered his voice. If someone were at the door, he wouldn't be overheard. "I'm going to give her a house and an income so that she doesn't need to remarry."

CHAPTER 4

$\mathcal{S}$lade blinked. "Pardon?"

"You heard me." Hughe took great pains to remove his gloves, pinching each finger carefully and studying the act intensely. "I've taken a liking to her."

"You wish to make her your mistress?"

Hughe laughed loudly, ending in a snort. "No, dim wit. I'm simply going to fund her until she finds a suitable husband."

"Ah, well, that may not be too long."

Hughe paused, one glove half off. "You've found her a husband?"

"Not yet. But if she doesn't find one while in London, I'm afraid she'll have to wed the blacksmith from our village. I'll have her married off within—"

"The blacksmith! Have you gone mad?" Hughe completely forgot his gloves and thumped his fist down on the desk. "You cannot allow that. *I* cannot allow it."

"It's not my choice, my lord, but hers!" Slade protested. "The blacksmith is a strong fellow who runs a strict house. Cat accepts the need for a firm, husbandly hand. Indeed, I've discussed it with her and she is amenable. The smith will know better than me how to keep a woman like Cat in her place."

Hughe was so shocked he didn't know where to start. He simply stared at Slade, expecting him to burst out laughing and admit that it was a joke. He did not laugh.

"She won't be marrying the blacksmith," Hughe said, managing to sound light when all he wanted to do was thump some sense into the fool. "I'll give her a cottage and an income until such time as she finds a *suitable* husband. I'll ride to Slade Hall as soon as it's settled in a week or two. In the meantime, you are not to mention it to Lady Slade. Understand me? Not even a whisper should reach her ears."

Slade held up his hands. "Of course. But, my lord, are you quite sure? What if she gets too comfortable living off your income and in your cottage? What if she decides it's better than marriage?"

Hughe shrugged. "Then so be it."

"My lord, you cannot be in earnest!"

"I am. What is it to you? You don't care for her. You said yourself you cannot afford her. I can."

"What do you expect in return?"

An easing of his conscience. "Nothing. Oh, a little gratitude and a prayer for me when she remembers. My soul might yet be saved."

"I'm not sure this is a good idea." Slade leaned forward again, and seemed to be preparing a speech of utmost importance. Hughe silently groaned and wondered how long he had to listen to him. "Women *need* to be married, my lord. It's the only way to keep them in check. Particularly ones like Cat. She's too headstrong." He lowered his voice. "She has *opinions*."

Hughe pulled a face. "Good lord, no." He gasped. "Not *opinions*." He needed to employ every ounce of his acting skills not to laugh.

Slade seemed satisfied that Hughe understood him. He sat back and gave an emphatic nod. Behind Hughe, a swish of skirts announced the arrival of a woman. Cat? Even so, it didn't divert Slade from his topic. "Let them do as they please and they become lazy, spiteful creatures," he went on. "Women of strong mind need a strong husband with a heavy hand. They ought to know their place or all mankind suffer the consequences."

Spoken like a prick who knew women not at all. Hughe curled his fingers around the chair arm to stop himself slapping some sense into Slade. "They ought to know their place," he said, summoning every foppish thought he could muster. If he were to deflect Lady Slade's desires, he needed her to think him a fool. He gave a tinkling laugh for good measure. "I agree with you there. But I think their place ought to be in their husband's bed."

He had the satisfaction of seeing Slade's face turn bright red. Behind him, the skirts shushed gently. He wondered if Cat was blushing too.

"A woman's sole purpose ought to be to please her husband in *every* way." He winked at Slade.

"What about obedience?"

"Of course. Surely wives are not that very different to dogs. I may not have a wife, but my kennels are full. That makes me an expert."

The shushing drew closer and stopped right behind him. He turned around and smiled up into the flushed face of Cat, standing with hands on hips. Her eyes flashed, their shade a remarkable violet-blue. His smile broadened.

"Good afternoon, Lady Slade. What a pleasure to see you again. Are you well?"

"I am well," she spat. "For a dog."

"Ah. You heard that." He turned back to Slade. "I don't know why they always get so upset when I mention dogs. I'm very fond of them."

Cat couldn't believe what she was hearing. She'd been merely passing by when she overheard Slade lamenting women having opinions. She'd known he was referring to her and had wanted to hear Oxley's protest on the subject. But he had agreed with her brother-in-law. This was not the same Lord Oxley who'd rescued her and kissed her. This was some boorish buffoon who'd taken over his body and said the most idiotic things. She wasn't sure whether to ignore him or retaliate on behalf of all womankind.

Actually, she was sure. Comments like that couldn't be left unchallenged.

"My lord, it's so good of you to visit us," she said, sickly sweet. If she was going to fight with him, she needed to do it on his terms.

"I know," he drawled.

"Tell me, does your future wife know that she'll be kept in a kennel?"

He studied her from beneath lazy, half-lowered lids. "You're mistaken, dear lady. I have no plans to wed yet."

"No? But an earl must breed! If a wife's duty is to her husband, then surely a man's duty is to beget heirs upon his wife. Dozens of them. After all, what else is he put on this Earth for? He has little other purpose except prancing about in elaborate costume, turning a fine leg. Of course every gentleman should present himself in the best light for the sake of his good name, but there *must* be more to it, don't you think? We've all been put on this Earth for a reason, my lord, you included. I do wonder, however, what is *your* purpose if not to strengthen the Oxley line? Hmmm?"

"I do plan on marrying, dear lady. All in good time."

"You are how old, my lord?" She swept her gaze over him, taking in the bright blue cape, the velvet shoes with silver buckles, so inappropriate for outdoors, and the rings on his fingers. But his face held a different story. The fine lines crinkled around his pale, intelligent eyes and she could swear his lips were curved at the edges ever so slightly. Was he laughing at her? At himself? She did not understand him one bit. He was a mystery that she dearly wanted to solve. "Nearing five and thirty, I'd wager," she went on.

"Cat!" Slade snapped. "Enough of this."

Oxley pouted. "I am not yet thirty."

"Really?" Cat said. "Dear me. You ought to spend less time in the sun. It's not good for the skin."

"Indeed, my skin does not feel as silken as your own, dear lady."

Her next insult turned to ash in her mouth. How could a man be so rude and yet so flattering at the same time? "You have not touched my skin."

"I assisted you last night."

"We both wore gloves."

"Assisted her with what?" Slade asked.

"It is a guess," Oxley said, ignoring him. "I can tell your skin would be a delight to touch."

"Ha!" She crossed her arms and refused to look at the too-handsome face with the dancing eyes and teasing mouth. It was no wonder he had women falling over themselves to become his next mistress. For a moment she'd wondered how such a fop had gotten so many beautiful women into his bed, but she had to concede that he could be utterly charming, foppishness notwithstanding.

The landlady had assured her that Oxley was a well-known breaker of hearts, the most recent being a woman by the name of Lady Fitzwilliam who was apparently both furious and distraught in equal measure at being cast aside on this very visit to London. Cat tended to believe the landlady's account since she housed so many lesser nobles when the court was at Whitehall and gossip was, after all, the currency of many.

"Excuse me, gentlemen," Cat said, backing toward the door. It was time to retreat. She was losing the exchange rather badly and she did not like the insulting tone in her own voice. It was not how she wanted to fight her battles.

Oxley stood and bowed to her. "Good afternoon, Lady Slade. I hope we meet again."

"I doubt we will," she said. "We're leaving in the morning and I have no plans to attend court tonight."

He bowed again. When he straightened, he had an odd smile on his face. A knowing, secret smile. What was he up to?

LORD SLADE COULDN'T BELIEVE his luck. Not only was he finally home again after suffering through an interminable visit to filthy London, but he'd almost secured an agreement with Lord March-ment. A very lucrative agreement. All that ass-licking—quite literally—had gotten results. Having Cat taken off his hands was an advantage he'd not anticipated, although he'd only believe it when he saw Oxley riding through the gatehouse, money in hand. He had a suspicion that the earl would change his mind, or simply forget having made the offer three weeks ago. He seemed the fickle sort.

On the other hand, there were a great number of things that didn't make sense where Oxley was concerned. For one thing, according to Cat, he'd saved her life. Added to which, there was intelligence in Oxley's eyes that could not be masked by a loose twist of the hand or a colorful hat. Oxley's duality had got Slade thinking. He took his thoughts to Hislop, a man with a keen eye for people.

"What do you think of Lord Oxley?" he asked Hislop as they finished their daily briefing. Hislop was useful for getting things done, not only with the estate, but with the household servants too. They now worked doubly hard for less pay. Slade assumed he'd threatened them with bodily harm. He didn't care. They were replaceable, and Slade Hall was in no position to be generous thanks to his clod of a brother.

Hislop put one booted foot on the edge of the desk and leaned back in his chair. Slade eyed the muddy sole, but said nothing. One did not tell a man like Hislop to lower his boot. He was a tall fellow and thickly muscled. A menacing gleam in his eye and the white scar slicing through his beard were usually enough of a deterrent to anyone who considered defying Slade's authority when Hislop was by his side. For those for whom it wasn't, his blade and fists were. Despite his tendency to use violence to solve everything, there was something alluring about Hislop too. Or perhaps it was the quick temper that made him so. Slade was as drawn to him as a moth to a flame. He knew Hislop might prove dangerous one day, but at the moment, he didn't care.

"He's hiding something," Hislop said in that no-nonsense manner of his. He didn't give his opinion unless asked, but when he did speak, it was always to the point. "I've thought it ever since you pointed him out to me. No man with that much physical presence can be so ridiculous."

"I agree. I also think he's hiding something interesting and of particular importance to me. "

Hislop narrowed his yellow eyes. "You think he's the assassin, don't you?"

Slade's heartbeat quickened, but whether from hearing it voiced aloud or from Hislop's intense stare, he couldn't fathom. Perhaps a little of both. "I don't know. He could be. Cat told me he asked some questions about Stephen's death, but that could have been curiosity. That's why I devised a little test, that day he came to me in London. I asked if he'd been to Slade Hall and he mentioned being in the woods two years ago. I asked if that was before or after the flood and he said before March Ninety-seven. But he couldn't have come then. There was indeed a flood, but I lied about the date. It came at the end of Ninety-six. The entire area was under water for the first four months of Ninety-seven."

"Perhaps he was mistaken about the timing of his visit."

Slade stroked his chin. "Perhaps. He did seem a little distracted during the conversation. There's something else that I find interesting. He's bloody rich."

Hislop shrugged. "He's an earl."

"That doesn't entitle him to wealth. Of course, you wouldn't understand."

A muscle high in Hislop's jaw bunched. Slade swallowed. Perhaps he shouldn't have been so condescending.

"I know for a fact that Oxley has been granted no exclusive licenses," Slade went on. "Admittedly he has extensive land holdings, but..." He shook his head. "I do wonder if he has another income source."

"Perhaps that's why he's sniffing around your sister-in-law," Hislop said. "If he is the assassin, he might have learned something that raised his suspicions about your brother's guilt."

"How could he? Stephen killed Crabb in cold blood. I made

sure he did, just like I made sure there were enough clues for the assassin to find that out for himself."

"True, but by all accounts, the Assassin's Guild do not like anonymous clients."

"Then accounts must be wrong, because they cannot know it was us. No one has accused us."

"Not us, Slade. You." Hislop's smile turned predatory. The man ought to be careful. If Slade was uncovered as the person who commissioned Stephen's death, then he would make sure Hislop was found guilty too.

Slade tore his gaze away from that handsome, dangerous face with its scars and eyes that burrowed into a man's soul. "We need to find out whether Oxley is the assassin or not."

"And if he is, whether he suspects he was manipulated into killing your brother by none other than yourself."

Slade swallowed. He didn't like to hear it put so baldly. Of course Stephen had deserved to die. He was ruining the estate and the Slade name with his gambling obsession and neglect. Their father would have understood the need for action. No heir had been produced and neither Cat nor Stephen grew younger. If Slade had waited then time would have run out. This way he was still young enough to fix the estate problems, wed and produce his own heirs.

But if Oxley turned out to be the assassin and he suspected he'd been manipulated into killing a man, everything could have been for naught. The Assassins Guild was ruthless when it came to dispensing justice. "What did you do with the money the mayor gave you?" he asked Hislop. Money the assassin had anonymously stipulated was meant for Cat, no doubt to ease his conscience. But Cat hadn't needed it as much as Slade. After all, a woman would only waste it on frivolities. He'd made sure Hislop intercepted the purse and sent the mayor on his way with assurances that it would reach Cat. The mayor had either been too frightened of Hislop or too lazy to find out whether his errand had been dispatched according to the wishes of the fellow who'd given him the purse.

"Paid your debts, like you asked."

"Good. Good. But I do wonder if we should have given some of it to Cat. Perhaps Oxley wouldn't be coming after us now if we had."

"We don't know if he is," Hislop said with impatience. He crossed his long, powerful legs, causing the straps of muscle visible beneath his tight breeches to cord and relax. Slade swallowed heavily. "We don't know for certain if Oxley is the assassin. There's no proof."

"No," Slade said quietly, lifting his gaze to Hislop's face. "But why else is he offering to house her and give her an income? It doesn't make sense."

"Maybe he wants to fuck her."

Slade snorted and Hislop laughed at his own joke. Nobody wanted to tumble scrawny, plain little Cat. Slade quickly sobered. He frowned in thought and studied the ledger open before him. He hardly saw the numbers, however. The problem of the unknown assassin kept eating at him. Not for the first time, he wished he'd killed his brother himself. He'd allowed damned sentimentality to get in the way. He wouldn't make the same mistake twice.

"We need a plan," Hislop announced, getting to his feet. "One that will tell us unequivocally if Oxley is the assassin or not."

"What do you have in mind?"

"We have the perfect arrangement staring us in the face."

Slade looked at him askance. "What are you talking about? What arrangement?"

"When is a man at his most vulnerable?"

"When he's asleep?"

"Not to kill him, to learn his secrets."

Slade frowned harder. He couldn't think of any situation. When a man was awake, he could hold his tongue under torture if he had enough courage and conviction. He shrugged. "I don't know."

"When he's fucking."

Slade shook his head. He'd never understood how some men

could let their guard down with a woman, or man, in bed. Fools, all of them. He would never be so weak. "Go on."

"We need to speak to Oxley's mistress," Hislop said, pacing the large study with long strides.

Slade licked his lips. "We could have her ask him subtle questions or sneak about his rooms when he's asleep. But how can we gain her trust? What if she won't do anything against him? We can't pay much."

Hislop stopped in the middle of the study and gave Slade one of his sly smiles. "That's where your sister-in-law comes into play."

"Cat? But what if he doesn't want her as his mistress? He's hardly likely to cast off his current woman for her skinny bones."

"I admit it's a gamble, but if she tries harder, it might happen. Tell her she must throw herself at him. Men like Oxley can't resist any woman if she's overt enough. Besides, she doesn't need to be a long-term mistress, just for a few nights."

Slade wasn't convinced. Cat was much too ordinary for the sophisticated tastes of a gentleman like Oxley, even if she lifted her skirts and painted an arrow on her belly pointing to her womanly parts.

"Trust me," Hislop said. "I know men like Oxley. He won't be able to say no to her. Besides, he must be interested or he wouldn't have flirted with her."

"They've flirted?"

"God, Slade, do you know nothing about relations between men and women?"

Slade didn't, but he trusted Hislop. If he thought Oxley would take Cat then Slade believed him.

Good. It was settled. He always knew Cat would have a use one day. "The problem will be getting her to agree to it."

"I have a way. Make sure she's here after dinner this afternoon." He strode out the door, not answering a single question that Slade flung at him.

* * *

CAT HAD SUCCESSFULLY AVOIDED Slade since their return home. As usual, he and Hislop had gone about their business, leaving her to go about hers. With the weather warming up, she ventured into the village to visit friends or tend the gardens. With fewer servants to help out since Slade let most go, it was up to her to maintain the orchard and kitchen garden. There had been no more talk of marrying the blacksmith, or indeed any other gentleman, but instead of lifting her spirits, his silence on the matter unnerved her.

Perhaps now she was about to find out why that silence. He'd summoned her to his study. Unfortunately, when she entered the sparsely furnished chamber, he wasn't alone. Hislop was present and another man she knew as Wright, a grizzly, thick-set laborer from the village. He sported a fresh cut across his face, as if he'd been sliced by a blade only recently. His right shoulder seemed to sit a little lower than the other, too.

She eyed Hislop. The man's fingers flexed. He did not bow or acknowledge her in any way that a man in his position should. Wright tugged on his forelock and nodded a greeting.

"Ma'am," he said.

"That looks nasty, Mr. Wright," she said, scrutinizing his face. "How did it happen?"

He lifted his heavy lidded gaze to Hislop and winced. "Accident."

She knew she would get no answer from him. The threat of Hislop was too great. She suppressed a shudder. "Why have I been called in here?" she asked Slade. "Surely the wise woman can see to this poor man's injuries."

"There's something you need to hear," Slade said without rising from his chair. He was the only one sitting. Nor did he offer a chair to Cat. "It's about Stephen."

She promptly sat. She rarely thought about Stephen lately, and had certainly not expected to have a conversation about him now. Wright was the man who'd thrown cold water on the accident theory. He'd voiced his concerns to her at the time, and she'd raised it with Slade. He'd not listened of course. So why had he summoned the fellow now?

"Tell her," Slade ordered Wright.

Hislop kicked him in the shin and Wright grunted. "I remembered something about that day he died," Wright said, rubbing his leg. "Something new."

"Oh? How convenient." Either it was an outright lie or Wright had witnessed something at the time, but Slade had kept him quiet with a few coins and perhaps a promise not to have him arrested for poaching. If Slade had paid him off, why this display now?

"Aye," Wright said with a glance at Hislop. "The memory works in strange ways."

"Go on," Slade said, sounding bored. "Get on with it. Tell her about the man you saw."

"You saw someone?" She stared first at Wright then Slade. "Why was I not told?"

Slade stretched his neck out of his lace collar. Hislop bared broken teeth. "What business is it of yours?" he snapped.

"I was his wife!"

He lifted one massive shoulder and looked away from her to Wright. The laborer swallowed heavily. "Keep talking," Hislop said.

"I saw two men," Wright went on. "I overheard them talkin', too."

She waited, every sense alert to signals Wright gave off. If he lied, he was very good. If she had to put a wager on it, she'd say he was telling the truth. "What did they look like?"

"They were dressed like normal folk." He indicated his own clothing. Apparently patched up rags passed as normal in his view. "Both wore hoods that covered their faces. Both were tall, but one was a giant. Much bigger than me or Mr. Hislop here."

That certainly was big. Hislop had to bend to enter most doorways and his shoulders were like boulders. "He was the one carrying quiver and bow, but if he shot Lord Slade, I didn't see him do it."

Cat swallowed the bile burning her throat. Her husband was

gone. She'd mourned him, despite learning how he'd left her destitute and at the whim of his merciless brother. She would not shed any more tears for him.

"The other fellow's hood came off after," Wright said. "I only saw his back. His hair was short and the color of wheat left out in the sun. Then I heard him call the giant somethin'." He screwed his face up. "Tole, Gole." He shrugged. "I was too far away to hear proper."

"Why are you telling me this now, Mr. Wright?"

Wright lowered his gaze, but not before it flicked in Hislop's direction. He touched the cut on his cheek. His fingers came away bloody. "Thought it was time to get it off my chest."

Cat's heart raced. She was almost sure now that Hislop had forced him to keep silent. Until now. But why?

Oh God. Surely not. Surely he had nothing to do with the death? If he had, then that meant Slade was behind his own brother's murder. He couldn't be that heartless. Could he? And if he were responsible, why was he forcing Wright to tell her now?

She mustn't show any sign that she suspected Slade's involvement despite her insides grinding like a millstone. She entwined her fingers in her lap and squeezed until she was able to muster some courage. She had to get out of there and avoid them, just as she'd managed to avoid them since returning from London. There was nothing she could do now except hope and pray that this would all blow over.

She made to get up, but Hislop forced her back down with a heavy hand to her shoulder. She glanced up at him and he winked. Winked!

"You may go," Slade said to Wright. "Cat, stay."

Like a good dog, she stayed. She was reminded again of the conversation in London with Slade and Oxley about wives and dogs. It was an absurd time to think of it. Must be her mind playing tricks as she struggled to suppress her fear. Lord, what she wouldn't do to be with Oxley now. Fop or not, at least he made her feel safe.

Wright shuffled out and Hislop shut the door. She studied her hands in her lap and prayed that she was mistaken about Slade and Hislop having something to do with her husband's murder. As much as she wanted to flee, she also wanted to know why they'd allowed her to hear Wright's evidence now, after silencing him back then. None of this was making sense.

Yet she asked no questions and waited for Slade to speak, just like a good woman should. Or should that be a good dog?

"Wright came to me with his story only today," Slade said idly.

Liar.

He leaned back in his chair and stretched his legs out under the desk. "Immediately, it set off bells in my head. You see, I had something of a revelation in London. Something that worried me at the time, but after hearing Wright's confession, got me even more worried. I think I'm right."

"Right about what, my lord?"

"Just listen," Hislop muttered. "Don't interrupt."

She wanted to remind him that he spoke to a lady, but he had too much influence over Slade. The simple fact that Slade didn't defend her honor proved it.

Slade stroked his chin. "I think the blond fellow Wright spoke of was Lord Oxley."

"What?" she exploded. "Don't be absurd. He's no murderer! He's an earl!"

She did not see Hislop's hand until it was too late. He hit her across the cheek, almost knocking her off the chair. She cried out and clutched her stinging face. She shrank away from Hislop, but he didn't try to hit her again.

"I told you not to interrupt," he growled.

She bit back a thousand savage responses. None of them would do her any good now. The game had suddenly changed. It would seem Slade and his man had an interest in taunting her where before they simply ignored her. What game did they play? And how could she ever feel safe in her own home again?

"As I was saying," Slade went on as if his sister-in-law had not just been back-handed by his brute. "I have reason to suspect that Lord Oxley is a killer." He held a finger in the air. "For one thing, he's not what he seems. I'd wager he's no fop. No dandy ever had so many mistresses. No dandy could scare off a couple of thugs. No dandy would have the respect of the queen. Her Majesty may flirt with them, but there's more than that between her and Oxley, by all accounts." He held up another finger. "Second, he's taken an uncommon interest in you. Why would he do that unless he's got a reason?"

She couldn't think what that reason would be either. She was under no illusions that a gentleman of Oxley's pedigree had an interest in *her*. But Oxley was no murderer. Why would he kill Stephen? What could a wealthy and influential earl possibly have against a little known baron?

She didn't ask, but it was almost as if Slade could read her mind. "It may have something to do with a woman they shared," he said. "I know little about it, but I believe Oxley doesn't like other men fornicating with his mistresses."

Cat bristled. She knew Stephen had other women, but did he have to be so blunt about it? The man was crass as well as heartless.

He held out his hands, palms up, as if laying his evidence in her lap. "What do you think, Cat? Is love reason enough to kill?"

She lowered the hand that still touched her burning cheek. There was no blood, but she would soon sport a bruise. "I don't think Oxley is a murderer."

"Are you saying your lord and master is wrong?" Hislop drawled.

She eyed him warily. "Why are you telling me your theory?" she asked Slade.

"Ah." He smiled. At least, she thought it was a smile. His lips became crooked and the corners lifted. "This is where it becomes interesting. You see, you are going to become his mistress."

A bubble of laughter escaped her throat, but quickly vanished as Hislop raised his hand. She flinched, but he did not strike her. "He wouldn't want me," she said.

"He will." Slade sounded so convinced that she wondered if he knew something she did not. "And when he does, you're going to spy on him for me."

She kept her initial protest to herself while carefully watching Hislop out of the corner of her eye. "Am I?"

"You're going to learn his secrets. Find out what his movements were at the time of Stephen's death. Find out when he came here. Look for correspondence." He flipped his hand in the air. "Anything. Then report it back to me."

She smoothed her hands over her skirt then slowly rose, so as not to startle Hislop into hitting out again. "I'll consider your suggestion. Thank you for keeping me informed of your thoughts, my lord. I appreciate it." She'd never been so formal with him. Never treated him as if he were so far above her. But everything had changed now. Hislop had seen to that.

"Good girl," Slade said, returning to his ledgers. He pulled his inkwell closer and plucked up the pen.

She backed away toward the door, not taking her gaze off Hislop. The brute smiled at her. His tongue flicked out over his lower lip. Her insides recoiled, but she did not turn away from him.

"There is only one problem," she said as her fingers closed around the door handle. Slade didn't even look up from his papers. "How will you reintroduce us? He lives on his estate most of the time and I live here. We're hardly likely to meet again."

Finally, Slade did look up. He had that odd smile on his face again. "That's where you're mistaken, dear Cat. He's arriving tomorrow."

CHAPTER 5

*C*at watched Lord Oxley ride up on Charger from her bedchamber window situated in the only remaining tower of the old fortified manor. That part of the house was over three hundred years old, with the drafts to prove it. In summer, however, it was pleasant enough, with magnificent views over the countryside and down to the village. She could see Oxley and his entourage for miles before they reached the gatehouse.

She'd not expected him to come at all. Surely Slade had said it to tease her. Or perhaps he was in earnest and it was Oxley who was joking, by pretending to come when in fact he had no such intention. Yet here he was, riding on his beautiful white horse, dressed in crimson and black with a crimson hat, six servants in tow. They were met by the Slade servants and immediately a flurry of activity surrounded the earl as his vast amount of luggage was offloaded from the cart and carried inside.

Oxley himself was met by Slade. The two greeted each other formally. Then Oxley suddenly looked up at her with those ice-blue eyes, as if he knew she'd been there all along, watching him.

She stepped back from the window and pressed a hand to her thumping heart. Why was she reacting like a coy maid? Why did he make her blood hot and her pulse race? He was a fool. A fop.

Perhaps her reaction was due to nerves. After all, Slade was about to offer her to Oxley like a pheasant at the dinner table.

Well. It was time to venture downstairs and see if Oxley would agree to the scheme. His refusal was her only hope. She didn't dare say no to Slade's face, with or without Hislop present.

She wound her way down the spiral staircase and found both gentlemen on their way up to see her. It would seem they weren't about to waste any time in getting to the point.

"Good afternoon, my dear Lady Slade." Oxley was about to bow when he spotted her bruised cheek. He lifted a hand as if to touch it and Cat was reminded of his gentle fingers brushing her hair aside that night he'd saved her, and the soft touch of his gloved thumb as he wiped away her tears. It sent a rush of tingles through her body that warmed her all over. "What happened?" he said, no trace of the fop in his blunt voice.

"Nothing," she said.

"Walked into a door, silly chit," Slade said with a snort.

Oxley studied her for some time until his cool eyes shuttered. He suddenly laughed. "You ought to be more careful, my lady. Those vicious doors are everywhere!" He'd dispensed with the hat and his blond hair gleamed from the sunlight streaming through the window. "It's indeed a pleasure to see your beautiful face again."

She curtsied and accepted his praise without so much as a roll of her eyes this time. She was in no mood for teasing. "Would either of you like to tell me what this is all about?"

Oxley straightened. He frowned and tiny lines bracketed his mouth. His eyes danced, however. She may be in no mood for teasing, but she got the feeling he was. "My lady?"

She turned to Slade instead and forked an eyebrow at him. "Well?"

"Allow Lord Oxley time to settle in, Cat," he chided her. "See how eager she is to speak with you, my lord. She's champing at the bit."

Oxley grinned. "So she is. Well then. Allow me to change into more comfortable clothing and then I'll come to you both. I'm so dusty!"

Slade beckoned the hovering manservant. "Take Lord Oxley to his rooms. See that he's made comfortable."

Oxley bowed to Cat then followed the servant out. Once he was gone, Cat said, "Are you going to make me wait longer before you tell me why he's here at all? Did you invite him with the purposes of offering me up as his mistress?"

"Now, Cat. You know Hislop and I only thought of that scheme yesterday. Oxley's had this visit planned since London."

"London! Why didn't you tell me?"

"He told me not to."

"Why is he here?"

"His reason for coming is not important."

"It is to me."

"The real concern is our plan," he went on as if she hadn't spoken. "Try to look a little more appealing." He pulled down on her bodice at her bust, attempting to lower it.

She stepped out of his reach. She had wanted to slap him, but even though Hislop wasn't nearby, she didn't feel brave enough. "Don't."

His nostrils flared. "Change into something more appropriate then meet us in the great hall."

"More appropriate?" She looked down at her black gown. "Oxley knows I'm in mourning."

"I'm not referring to the color, but the cut. It should reveal some flesh. Must I explain everything to you?"

"I will not wear anything more revealing, thank you. Kindly keep your opinions on my dress to yourself."

She was about to argue when Hislop appeared as if he'd emerged from the stone walls themselves. "You heard him. Change."

She touched the bruise on her cheek then turned and headed back up the stairs. She was not fool enough to argue with *him*.

Hislop and Slade's footsteps retreated in a different direction, giving her pause. She rested her palm against the cool stones of the stairwell wall and drew in a deep breath. She would not wear a low cut gown to seduce Oxley. She didn't possess any low cut gowns, nor would she be party to the mad scheme. Lord Oxley was no killer.

Instead of continuing upstairs, she walked quickly to the great hall, the first room Oxley would have seen upon arrival. Once settled on her favorite chair by the window, she picked up her sewing and completed a few stitches. It wasn't Oxley who entered first, however, but Slade and Hislop, followed by the maid carrying a tray. She set it down and rushed out again, not making eye contact with anyone.

Slade strode across the room and stood over Cat. He pinched her sleeve at the shoulder and tugged, almost pulling out the pins that held the sleeve in place. "What's this? I told you to change."

"There was nothing more appropriate in my wardrobe. You sold my loveliest gowns, my lord. They were the only low-cut ones I had."

"Then alter one! Tear off a piece!" he spluttered, flinging his arms in the air. The sight of his uncharacteristic blustering unnerved her, but not as much as Hislop's narrowed eyes. Menace lurked in them.

"I am." She indicated her sewing.

Hislop snatched the gown out of her hands. He held it up to see that she had indeed been working on the bust area. When he saw that she had, he grunted and flung it back at her. She caught it and met his glare with one of her own.

"When will it be ready?" Slade asked.

"Tomorrow."

"That's too late," Hislop snapped. "Work faster."

"I cannot work any faster. Not on my own. If I had a maid—"

"We can't spare any."

"We?" She lowered the gown and summoned all her courage into a glare that she pinned on Hislop. "You mean *Lord Slade* can't."

Hislop's top lip curled in a sneer. He stepped toward her and

Cat shrank back, regretting her outburst. What had come over her? Damned, foolish pride, that's what. And now she was going to receive another slap for it.

To her surprise, Slade put up his hand to stop his man from striking her. Hislop seemed just as surprised. He growled low in his throat, but it wasn't clear if his frustration was leveled at Cat or Slade. He stalked away, but did not exit the great hall.

Slade squatted beside her. "Listen to me, Cat. I know you're upset by our reduced circumstances. I am too. We shouldn't have to bow and scrape. You shouldn't have to wear dull clothes and I shouldn't have to…work so hard to climb out of the mess my brother left behind. None of this is your fault, or mine. Blame Stephen, but only partly. He could have found a way to be clear of his debts, but was unfortunately taken too soon. If you want to blame anyone for this, blame his killer."

Ah. She was wondering when he would get around to the task he'd set for her. "I do blame his killer," she told him. "I hate him. I hope he'll be dealt justice. But I do not think Lord Oxley is the murderer, and I will not try to trap him in such a manner."

He thumped the back of her chair with the flat of his hand, very near her shoulder. The thud brought Hislop striding back, a vicious scowl on his face. Cat's fingers tightened around the needle.

"You're a stupid girl!" Slade growled. "Listen to me. I know what happened. I know Oxley killed him. We must make him pay for… all of this!" He grabbed the gown she was pretending to alter and snatched it from her hands. Pins scattered across the floor and a ball of thread rolled away, leaving an unraveled trail behind. He shook the gown in her face. "Where is your loyalty to the Slade name? Where is your loyalty to your lord and master? Well? It's time you did something useful around here and worked for your keep. You *will* flirt with Oxley today, and you *will* sleep with him tonight. Understand?"

"I do," she whispered. Ice-cold fear slithered down her spine, but she swallowed the lump in her throat and forged on. "I am angry at Stephen's killer. Very much so." That at least was the truth. If he were still alive today, she wouldn't be at Slade's mercy, or Hislop's. She would be secure, living a comfortable if uneventful life. She was utterly furious with the killer, and if she ever got to face him, she'd scratch his eyes out and see that he got justice for what he'd done. But that killer couldn't be Oxley. "My lord, what if he doesn't want me?"

"Make him want you. You're a woman. Do whatever it is women do to get men to fuck them."

She didn't gasp at his language or his tone. She was too busy watching Hislop, a menacing gleam in his eye, a cruel twist to his mouth. She flinched just as his hand struck out, grasping her gown at her chest. He jerked her to her feet as easily as if she were an empty sack. He lifted her up so that she was no longer touching the floor rushes, his fist twisting in the fabric, tightening it. His breath reeked.

She struggled to free herself, shoving at his massive shoulders. He did not let her go. She kicked him in the shin. He hissed in pain, but still did not let her go. He bared his teeth and laughed a brittle, cackling laugh.

"You shouldn't have done that." He leaned back and eyed the bridge of her nose. He was going to smash his head into her face!

"And *you* shouldn't have done *that*." Oxley's voice came from the doorway. It was not the lilting one of the fop, but the commanding one of her rescuer. He did not shout, but his tone was as forceful and cold as a blade to the throat. "Put her down."

Hislop slowly lowered her. Once her feet were on the ground, she ran to Oxley. He angled himself so that she was a little behind him. She blinked back at Slade and Hislop, both standing near her chair, silently fuming.

"Would anyone care to tell me what this is about?" Oxley asked.

"We're having a family discussion," Slade said. "It's none of your affair."

"That's where you're wrong." Oxley spoke lightly, but the thread of steel ran clear through his words. "Lady Slade is very much my affair now."

"I am?" she said. Did that mean he was going to make her his mistress? She wasn't sure whether to be flattered or offended. At the very least, it would have been nice to be asked. On the other hand, it would offer her protection, and at that moment, safety was her greatest need.

"Considering the situation here, I see no reason to delay our discussions." Oxley half-turned so he could see her, but also keep an eye on Hislop. The brute stood beside Slade, his hand on his sword hilt. "Lady Slade, I've come to offer you a house and your own income until such time as you remarry."

She blinked slowly. He'd spoken so quickly that she wasn't even sure she'd heard correctly. "What?"

"No," Slade said, stretching his neck. "I've decided I don't accept."

"You have no choice," Oxley said, sounding impatient. "This is an arrangement between Widow Slade and me."

"Wait." She held up her hands. Surely she was dreaming. "Am I supposed to rent this house from you? But I have no money." And yet he'd offered her an income too. Was that to pay the rent?

"It's my gift to you for as long as you need it."

Ah. Yes. So he did want her to be his mistress. "I accept," she said before she was even aware that she'd opened her mouth to speak. Perhaps she ought to have shown a little more reluctance and a lot more indignation at his impertinence.

His eyes crinkled in a smile. "How soon can you be ready?"

Slade stepped forward and Oxley responded instantly. He once more ensured she was safely behind him. He was unarmed, however. He must have assumed swords weren't worn in the house, as was usual. Only Hislop carried his rapier. He always did. If Hislop drew, Oxley didn't stand a chance.

She glanced around for potential weapons.

"Are you asking her to be your mistress?" Slade asked.

"No!" Oxley placed his hands on his hips and eyed Slade up and down. Now *that* was a show of indignation. "I expect nothing in return. Not even a peck on the cheek."

Oh. Well then. What was he offering? She was more confused than ever.

"She doesn't interest you in that way?" Slade asked.

"I, er..." Oxley cleared his throat and his cheeks colored. It would seem the suggestion that she be his mistress had offended *him*. Did he find the thought of bedding her so abhorrent?

Slade winked at Cat and tugged on his collar then nodded at Oxley, now studying his shoes. She shook her head. She would not force herself on a man who didn't want her. Pride was all she had left in the world and she would hang onto it for as long as she could. She ignored Slade.

Slade clicked his tongue and blew out a breath.

Hislop, however, smiled. Cat's insides churned at the sight. "You forget that she is Lord Slade's sister-in-law," he said, coming to stand at Slade's side. "He is entitled to see her whenever he wishes. And I know how my Lord Slade enjoys her company. He and I will be happy to call upon her in her new home since we'll miss her terribly. We'll be sure to visit often. Won't we, sir?"

Slade quickly nodded. "Very often," he said. "She will not be allowed to become lonely. I might even set my man to live nearby, to be sure she has everything she needs. We're family, after all, and family must look after one another."

It was a slick move, and one that could have backfired on them if Oxley was a less astute man. They were bargaining on his compassion and his desire not to see her harmed. She'd never met such a champion of women before. To think that a man like him cared about a poor, plain baron's widow! She wondered if he tried to save all the women he met, or whether she was just fortunate. She had the absurd notion that he kept cottages all over the country, each one housing a lady in need of protection.

"The house is out of the way," Oxley said slowly, as if measuring each word carefully. "I won't even bother telling you where it is."

"You will," Slade said. "I have a duty to her. If you don't then I'll have to tell the relevant authorities how my sweet sister-in-law was abducted against her will."

The air in the great hall thickened. Cat felt like the walls were closing in on her, suffocating. She might never get away from Slade and Hislop, not even with Oxley's influence and protection. He couldn't afford the scandal of an abduction story. Slade was right. The authorities would investigate and she would be found. She couldn't escape.

Tears sprang to her eyes, hot and burning. Slade saw them. Hislop too. He grinned. Her only recourse was to do as they said, and throw herself at Oxley. They would be satisfied with nothing less than her being his mistress and doing their filthy spying for them.

She swallowed the lump in her throat and slipped her hand inside Oxley's. Startled, he looked down at their linked hands, then up at her face. She thought she saw him wince, but that couldn't be it. She wasn't holding him that tightly. He could easily remove his hand if he wanted to. He didn't.

"My lord, I have a proposal for you," she said quietly. She didn't want Slade and Hislop to hear, but she knew she had to say it in front of them. They would not be satisfied unless they heard her offer herself to Oxley. "I cannot take your house and money without giving something in return." She swallowed again. Why was this so hard? She quite liked the fellow. He was handsome, well built, and charming most of the time. Lying with him in his bed would be pleasant. Yet it was so difficult to say those things to his face.

Slade cleared his throat. She glanced at him and he urged her with a nod.

Cat squared her shoulders and thrust out her insignificant chest. "I would like to thank you properly," she forged on. Her voice didn't sound at all like her own. It was throaty, sensual. She ran her hand along Oxley's arm, up his neck above his ruff to his chin. She trailed her fingertips across his jawline and smiled as a muscle pulsed there. He swallowed audibly. His gaze connected with hers. His eyes turned darker, smoky, not at all icy. She wasn't sure if it was desire that she saw in them or not. It could have been confusion or distrust. He gave no response. No bending of his head to kiss her, no pushing her away and ending the farce. There was more work to be done yet.

She lifted both arms and teased his hair, curling the lock at his ear around her finger. She gently pulled his head lower then stood on her toes. Her mouth was at his chin. His breath warmed her. It was just like that night again. The memory of their kiss slammed into her and she was back in London once more, being held by him, kissed by him beneath the shield of darkness. She wanted to feel what she'd felt that night. Wanted his arms surrounding her, his lips on hers, as soft as down, as heady as strong wine. Wanted him to caress her.

She pressed her hands to either side of his face to angle it down. She drew him closer until her mouth touched his. She parted her lips.

"Blast," he muttered, drawing back. He grasped her hands and lowered them to her sides, then, without looking her in the eye, he turned away. His chest rose and fell with his deep breaths. His head lowered.

He had rejected her. He didn't want her. Didn't like her in that way. What he felt for her was pity, that was all. He felt sorry for her living with Slade and Hislop. He did not want her as his mistress, even when she was offering herself to him.

She didn't want to look at his powerful shoulders sagging anymore, but she didn't want to turn to see Slade's reaction either. His plan was falling apart. She had tried to give herself to Oxley and failed. There was only question remaining now:

When would he make her pay for the failure?

Hughe drew in several deep breaths, but they failed to slow his rapidly beating heart. Even though he didn't face Lady Slade, her troubled eyes haunted him. He could still feel her hand in his, small and warm, trembling ever so slightly. She'd been frightened at first and reluctant. She wasn't throwing herself at him because she wanted to, but because Slade wanted her to. It would not go well for her if Hughe left and she had not secured him. Hislop would make sure of that. The thug had already marked her cheek. Next time, he would do something worse.

For the first time in his life, Hughe felt like events had spun out of his control. His pulse raced too fast, his head was dizzy with all the scenarios buzzing around inside. He was worried about Cat and he had no idea what Slade was up to. What did the cur hope to achieve by installing his sister-in-law as Hughe's mistress? Whatever it was, Hughe wouldn't let him succeed. He wasn't going to take Lady Slade as his mistress.

He was going to take her as his wife.

There was no other choice for a woman like her. Clearly Slade was not prepared to leave her alone. The prick could ruin her if he wanted to, and worse. Hislop looked like the sort of brute who would enjoy making her suffer for failing to entice Hughe into her bed. Slade seemed in earnest about crying foul too. Hughe's reputation could withstand accusations of abduction, but Cat's couldn't. She would never find another husband in good standing. No, there was only one way to save her from Slade that did not involve taking her as his mistress. It was to wed her.

He slowly turned, a stiff smile on his face. If he was going to do this, he was going to do it properly. He took her hand and dropped to one knee before her. She gasped. Slade and Hislop shuffled their feet. Hughe ignored them.

"My dearest lady," he began. Was that how it was done? He wasn't sure. He hadn't prepared a speech. He had known he would need to one day, but had hoped that time was months away, perhaps more if he could rein in his mother's matchmaking. "My dearest lady. Will you do me the honor of becoming my wife?" Just saying the words made his head ache.

"I, uh…"

"Say yes, you foolish girl." That was Slade. Hughe hardly heard him.

"But…are you sure, my lord?" she asked.

He laughed. God, no. He wasn't sure at all. So why the hell was he laughing? "Of course."

"Are you thick, girl?" cried Slade. "Agree to it before he comes to his senses."

"I am in full capacity of all my senses," Hughe said, more for Cat's benefit than Slade's. "I am in need of a wife. You are in need of a husband. I don't like young, silly girls. You seem sensible and I enjoy your company." All of that was true, he realized with a growing sense of satisfaction.

"In that case, yes," she whispered. "Yes, I will marry you, my lord. Thank you." Her fingers curled around his and held him gently but firmly. Claiming him.

He rose and offered her a fleeting smile that grew to a broad one when he saw the sheer relief in her eyes. Tears brewed in their depths, but he guessed they were happy ones. If he needed any more confirmation that he'd done the right thing, that was enough. She was free of Slade and Hislop.

He wondered if that had been Slade's plan all along—to be brutal to her to encourage Hughe's sympathies and stir his protective instincts. Then back him into a corner with no other way out but to offer marriage. Clever. Very clever. Hughe ought to call it all off and leave immediately, but he knew it would not go well for Cat if he did. Hislop looked like he *wanted* to hurt her.

Hughe linked his fingers with hers. "You're mine now," he murmured quietly so that only she could hear. "I'll protect you."

An errant tear escaped her left eye. She quickly swiped at it and gave him a wobbly smile.

"We'll leave tomorrow," he said. "Will you be ready by then, my dear?"

She nodded and slipped her hand from his. "I'll begin packing now." She gave an awkward curtsy, as if she didn't know what to do, and hurried from the great hall.

Hughe beckoned both Slade and Hislop with his finger. With a quizzical glance at one another, they obliged. Hughe bent his head forward, conspiratorially. Slade did too, to listen. Hislop did not.

"If either of you go near her," he said, directing his entire attention to Hislop, "I will slice off your balls and feed them to the dogs."

Slade swallowed audibly. "You have my word, my lord! There is no reason for us to harm her. No reason at all! How could you think such a thing?"

Hughe didn't bother answering. He watched Hislop from beneath his lashes and curled his hand into a fist. He ought to punch him for what he'd done to Cat. But he simply turned his back and left. Retaliation would only bring more danger to her door, not Hughe's.

He went in search of his servants to advise them of his plans, but got only as far as the courtyard. He paused and blinked up at the bright yellow sun. Bloody hell. How had he reached this point? Mere weeks ago he'd been blissfully carefree. Now he was betrothed.

How his friends would laugh when he told them. How his mother would berate him for his choice.

* * *

SLADE SLAPPED Hislop on the shoulder. "It went better than I expected."

Hislop glared at him until Slade removed his hand. "Oxley is more of a fool than we thought."

"Indeed." Slade rubbed his hands together, thinking hard. "Yet he was menacing. Did you see that wild look in his eyes? I thought he'd kill you with his bare hands when you went to hit her. Pretending to hurt her was a stroke of genius."

"I wasn't pretending."

Slade eyed his man warily. He could well believe that Hislop would have hurt Cat again; just because he wanted to, not for any ulterior motive. Ever since Slade had given him free reign with his fists, he'd been champing at the bit waiting for her to give him an excuse to hit her. "It was fortunate that Oxley's protective instincts overrode any sensible ones. He'll come to his senses soon enough and realize the poor match he has made. But you and I are both witnesses to his proposal. He can't back out now."

"The man's a fool," Hislop said again. "Your idea was clever."

Slade puffed out his chest. Indeed it was clever. Brilliant! He had only hoped to get Oxley to take Cat as his mistress. He'd never expected him to marry her! When he'd seen her reluctance to become his mistress, and the way Oxley reacted to the bruise on Cat's face, Slade had known what to do. Urge her further along that path, and when she failed, as he suspected she would, threaten to hurt her. Oxley would be forced to take her as his mistress just to protect her. But it would seem Oxley didn't want a mistress, he wanted a wife.

Even better. Now Cat could have access to all of Oxley House, not just his person. Given time, she would know for sure if Oxley was the assassin or not, and whether he suspected Slade had hired him to kill Stephen.

"Are you going to talk to her about what she needs to do next?" Hislop asked.

"No. She won't listen now. We've planted the seeds in her head and that's enough for the moment. If I'm right and Oxley is the assassin, she'll find out soon enough. And when she does, she'll come and tell me because she'll be too angry at her second husband for killing her first. Angry, frightened or sickened, it doesn't matter which. Just as long as she knows she can come running back here."

"The more I see of him, the more I think it is him," Hislop said, staring at the door through which Oxley had left. "The fop is definitely an act, which for some reason he wants to maintain. But he's no fool."

"Except when it comes to women."

Hislop grunted a laugh. "Aye, except when it comes to women."

CHAPTER 6

*C*at saw her betrothed very little on the journey to his Hampshire estate. He had no horse or carriage for her, so she had to sit beside the cart driver. Oxley rode ahead each day. She rather liked watching him from behind. He removed his cloak when it grew warm, giving her a nice view of his broad back and shoulders, straining the seams of his doublet. He moved effortlessly with the horse, and she found the gentle rocking of his body enthralling. She couldn't tear her gaze away, and anyway, why should she? He was almost her husband. She would be seeing more of him in the days to come.

The thought made her head giddy and her heart race. Every part of her tingled as if his hands ran lightly over her skin, exploring, teasing. She had not felt this much anticipation before her first wedding night.

They stopped to dine at midday and secured rooms in traveling inns along the way. She expected an earl of Oxley's standing to stay in grand houses, but he didn't approach any of the estate gates they passed. Indeed, he didn't even introduce himself to the various innkeepers. He simply asked for chambers and was granted them. They must have known him. She did spot him talking to one or two keeps and inn servants, their heads bent in quiet discussion. It was as if he were their equal and not on a higher level at all.

From time to time, he fell back to speak to her on the road. He asked how she fared, if he could get her anything, and what she liked to do, to eat and drink. She asked him about his house, his family and servants. She learned that his mother, the dowager countess, was the only member of his family living at Oxley House. Indeed, he was an only child with three other siblings dead and buried years ago.

Throughout all of these brief conversations, he spoke like the fop again, in a simpering voice that always sounded as if he were on the verge of breaking into laughter. He seemed to find amusement in everything, from the birds flitting past to the beggars sitting on the side of the road. He threw coins at all of them. Every single one, and there were dozens. His good humor grated after a while. She wished he would dispense with the ruse now that she'd seen the other side of him. Was he going to keep up his foppishness for their entire marriage?

After two days they reached Oxley House. She had expected it to be magnificent, yet she'd not envisaged it to be quite as grand as the glittering mansion nestled on a slight rise at the edge of a lush forest. It was a modern building, although off to the east on another rise she spotted an old castle keep, much like Slade Hall. The new Oxley House shimmered like a jewel in the sunshine. There was so much glass! She'd never seen any place with that number of windows before. She couldn't even begin to count them all. The main part of the house was three stories high, the towers at either end stretching to four. Decorative crenellations and a stone carving of the family crest topped the roofline, interspersed with dozens upon dozens of chimneys, shooting majestically into the sky. Fittingly, the house itself was a warm brick that appeared golden in the late afternoon sunlight.

"Welcome to your new home, my lady," Oxley said, drawing Charger alongside the cart. "I hope you like it."

"I do," she said on a breath. "It is a jewel, my lord." She had the urge to thank him again for rescuing her, but he'd asked her to stop the habit the day before. He'd insisted that *she* was doing *him* a favor by finally ending his bachelor days. She'd chosen to ignore the heavy way he'd said the word 'bachelor' and the dimming of the light in his eyes. It wasn't her fault that all noblemen must marry eventually.

"Drive up to the front door," Oxley said to the driver. "I'll be taking my bride through the proper way."

A dozen servants spilled out of the house as they approached. They greeted their master and he greeted them in return, before they efficiently went about their business of tending to the horses or taking trunks inside. Oxley helped her down from the cart and was about to escort her inside when a thin, crooked man, who must have been in his seventh decade at least, met them on the steps.

He bowed. Or that is, Cat assumed the nodding of his head was a bow. His back seemed to be permanently fixed in that crooked position, poor man. "Good afternoon, my lord. The guest rooms are already prepared for Lady Slade, sir."

How had Oxley organized it all from the road? He'd not sent any of his men ahead. If he'd sent word, it hadn't been with one of them. Cat felt rather relieved. The thought of arriving unannounced had made her feel a little sick. At least this way his mother would have fair warning to grow used to the idea of a nobody marrying her son.

"Guest chambers?" Oxley echoed.

"There has not been enough time to remove all of the dowager's belongings, my lord," the crooked man said.

Cat winced. Throwing the countess out of rooms that she must have occupied most of her life wasn't the best way to start their new relationship. "There's no hurry," she said. "Please allow Lady Oxley to move in her own time." Or not at all. A house of that size must have many bedchambers. Cat could live in one of them until Lady Oxley was ready to move of her own free will.

"Crane, this is Lady Slade," Oxley said. "Lady Slade, this is

Crane, my house steward. Anything you need, go to him. He's a marvel. Oxley House would fall apart without him."

The old man glowed under his master's praise, and he appeared to be trying not to smile. He bowed his awkward bow to Cat and she smiled back.

"I'm very pleased to meet you, Crane," she said.

"And I am pleased to meet you, my lady."

"She won't be Lady Slade for much longer," Oxley went on. "She'll be my wife. Catherine. Cat," he said, sounding out the word as if seeing if it suited her. He must have liked it because he smiled at her rather sweetly. "Can I call you that?"

"Of course, my lord."

"And you must call me Hughe."

Crane cleared his throat. "My lord, I ought to warn you that the dowager countess has been asking her friends about Lady Slade."

"And what has she learned?"

"Nothing, as far as I am aware. There hasn't been time for her letters to be answered."

"Good," Hughe said tightly. "She'll get to meet Cat first."

Cat's stomach sank to her toes. It would seem she had been right in assuming the dowager countess would find fault with her son's choice of bride. It was inevitable, she supposed, and worrying.

Hughe led her across the porch between slender columns and into the house. The inside was just as magnificent as the outside. The great hall was the most enormous room she'd ever been in, besides the Presence Chamber at Whitehall. A long oak table and bench seats occupied most of the space. A hearth fit for a giant yawned on one side, above which were mounted two crossed swords. Tapestries and screens hung on the walls, their vibrant colors brightening the room.

Cat was so busy admiring the great hall that she didn't see Hughe signal the maid to approach until she was at Cat's side.

He patted her arm. "Go upstairs and allow the maids to take

care of you. The journey has been long and you must be exhausted."

"Not at all," she said. Indeed, she felt like a child on her birthday, presented with an assortment of gifts to unwrap. She wanted to explore every nook, peek into every room, and speak to every servant to learn more about her betrothed.

"There should be a bath in your chambers and new gowns too," Hughe said. "Although I'd wager most are too big."

Perhaps she could leave the exploring for now. A bath sounded like Heaven, and of course she ought to try on all her new clothes. "Thank you, my lord. Hughe."

He bowed elaborately. "It's my pleasure! I cannot wait to see you in those gowns. I hope some are blue to match your eyes. If not, I'll have them made. Dozens of them." He was back to being the fop, but she didn't mind. Anything was better than Slade and Hislop.

She followed the maid up to her new bedchamber. It was larger than her room at Slade Hall and looked more comfortable, with an enormous canopied bed and thick mattress. The seat in the window embrasure was covered with deep cushions in crimson velvet.

Another maid emerged from the adjoining room and announced that her bath was ready. Cat gratefully allowed the girls to help her undress and sank into the water with a sigh. She could certainly grow used to this.

HUGHE CHANGED his clothes and reluctantly went in search of his mother, his good mood dampening somewhat at the thought of the discussion he was about to endure. He'd enjoyed seeing Cat's eyes light up at the sight of his home and the smile she'd bestowed on him when he told her about the bath. Had her servants never carried a bath up to her chambers at Slade Hall? Probably not. For one thing, that narrow spiral staircase with its unforgiving stone walls would not make it easy, and for another, he had seen so few servants. She'd not even insisted on bringing a maid with her. If she continued to be such an agreeable woman, he might not mind being married as much as he thought he would.

He found his mother in the high great chamber on the topmost floor, where she liked to spend most of her time. She sat sewing on her large throne-like chair, with her maids seated on lower chairs around her. They rose upon his entry and curtsied.

"Son," his mother said, holding out her hand to him. "You're home."

She sounded surprised, even though she would have seen his arrival through the windows. It irked him that she'd not come down to meet Cat, but perhaps it was better this way.

He kissed her cheek and held her thin hand in his own. She looked a little more tired than usual, her skin too pale, but her eyes were as sharp as ever. "Good afternoon, Mother. I hope I find you in good health."

"My health is as it always is."

It was her usual answer and told him nothing. He supposed it was better than listening to a catalog of ailments, but he would like to know if she felt unwell instead of hearing it from her ladies. At least his last absence hadn't been particularly long. With his friends and his latest target not far away at Sutton Grange, he'd been able to come home before heading off to Sussex and Slade Hall.

"Any news?" he asked. "Crane tells me the servants are all well." Hughe would speak to his land steward later to find out how his farmers fared, but the man was as efficient and capable as Crane, and he knew all would be in order.

"We have no news," his mother said. "Oxley House carries on well enough when you're not here. Indeed, it's on the few occasions that you do return that everything is thrown into disorder. You seem to bring madness with you, Hughe. No more so than this time." She said it sweetly enough, but he heard the coolness to her tone. So did her ladies, if their worried glances were an indication.

"Cat is looking forward to meeting you," he said.

His mother arched her eyebrow at him. "You're marrying a cat?"

"Her name is Catherine. She likes to be called Cat."

"Does she also like to live in the barn?"

"Mother," he said on a sigh. He'd known it would be like this, but still he'd hoped her relief at finally marrying him off would override any issue she had with Cat's status.

"When will you wed?" She continued stitching as if they weren't discussing one of the most important events of his life.

"Next week. Perhaps longer if I cannot return sooner."

"Not waiting for all three banns to be read, I see?"

"I've sent a man to obtain a special license."

"Is there a particular reason to hurry?"

Her ladies blushed and bent their heads lower over their sewing. "She is not with child," he said, not caring if he offended anyone by his directness.

His mother lowered her sewing to her lap and fixed him with a stare that had not become frail over the years like her body. "Then why are you marrying her?"

"Because I want to."

"And what is she bringing to the marriage?"

"Herself."

The tiny lines around her mouth drew together. "Who are the Slades? I admit to knowing nothing about them."

"A baronial family in Sussex. Cat is the widow of the second baron."

"Baron." Her huff told him what she thought about that. "And her own family?"

"Her father was a gentlemen farmer. He's dead, as is the rest of her family. She has no one in the world."

"Her husband's connections?"

"There is a brother-in-law, the new baron Slade. He's insignificant and takes out his frustration over that fact on his late brother's widow."

"Ah. Now I see."

He didn't know what she saw. How could his brief introduction to Cat's situation have told her anything of importance?

She took up her sewing again, effectively dismissing him. He would not be dismissed, however. He had to leave in the morning and he couldn't go with a clear conscience if his mother and Cat got off to a turbulent start.

He strode to the window and looked out upon the driveway and the knot garden to its left with the low hedges and roses in full bloom. Cat had told him she enjoyed being in the garden. If the weather stayed pleasant and his mother became difficult while he was away, at least she had somewhere to retreat to.

"You don't approve," he said, leaning on the window sill.

She took so long to answer he wondered if her hearing was failing. "Young men should not be allowed to choose their own wives."

"I don't see why not. I think I chose rather well."

She paused mid-stitch. She didn't say anything straight away, or make any sound at all, but somehow everyone in that room knew she was displeased. Hughe could hear the maids swallowing from where he stood as they glanced furtively at their mistress.

"Leave us," she told them.

They couldn't get away fast enough. They didn't even bother to pack up their sewing and just left it on their chairs. Hughe waited until they were gone before returning to his mother. He picked up the shirt one of the maids was working on and studied it without really noticing a single thing about it.

"I've got things to do," he said. "If you want to shout at me, get on with it."

"Don't," she bit off. "I allow your glibness most of the time, but not about this. It's much too important."

He set the shirt down on the table and sat on the chair. "Then let's be frank with one another. I am marrying Cat. I've promised her, in front of witnesses, and there's no going back."

"You can get out of a spoken agreement."

"I don't want to."

She pressed her lips together and laid her sewing in her lap. "I don't understand you, Hughe."

"You never have."

To his surprise, she flinched. How could that truth hurt her? They were very different people and she'd had little to do with him throughout his life. He hardly knew her, and she him.

"You've fought me on this issue for years," she said.

"Then you should be pleased that I've finally settled on a bride."

"But why her? I've presented you with so many options from the best families in the country. Beautiful, good girls, and some not so good ones too in the hope they could entice you. Yet none of them pleased you."

He shrugged. "I didn't particularly like them."

"You hadn't even met half of them!"

"Perhaps that was the problem."

"For goodness sakes. You cannot be expected to meet everyone, particularly when I don't even know where you are much of the time, and cannot arrange meetings at the drop of a hat. Your insistence upon being introduced to these girls was an impossible demand."

He shrugged again. There was simply nothing to say to that. She was right. He had wanted to meet his potential bride first, but he was rarely home and never divulged his plans to his mother.

She shook her head. "All of those lovely, eligible girls from excellent families, and you chose a baron's widow. And not even an important baron, but somebody I haven't even heard of."

"To be fair, there are a lot of barons, and her husband wasn't particularly fond of going to court. Secondly, I don't need a rich wife or a well-connected one. I have more money than I know what to do with and enough connections of my own."

"There's no need to boast."

Was there no pleasing her? "I think you get my point."

"I do not. Sometimes it's not about the money and connections they bring. How can I put this?" She searched the ceiling as if she could pluck the answer from the beams. "It's about legacy. The joining of two magnificent families serves to strengthen both and ensure the line remains healthy, long after husband and wife have passed on."

He knew all that of course, but he'd never been very good at doing the right thing. That was why he liked being an assassin. It was perhaps the least acceptable thing for an earl to do, and he reveled in his role. His friends too were not the sort a nobleman should have, but Hughe had never let that worry him. He knew he could trust them with his life and that was all that mattered.

"How many children does she have?"

Her question caught him off guard, although he probably should have seen it coming. Marriage was, after all, about getting heirs. "None."

Her eyes widened. She leaned forward as if she hadn't heard him correctly. "None?

"None."

"You chose a barren wife! Have you lost your mind?"

Sometimes he wondered that himself. "The lack of children could have been her husband's fault. Indeed, I think it may have been, since he had many mistresses and had no children from them either." He'd had his men ask the servants and villagers, and all had reported the same thing. Cat's husband had taken many women to bed over the years and there'd been no children born to any of them that could be attributed to him.

His mother conceded his point with a huff. "It's still a gamble."

"Would you have preferred I bedded her and waited a few months to see the result?"

She didn't answer and he wondered if he'd been right. He knew his mother wanted to ensure the Oxley line wouldn't end with him; she had told him as much on numerous occasions. It was why he felt sure she would come to accept Cat in time. She may not be his mother's choice of bride, but she was the only way he was going to get an heir now. Besides, Cat was amiable. His mother would have loathed sharing her home with a silly girl.

He stood and kissed her white lace cap. "Whatever you think of my actions, Mother, do not take it out on Cat. Be civil to her."

"I am always civil."

"Then be nice."

She said nothing and Hughe left, wondering if he could waylay their meeting a little longer.

* * *

CAT HAD EXPECTED the dowager countess to be a large woman who looked down on everyone else from a great height. From the answers the maids had given her, as they helped her dress in the dark green gown, Cat had thought her future mother-in-law would resemble a dragon. But she did not.

The woman Hughe presented her to in a pretty chamber on the topmost floor was feeble and small. One side of her face drooped and a walking stick leaned against her chair. Her pale skin was mostly smooth, except around her mouth, eyes and the bridge of her nose where wrinkles gathered. It wasn't any of these things that struck Cat, however. It was her eyes. They were so like her son's, as ice-blue as a frosty February morning. She did not rise when Cat entered, but did look up from her sewing.

Cat curtseyed low.

"You may rise," Lady Oxley said in a tone more imperial than the queen's, despite the slight lisp. "Sit."

Cat sat on the chair one of Lady Oxley's three companions vacated for her. Hughe gave Cat an encouraging wink. If he was nervous about this meeting, he didn't show it.

"You may go, Hughe," his mother said.

"I'd rather stay," he said.

"Nevertheless."

Cat caught his attention and gave him a reassuring smile. He bowed. "It would seem I'm not needed," he said.

All the women watched him go. The dowager's companions were about her age, which must have been fifty or so. They sat on chairs lower than the dowager's, their backs to the wall of windows that overlooked the front drive and the pretty views of Hampshire beyond.

"This is a lovely room," Cat said, meaning it. She could understand why the ladies had been here ever since her arrival, since the dowager was most likely not very mobile.

"Are your eyes good?" Lady Oxley suddenly asked.

Cat blinked. What an odd question. "I, uh, yes."

"Do you sew well?"

"Quite well." Cat's needlework was excellent, but she didn't think it a good time to boast.

The dowager handed her the garment she was working on. "It's a shirt for my…" She cleared her throat as if something had gotten stuck there. "For your betrothed. The light grows too poor for me to continue."

The daylight was indeed fading, but Cat could probably see well enough for another half hour at least. After that, if enough candles were lit, she could continue through the evening. She almost laughed at the thought. Of course candles would be lit and likely dozens upon dozens of them at that. By the look of the opulence greeting her in every room, the expense of candles could be spared. They wouldn't be tallow ones either, she'd wager.

"Has my son shown you around the house?"

"Crane has, my lady. Hughe was busy attending to estate matters."

She arched a brow. "'Hughe?'"

Cat blushed to the roots of her hair. "His lordship asked me to call him that."

The dowager huffed and turned her face away. Cat supposed meeting one's future daughter-in-law was taxing enough, particularly when that daughter-in-law wouldn't have been her first choice. Perhaps not even her hundredth.

The ladies resumed their conversation after a few moments of strained silence. Although they didn't specifically draw Cat into their chatter, she joined in anyway where it felt appropriate to do so. She only wished the dowager would, too. Whether she was always this silent, or whether it was only because Cat was there, she couldn't tell, since the lady had closed her eyes. Perhaps she'd fallen asleep.

When it grew too dark to continue sewing, one of the ladies rose and lit all the candles. Two kitchen maids entered, carrying trays laden with cheese, dried figs and small tarts for supper. Cat looked past them to the doorway, hoping Hughe would join them, but he did not. She ate with Lady Oxley and her companions and wondered when it would be polite to leave. She still had much investigating to do. She'd only tried on two gowns after her bath. One was far too big, the other, the green one she'd left on, was a better fit, although it was somewhat out of fashion.

"You didn't bring many belongings with you," Lady Oxley said, rubbing crumbs from her fingertips. "Only one trunk." So she *had* seen them arrive.

"I brought only what I needed."

"Hmmm."

What did that mean?

"Where did you meet my son, Catherine? May I call you that?"

"I prefer Cat."

"I don't."

Cat sucked in a breath along with some patience. "I met him at Whitehall. Didn't he tell you?"

"You've been to court?"

"Twice."

"As often as that?" The sarcasm dripped from her tongue like poison.

Cat concentrated on her food. She would not be drawn into an argument with this woman. She had a feeling she wouldn't win and it would only make her blood boil more.

"I would have gone more often but Lord Slade didn't like court. He preferred hunting."

"Most men do."

"Hughe doesn't seem to. Does he hunt? There looks to be a lovely forest out there. Is it well stocked?"

The dowager arched her brow again. "It is, but my son doesn't hunt often. He's got more important things to do than pursue animals."

"Of course. I'm sure the estate keeps him busy."

Lady Oxley picked up her wine and pressed the glass to her lips. "Oh no, Catherine. Didn't he tell you? His land steward takes care of the estate. That frees Hughe to pursue...other interests."

Cat lowered her gaze to her trencher. She no longer felt hungry. The last two days had been so pleasant that she'd forgotten about Hughe's 'other interests'—his mistresses. Of course, it was unlikely he'd give them up and she had no right to ask him to do so. Still, she hoped, in time, that he would find all he needed in his wife at home. She lifted her gaze to Lady Oxley's. "Other interests," she echoed, "but not animals."

Lady Oxley flinched, wrinkling her nose. Cat frowned back at her. She got the feeling the dowager hadn't meant to imply that he was pursuing *females*. So what had she been referring to?

"If you'll excuse me," Lady Oxley said. "I'm tired." One of her companions handed her the walking stick then two of them helped her to stand. "Good night, Catherine. I hope the bed is to your liking."

"Thank you, my lady. Good night."

Lady Oxley's ladies flanked her as she slowly hobbled out, leaving Cat alone. After a moment, she picked up one of the candelabras and blew out the others.

She found her way back to her rooms easily enough. Her two maids were sitting together in one of the lesser chambers, altering her new gowns. She sat with them for a while and helped until she sent them off to bed when the younger one yawned.

With both girls sleeping on the truckle beds on her bedchamber floor, Cat doubted Hughe would visit her, so she was surprised when a knock on her door sounded.

"It's me," Hughe called out.

One of the maids opened it and let him in, but he stepped only as far as the end of Cat's bed. "My apologies," he said. "I lost track of time. I had hoped to speak with you tonight, but I see I've woken you. I can only apologize for the intrusion over and over."

"Please, don't," she said, laughing. "It's quite all right." She wanted to tell him he could visit her any time, but she didn't think she knew him well enough for that. Besides, her maids were there and the wedding hadn't yet taken place.

"How did your meeting with my mother go?" he asked.

"As well as can be expected."

"As badly as that?"

She grinned. "It went well enough. She just needs time to adjust to having me here. I'm of the opinion that she wasn't expecting you to bring home a bride."

"True. Usually it's a batch of letters and a new piece of jewelry. Cat," he said, growing serious. "I have to leave tomorrow."

Leave? Already? "Oh." It wasn't her place to ask him why or to plead with him to stay, but she had to bite her tongue to stop her questions.

She waited for him to offer more information, but he didn't. He came around to the side of her bed and took her hand. A jolt of heat and something else whipped through her, setting her body alight. They'd touched before, but either one or both of them had always been wearing gloves. Not this time. To her surprise, his hands weren't soft and fine, but strong and calloused. They weren't a dandy's hands. He bowed then pressed her knuckles to his lips. Now *they* were soft. Warm. She would like to feel those lips on other parts of her body, trailing kisses down her throat, her breasts, her belly, her thighs.

Her breath hitched, the sound audible in the silence.

Hughe jerked upright as if she'd flicked him off. His back and shoulders were as rigid as marble. Perhaps he had been as shocked by the connection as she was. It was too dark to see his eyes, but she imagined them to look smoky with desire and pent-up passion, only because she knew her own told a similar story. Her entire body tingled and it hadn't even been a proper kiss!

"I'll be gone for a week or more," he said quickly, returning to the foot of her bed. He sucked in a deep breath that seemed to ease his rigidity, and flopped down on the mattress near her feet like a rag doll. He lay across ways, his elbow bent and his head propped up on his hand. "We'll wed upon my return and celebrate with a grand feast. There won't be time for most of Mother's friends to get here, but believe me, that's a blessing! It'll be the servants and villagers and a few of my own friends who will absolutely adore a little Cat like you. It'll be quite the party, my dear! I love parties. Don't you?" He patted her toes beneath the covers and stood. "Good night, dear betrothed. Sleep well. See you in a week."

He swept out of her bedchamber before she could utter a word. She blinked after him, wondering what had just happened and why she was still feeling like she'd been hit over the head after such a simple, chaste kiss on the back of her hand.

"Is he always like that?" she asked her maids.

"Don't know, my lady," one said. "He's not at home much and when he is, we see him rarely."

Cat sank back into her pillows with a deep sigh. Once they were wed, would she only see him when he came to her chambers to perform his husbandly duties? And would that be immediately before or after he visited his mistresses?

CHAPTER 7

*H*ughe wasn't gone for a week. He was away for three, although he did write from a village called Sutton Grange to inform Cat he needed to stay longer to attend a wedding. She had much to do in that time, from sewing a new gown to meeting all the servants to preparing for the wedding feast. The entire household was giddy with excitement about the upcoming nuptials between their master and his mysterious betrothed. Cat took great pains to become less mysterious, and she thought she succeeded where the servants were concerned. She had even managed to win over the dowager's companions, who now actively drew her into conversation.

The dowager herself was another matter. She became quieter, rarely engaging in conversation with anyone. She sat in her enormous chair like a queen holding court and either sewed or closed her eyes and slept.

"Are you ill, my lady?" Cat asked her the morning before her wedding was to take place. The sun shone through the windows like a beacon, turning the dowager's silvery hair even whiter. The weather had been fine all week and looked set to continue for the wedding.

"I am quite well," the dowager countess said, without looking up from her sewing.

"Are you worried that Hughe has not yet returned? I admit to being concerned myself. Will he be home in time for the ceremony, do you think?"

"He will be. My son may be many things, Catherine, but he does not give his word lightly. If he promised you that he will be back in time then he will be."

Cat bowed her head. "Of course. I do not doubt it." She returned to her sewing, aware that the eyes of the ladies were on her. All except the dowager's. The stiff old lady was proving to be more difficult to win over than Cat had expected. Even so, she kept trying.

Cat pressed a hand to her stomacher. "I admit that I'm a little anxious now that the wedding is so close."

"Why?" Lady Oxley asked. "You've been married before. You know what to expect in the marriage bed."

Cat's face colored. This was not the sort of conversation she wanted to have with her future mother-in-law. "I do."

"If you are worried that my son will not treat you well after you're married, then let me assure you that he is a gentleman. He doesn't hurt women."

Cat gasped. "I never assumed he did!"

"It makes him a rarity." Lady Oxley punched her needle through the fabric and jerked the thread through so hard that it snapped. With a click of her tongue, she threw the garment into her sewing basket.

The ladies bent their heads lower over their needlework, but Cat watched her future mother-in-law through her lashes. Had Hughe's father been a heavy-handed husband?

"Speaking of how rare he is," the dowager said, finally meeting Cat's gaze with her own cool one. "Did he tell you that he made a new will before he left?"

Cat's heart ground to a halt in her chest. "He's ill?" she whispered.

"Of course not. He likes to be prepared for all eventualities, even that one."

Cat's heart restarted and she drew in a deep breath. "I see." She didn't see at all. She wasn't yet his wife. They shouldn't be having this discussion.

"He told me all about it," his mother said, "since it affects me mostly. You see, under his old will, if he pre-deceased me, I would inherit everything except this house and the surrounding Oxley lands. His cousin, the heir, would get the entailed estate only, which makes up less than a quarter of Hughe's fortune. All Hughe's other properties and interests would be mine. It all goes to you, now."

Cat blinked at her. He had made provisions for her already? "You mean it comes into effect after our wedding," she clarified.

"No, Catherine, I mean from now. From the moment that will was signed by witnesses, as it happens. If my son dies, you inherit the majority of his wealth. He has made provision in his will for me to live in Dower House, at the edge of the village until my death, but you will be the mistress of it and everything else not entailed." She leaned forward a little. Her droopy eye twitched at the corner. "Whether or not you have children."

How remarkable. Cat was Hughe's heiress and they'd not even wed yet! Not too many gentlemen would be so generous to their widows, let alone a fiancée. Stephen certainly hadn't. It meant Cat didn't have to remarry when Hughe died. It meant independence and security forever.

She took a moment to collect her thoughts. The news had rather scattered them.

Lady Oxley gathered up her sewing once more. "Of course, there will be children."

"Of course," Cat muttered, hardly listening. "God willing."

"It is, after all, your duty."

That brought Cat's thoughts snapping back to the conversation. She had to remember to keep her wits about her when in

Lady Oxley's company, or risk being cut down to size with a few choice words. "I am aware of that," she said.

"You eat like a bird," the dowager went on. "Be sure to change that. Fatter women bear children more easily and I have it on good authority that your hips are narrow."

Cat's jaw tightened. "Did you question my maids?"

"They're loyal to me."

One day, hopefully soon, they would be loyal to Cat. She would make sure of it. "Dear Lady Oxley," she said with a sweet smile, "you didn't need to speak to my maids. I would have gladly shown you my hips if you'd only asked."

One of the ladies snickered, but quickly suppressed it when the dowager glared at her.

Fortunately they were all spared Lady Oxley's retort when a maid burst in, her face flushed. "Lord Oxley has returned! He comes now."

Cat stood and crossed to the window. A string of horses followed by two carriages and a cart wound its way like a languidly flowing river up the drive toward the house. Oxley led the way on Charger.

"There are people with him," Cat said, peering down at the riders. All sat tall in their saddles, but one was larger and broader than the others.

"His friends," Lady Oxley said, her tone grating. "So that's where he went."

Cat excused herself and headed down the stairs. She ought to greet her betrothed and his friends as they entered the house. Indeed, she was curious about these gentlemen. It would appear his mother didn't approve of them. Since she didn't approve of Cat either, that made her doubly curious.

She reached the front porch just as Hughe and his friends dismounted and the carriages drew to a stop. Before Cat could see them properly, Hughe bounded up the steps and kissed her on both cheeks.

"My dear! Are you well?"

"Very well, thank you," she said. "How were your travels?"

"Uneventful."

"Uneventful?" echoed one of the men from behind him. "You call my wedding dull?"

"I didn't say dull, I said uneventful. In my book, that's a blessing." Hughe presented the man who'd spoken as Mr. Edward Monk. Mr. Monk's soft gray eyes sparkled at Cat. He bowed and presented his wife, Elizabeth, a pretty woman who smiled warmly at Cat.

A handsome fellow came up the steps, holding a baby, his beautiful wife on his arm. Both sported the most charming smiles as they greeted Cat. Hughe introduced them as Orlando and Susanna Holt. She was instructed to call them all by their first names, because apparently Hughe did.

"So you are the woman who secured the most ridiculous earl in the country!" Orlando declared. "I admire you for putting up with him, my lady." He winked at her and she grinned back.

Hughe grunted. "I seem to recall saying the same thing to your wife when I first met her."

"It is an exercise in patience on occasion," Susanna said with a teasing sigh. "Pay them no mind," she said to Cat. "They're the most frustrating men when they're together. It's best to ignore them until they get it out of their system."

"I'll be sure to remember that," Cat said. "Are you staying long?"

"Only for the wedding. We must return to our farm in a few days."

"We'll remain," Elizabeth Monk said. "Indeed, our new home is your gatehouse."

"Marvelous!" Cat said. Finally some company of her own age! Although the dowager's companions were amiable enough, it would be nice to have a friend nearby. "You must long to settle in."

"I do," Elizabeth said, looping her arm through her new husband's and smiling up at him. He returned the smile and Cat's heart flipped at the love she saw in his eyes.

Another man approached. He was the large fellow she'd spotted, with mountainous shoulders and a broad chest like an ancient gladiator. He had dark skin compared to his friends and black eyes that took in Cat with a brisk, assessing sweep. It wasn't until his friends parted that Cat saw he held the hand of a smallish woman at his side. She left him and came up to Cat.

"It's wonderful to meet you," she said, kissing Cat's cheek. "We do apologize for landing on your doorstep covered in dust. Oxley House is magnificent, isn't it? So many windows!"

Cat laughed. The woman's enthusiasm was contagious. She liked her instantly. She liked all of them.

"This is Lucy Coleclough and her husband," Hughe said. "Call him Cole. Everyone does."

Cole. Why did that name sound familiar?

The dark man nodded, but didn't smile. "Pleased to meet you, Lady Slade."

"Cat," she corrected. "It's my pleasure to meet all of you. Welcome to Oxley House."

It was obvious from their reactions that the three men had been there before, but not their wives. It made her wonder how long they'd each been married, and how their husbands knew Hughe. They were not the sort of men she'd pictured as his friends. None had been introduced with a title, and none were fops like he could be on occasion. Indeed, she'd never met three more masculine men in her life, except perhaps for Hislop. Unlike that horrid toad, they were all amiable. Even the big Cole didn't seem threatening, considering his size. Perhaps if he'd been alone she would have been scared, but his wife's vivaciousness softened him. Such a friendly woman could not love a cold-hearted fellow, and by the looks of things, she seemed to adore him and he her.

"Congratulations on your wedding," Cat said to the Monks. She supposed Edward would be considered a retainer if he were to live in the gatehouse. She wished she'd inspected it to ensure it was ready and comfortable for a woman to inhabit.

"It has been the year for weddings," Hughe said on a sigh. "First Orlando and Susanna, then Cole and Lucy, and now the Monks. I was feeling quite left out. But not anymore." He took Cat's hand and rested it on his arm as Elizabeth did to Edward. "I have secured a lovely bride of my own to cherish."

Cat smiled, even though her heart took a dive in her chest. It was all a performance. Every one of them knew it too, because none met her gaze. They must have been told about the odd circumstances of the betrothal. Not a single person would think that Hughe had fallen madly in love with such a plain woman after a brief encounter.

Cat extricated herself from her husband's arm and touched the little foot of the baby protruding from the blanket in his father's arms. "He is quite a lovely little fellow," she said to Susanna. "What's his name?"

"George. Would you like to hold him?"

Cat accepted the little bundle from his father and stroked his soft cheek. She gently rocked him and smiled when he gurgled. She looked up to tell Susanna again that he was beautiful, but caught Hughe watching her, an odd look on his face. She couldn't quite decipher it. Wonder perhaps? She'd not thought him the sort of man enamored of tiny babes, but she could have been mistaken.

"Is everything set for the wedding?" Lucy Coleclough asked. "If not, then we are happy to help in any way we can."

"There's nothing to be done," Cat assured her. "The Oxley servants are very efficient."

"Hughe got them organized, eh?" Orlando said. "That's like him."

"It is? I rather thought it was Lady Oxley's doing."

Orlando and Edward laughed. Cole grunted. "Don't let the limp facade fool you, Cat," Orlando said. "Behind that simpering smile is a man whose ruthless efficiency can accomplish the most complex task in the blink of an eye."

Hughe's lips flattened as he stared at his friend. The cool eyes turned icy and seemed to convey a message that caused Orlando's smile to shrivel. Edward shifted his feet and Cole looked away.

Their wives glanced at one another. Cat got the distinct impression that she was the only one not privy to a secret.

Then Hughe suddenly turned on a bright smile. "I'm sure you all wish to rest after our journey." The hovering servants took that as a signal to approach the guests. "Your trunks should already be in your chambers, dear ladies. Be sure to ask for anything you desire and it will be granted."

Cat passed the baby to his mother and watched them leave. She was left alone in the great empty hall with her betrothed, and suddenly didn't know what to do or say. It was a rude reminder that they were still very much strangers.

"I hope the last few weeks haven't been too trying," he said to her in a formal tone that made her heart sink. She longed for some sort of intimacy, especially after seeing the way he treated his friends and they him.

"Not at all," she said. "I thought about you every day," she ventured.

"And I you. My mother didn't test your patience?"

He wanted to discuss his *mother*? What did Cat need to say to get him to notice *her*? "She has been of great assistance in preparing my wedding gown."

"Hmmm." It wasn't the answer she wanted, but it was all she would get. Cat didn't want to cause difficulties between mother and son, and anyway, she thought the dowager had been quite restrained in her opinions considering she was about to lose her status of mistress of the house to a woman she considered far beneath her.

"Do you want for anything?" he asked. "Be sure to let the servants know what you like and they'll fetch it for you."

"Everything is perfect. Thank you, Hughe. I am glad you're back safely." She bit the inside of her lip, unsure how to say what she wanted to say. How did a lady go about asking her intended to come to her bed? "I missed you."

He smiled. "And I missed you. Your company delights me."

She took his hand and was glad that he didn't try to avoid the connection. "I hope to get to know you better."

"Of course you will! We have a lifetime together."

Her smile grew tight, her insides hollow. He didn't understand her meaning at all. "I would like to get to know you...intimately."

The muscles in his face changed. The slackness vanished, his eyes opened just that little bit wider, and his mouth turned serious. She was beginning to recognize that these signs signaled the shedding of his foppishness.

"And I you," he murmured. "Very much."

She stepped closer and cupped his face. His eyelashes fluttered closed and he breathed deeply as if he could inhale her essence. It thrilled her, bolstered her confidence. Perhaps he did desire her after all. She desperately wanted him to. To have such a man as this *want* to be in her bed would fill her so completely that she might burst with the fullness in her heart. Yet surely she was dreaming.

"Beginning tonight," she said in a throaty voice.

His eyes opened and he gently withdrew her hand, kissed it then let go. She thought she heard a little sigh, but she could have been mistaken. "A gentleman ought to stay away from his betrothed on the eve of their wedding," he said. "I dare not keep you awake the night before such a long day. It's only one night, Cat."

Then what did one night matter? She kept her disappointment hidden behind a smile. "Of course. I understand."

"Tomorrow night. I promise. For now, I must see my mother or I'll be the worst son in the world."

She watched him go with a sinking heart, unsure what to think. She had just invited him to share her bed, but he'd refused. What sort of man did that? Tomorrow night was only one more night, yet it felt like a lifetime away. She hadn't realized it, but she now knew that she desperately wanted to hold her husband in her arms and be held by him in return. She wanted to be kissed by him again and again, and wanted him inside her, claiming her.

She had fallen in love with him, and fallen heavily. Not having that love returned was going to make for a very long and unfulfilling marriage.

* * *

CAT GAVE up trying to sleep some time after retiring for the night. All was in order for the morning, yet she couldn't stop thinking about the wedding, about Hughe, about the life ahead of her as Lady Oxley. About their wedding night.

Did he desire her or not? Was that smokiness in his eyes genuine, or was he playing a part? He was a most mysterious man. Added to which, she got the feeling his friends knew something about him that she did not. It was vexing.

She tossed and turned until she could stand it no longer. She threw a house coat around her shoulders and slipped quietly out of her bedchamber, careful not to disturb the sleeping maids.

She lit a candle and made her way to the stairs with the intention of going up to the tower room where she could look out at the night sky. It was what she'd often done from her chamber at Slade Hall to settle her nerves. The stars and moon were a peaceful reminder that the world continued on, no matter what happened in the lives of mortals below.

She didn't reach the stairs, however. Light flickered from beneath Hughe's study door. Deep male voices came from beyond, loud enough for her to hear if she put her ear to the wood. She only did it to see if she *could* hear, but when she heard her name, she paused. If they were discussing her, then she ought to know what they said. She might learn something about her future husband.

"When are you going to tell Cat?" Edward Monk asked.

There was a long pause before Hughe answered. "I'm not."

"What?" Orlando spluttered. "Are you mad? Tell her, man!"

"She has a right to know," came Cole's deep, commanding voice.

"I beg to differ." Hughe met his tone with a steely one of his own.

"Husbands and wives shouldn't have secrets from one another," Orlando said. "Trust me when I tell you, it never ends well."

"It ended well enough for you," Hughe said.

"After more drama than I care to endure again, and then I did tell her."

"Your situation is not as bad as mine."

"Stop playing the fool with her," Edward said. "She doesn't deserve to think her husband a fop when he's not."

"He's right," said Cole.

Hughe snorted. "An expert on women's opinions now, are you?"

"More so than you, it would seem. Holt's right. Tell her. Tell her everything or your marriage won't go well for either of you."

"Christ, this is an ambush," Hughe muttered so quietly that Cat had to strain to hear him. "Listen to me. It seems I have to explain some matters to you dim-wits. Your marriages are based on love and trust. Mine isn't."

Cat felt like a hole had been punched in her chest. She bit her wobbly lip and willed her tears not to spill. He was right. Of course he was. Hughe hardly knew her, it wasn't fair for her to expect him to love her just because she already loved him.

"You might grow to love her in time," Edward said. "She seems like a nice sort."

"She is nice. That's why I'm marrying her. I needed a nice, agreeable wife of *my* choice. Besides, I had to do it. You all know why."

Had to? Why did he have to? Because he was worried about leaving her with Slade and Hislop?

"But things are different for me than they are for you," he went on. "My marriage will be different."

"It doesn't have to be."

"It does. It was my duty to marry, but the other part of my life must remain separate."

Did he mean his mistresses? As if her heart didn't hurt enough, now it felt like it was being pierced with a needle over and over.

"I am not the romantic type," he said. "Not like all of you."

"Are you calling *me* a romantic?" Cole growled. Cat pictured the big brute leaning over Hughe, fists poised to thump him.

"As it happens, I am," Hughe said. There was a commotion inside that had Cat worrying about her betrothed's handsome face. Fortunately, his grunt was one of laughter, not pain. "Marriage is making you slow, Cole."

"I won't miss next time you call me a bloody romantic."

"My point is, I am not the sentimental type. You were right earlier. I am ruthless."

"Aye," came Orlando's heavy answer. "You are that. None of us doubt it."

Cat swallowed. His tone worried her. In what way was Hughe ruthless? He'd been nothing but gentlemanly to her. And yet she remembered the way he'd dealt with her attackers in London, and Hislop when he'd threatened her. Not even that cruel man had dared challenge Hughe. These three gentlemen, his friends, must have seen what she'd seen in Hughe's eyes at those moments—a cold, calculating anger that he barely had under control.

"Yet that doesn't mean you can't fall in love with your wife," Orlando went on. "Indeed, I'd like to put a wager on it."

"Don't," Hughe snarled. "Don't treat this lightly, or her. If you want to know the truth, then I'll tell you. I won't fall in love with my wife because I don't find her desirable. You've seen the sort of woman I take to my bed. Cat is the complete opposite."

Cat reeled backward. She blinked at the door, but it wasn't enough to keep the hot tears at bay. She swiped them away, only to have more take their place. His words raked over her skin like a sharp trident, tearing at her, wanting to gouge out her aching heart. She clutched her housecoat over her chest—her flat, pathetic chest—and fled. She ran back to her room, slipped under the bedcovers and cried softly into the pillow.

* * *

HUGHE FELT sick and a little lightheaded. The wine was too strong. He'd opened one of his best to share with his friends, and this was how they repaid him. By forcing him to say things he regretted as soon as the words were out of his mouth.

Yet he couldn't take them back. Not now and not in front of them. They were so smug with their troubles behind them and their lovely wives tucked up in their beds, waiting for them to return.

Christ. Cat had wanted him in her bed tonight too. He could have had his own lovely wife waiting for him. Could have eased the ache that had set up residence in his groin ever since catching sight of her on the front porch that afternoon. He'd not thought little Cat would take his breath away, but she did. Every time she touched him, he felt something shift inside him. Every time she smiled, he wanted to smile back. Every time desire filled her eyes he wanted to take her and kiss her and make her his own.

But he did not. Tomorrow night he could, but he was going to be ready for her then. He was not ready for her tonight. Not after drinking a skinful of strong wine. He knew he couldn't keep his heart closed and his mind on the task of making an heir while he was drunk. Duty. That's what this marriage was about. Duty, heirs and making sure she never found out he married her because he felt guilty for killing her first husband.

"Congratulations," Monk said with a shake of his head. "That was possibly the most foolish thing I've ever heard you say, and you've said a lot of foolish things."

Hughe watched Cole's fists, just in case he decided to use them again. He'd dodged the first blow, but only just. Love and marriage hadn't made him slow in the least. He was as dangerous as ever. "Cat is the opposite of what I like in a woman," Hughe said. "The evidence is before you in Lady Fitzwilliam, Lady Crewe, Lady Duckworth—"

"Enough," Orlando said, sounding bored. He refilled Hughe's glass.

Hughe threw it down in one gulp. If ever there was a night he needed to drink to excess it was tonight. He was getting married in the morning. Married! Tomorrow night and every night he was in Cat's company, he was going to remain as sober as a monk. He eyed Monk and snorted. Damned romantic fool.

"The thing is," Orlando was saying, "you're not with any of those ladies anymore." He smiled slyly, as if he'd won an argument. So did Cole and Monk. "Which proves that they're not your type after all."

Hughe dug his hands into his hair and held onto his aching scalp. "Stop talking in riddles."

"You could have had any unwed lady in the kingdom, yet you chose Cat, the very woman you should have stayed away from after assassinating her husband."

"No. I told you. That's *why* I married her."

Orlando, the pretty prick, laughed. "You *chose* her, Hughe. Open your eyes—"

"If you tell me to look into my heart, I'll thump you. I know why I chose Cat. She was in a bad situation, thanks to me."

"And me," Cole said. "Should I marry her too? I'll warn you, Lucy won't like that. She might look sweet, but I wouldn't cross her on this if I were you. She's grown quite attached to me."

He sounded so annoyingly smug. They all did. They thought Hughe was like them, when he wasn't. He wasn't soft, he wasn't romantic, and he had certainly never loved anyone, nor would he. Not even his mother. Now *that* would shock them if he told them.

"She's not the sort of woman I like to keep me warm," he said again, yawning. Maybe if he kept telling them that, they'd give up and leave him alone. He was tired. Tomorrow, his life changed forever. He needed to sleep to get through the madness.

"That's what we're trying to tell you!" Monk said. "You chose her to marry, not to fuck."

"I do want to fuck her," he slurred. Too late, he realized he'd said too much. He'd given them more ammunition. Damned wine.

His friends laughed. "Get up," Cole said, rising. "I'll carry you back to your bedchamber like the pathetic boy you are."

"No," Monk said. "Let him find his own way." He winked at Cole and Cole smiled back.

Hughe had the distinct feeling he'd missed something important. Not surprising, since he was too drunk and too tired to think straight. Maybe he'd even nodded off for a moment or two.

Orlando opened the door and somebody took him by the elbow and steered him out. Despite saying they wouldn't escort back to his own rooms, Cole marched him away from the study. He let Hughe go just outside a door then deserted him. They all did.

It took another moment before Hughe realized whose door he stood outside. Cat's.

The pricks. They'd done that on purpose. Well, more fool them because Hughe wasn't drunk enough to do something *that* foolish. He wasn't going inside. Cat would be asleep and he didn't want to disturb her before her wedding day. He meant it earlier when he told her she would need her strength. It was going to be a long day tomorrow. He was only ever going to marry once and he was going to make sure the wedding feast reflected it.

But first, perhaps he could take a peek at his betrothed's sleeping form.

He opened the door. The two maids snored softly on their truckle beds, but there was another sound that had his heart stopping. He strained to hear. Perhaps he'd make a mistake. He hoped he had.

But there it was again, the soft gasps of someone sobbing. Cat was crying.

CHAPTER 8

*H*ughe crept to the bed, mindful of not waking the maids. He was good at creeping. He'd done quite a lot of it over the years. Usually when he reached his target, he would slit their throat, but this time he lay gently down on the bed behind Cat. She didn't move, but she must have known he was there. Her tears ceased. Her breathing seemed to have stopped too. She was as still as a stone, but even through the bed linen separating them, he could feel her warmth and softness. He sidled closer until her back was against his chest and rested his hand on the curve of her hip. A shudder rippled through her and he had an urge to hold her until it subsided. He circled his arm around her, trapping her against his body.

"Poor little Cat," he whispered in her ear. "Don't cry." He nuzzled into her neck and breathed in her scent. She must have bathed in rosewater. It was intoxicating and filled his head completely. Or perhaps he was still reeling from the effects of that damned wine. He trailed his fingers lightly up and down her bare arm. The skin was soft, silky. He'd known it would be.

Other parts of her would be soft too. Like her throat, her nipples, the inside of her thigh. He grew hard thinking about touching her there, licking her, testing just how silky she could be. His cock felt hot and thick, the ache almost unbearable.

He shifted to alleviate the pressure in his groin, but ended up with her arse right *there*. God's blood, she had the most delectable little behind. He wanted to slide his cock against it, slip underneath her—

No. Not tonight. Not while she was upset. It was the eve of their wedding no less! She wouldn't want a great oaf of a drunkard prodding his hard cock at her. He must restrain himself, no matter how much it hurt.

He sighed against her and kissed the back of her head. She seemed to relax a little into him, which only served to harden him more. He lay there, frustrated beyond belief, and tried to think through the fog left behind by the wine.

How had this happened? When had he begun to desire Cat? Perhaps it began in London when they kissed. Or when she flirted with him with wit and words. Or when he'd seen the bruise Hislop had inflicted or when he'd seen her holding little George Holt. He wasn't sure. It had happened in small increments over time to take him by surprise.

Bloody hell. He tried to tell himself that desiring his wife was good for their marriage, but only a fool would believe that. Desiring Cat now would cause complications. He was supposed to keep his distance from her. Supposed to keep her happy, do his husbandly duty to get her with child, then leave her alone. He'd killed her first husband! He'd been the architect of her poverty and misery. She would hate him if she learned the truth, perhaps fear him too, and he couldn't bear that. Not now that he'd begun to like her.

"Don't cry, my little Cat," he murmured. She must be upset because of his mother. She could be a dragon when she wanted to be. He'd been the target of her waspish tongue on many occasions and knew what she was like. He was used to her ways, though. Cat was not. "I'll have a word with her in the morning. She won't dare to speak to you like that again."

Cat frowned. He thought she was crying over something the dowager said? Did his drunkenness make him blind as well as stupid? Perhaps it did. She'd seen what too much wine could do to a man. Although, to be fair, when Stephen was drunk, he would come to her bedchamber and tumble her roughly until he reached satisfaction. Hughe did the opposite, despite the rod prodding her rear. If only he would give in to the urge. If only he wanted her enough to take her before they were wed.

Clearly he didn't, or that erection would have been sated by now. Hughe might like her, he might want to comfort her when she was upset, or protect her when she was in danger, but he did not want more. He did not return her love.

His breathing deepened. His hard chest rose and fell against her back to an even, steady rhythm. His manhood deflated and the arm circling her grew heavy. He was asleep.

Cat closed her eyes and tried to sleep too, but her aching heart kept her awake for some time. She must have succumbed eventually, because the next thing she knew her maids were rousing her and Hughe was gone.

It was their wedding day.

* * *

THE WEDDING of Lord Oxley was held in the family chapel in the presence of the groom's intimate friends, some neighboring farmers, a few villagers and the higher servants. The lack of nobility was noted, but everyone there chose to dismiss it as inevitable since the marriage happened quickly. The ceremony itself was a somber affair, but the revelry at the feast afterward made up for it.

By the end of the day, when it was time for the bride and groom to retire to their chambers, many of the villagers, farmers and servants were dead drunk in Oxley House's great hall. Some had fallen asleep under the table, or out in the garden since it was a lovely evening. The village alderman still sat at the table, his head on his trencher, snoring into a pile of pheasant bones. The dowager countess had picked her way around them earlier in the afternoon and disappeared with her ladies into a quieter part of the house, displeasure written over her face. It was rumored that she was displeased with more than just the drunks, however. The lack of noble guests, for one thing, and her son's choice of bride for another.

But her stern countenance didn't put a dampener on the event. Everyone seemed to be enjoying themselves, and if anyone noticed that Lord Oxley's friends remained sober, they didn't care. If anyone noticed the new bride's sad eyes as she looked up at her husband, they didn't say so. What they did comment upon was how pretty she looked in her wedding gown. Prior to that day, most of her dresses had been too large for such a slight figure, but the blue satin gown fit her like a glove and showed off her tiny waist.

The couple was sent upstairs with a bawdy song that roused the drunks and would have made the dowager countess's lips purse if she'd still been there. The new Lord and Lady Oxley waved at their guests from the landing, then Lord Oxley picked up his new bride and with a "Whoop," carried her out of sight.

Hughe set Cat down on her feet just inside her bedchamber and shut the door on the cheering crowd. "They'll quieten soon," he said with an apologetic smile.

Cat had hoped to be taken to his rooms, but it would seem he preferred to bed her in hers. She still resided in the guest chambers, where she'd been since her arrival. His mother was yet to move out of the mistress's apartments. Cat didn't mind. She liked these rooms. They were closer to Hughe's.

"At least we're alone," she said. The maids had been given the night off, their beds tucked away. They'd lit enough candles to see by and strewn extra lavender among the rush matting. The bed covers were turned down, inviting.

"Do you need help undressing?" he asked.

She turned her back to him. "There are pins there," she said, pointing to her lower back where skirt met bodice. "If you wouldn't mind."

He unpinned her. The skirt, underskirt and forepart fell away. He collected the items and the sleeves she handed him and carried them into her wardrobe.

"Did you enjoy the feast?" he asked, returning. His gaze didn't quite focus on her, but a little past her, as if he couldn't even look at her. This was going to a tortuous coupling then.

"I did," she said. "The food was plentiful and delicious. Your friends and their wives are a delight. I'm so glad they came, and that the Monks will be staying. I know I'm going to get along with Elizabeth."

"They all like you," he said, standing before her. "Do you need help with the bodice?"

"No, thank you." She untied the laces down her front and separated the two pieces. He took them from her and carried them into the wardrobe too. She stood in her long shirt and slipped off her shoes. Hughe helped her with the necklace he'd presented to her that morning. It was an exquisite gold chain with a large oval sapphire at the center and smaller sapphires at intervals along the chain. She hadn't noticed until he'd taken her hand in the chapel that the sapphire ring he always wore was missing. It was then that she realized the gem now occupied the center of her new necklace.

She removed the matching earrings that he'd also given her that morning, and the rings. The jewels were a sharp reminder that she had done very well out the union and he'd fared poorly. She'd brought nothing of value to the marriage.

"Would you like me to disrobe before you remove your shirt?" he asked.

"I think that would be best."

It was all too formal, too awkward, too wrong. She wanted him to tear at her clothes, eager to see the package inside. She would have settled for a gentle unlacing. She hated this passionless process, as if he were ticking off each garment from a list. There was no desire in his voice, no heat in his eyes, not even an erection.

Unlike the previous night. Clearly he only desired her when he was too drunk to see properly.

At first she didn't watch as he removed his clothes, but then she decided he was her husband and she had a right to see him naked. She *wanted* to see him naked. She wasn't sure how many more opportunities she would get. By all accounts, he was rarely home.

He shed his doublet, jerkin, shoes and breeches, and, like her, stood in only his shirt. He gathered up the sides and drew it over his head without further ado. He stood there, entirely, gloriously naked, the shirt bunched in his hand. Her breath escaped in a *whoosh*. Her heart tripped over itself. She'd never seen a man like Hughe before. To put it baldly, her new husband was as magnificent as any life-sized statue of a god. Muscles corded across his shoulders and rippled down his arms. The skin looked as smooth as marble, but golden, not pale. A sprinkling of hair the same shade as that on his head covered his broad chest and arrowed down his torso to his manhood, jutting out from its nest.

Cat blushed to the roots of her hair. He hadn't been aroused when he'd first removed his shirt, but after her admiring gaze, his member came alive. Perhaps it needed attention to get started. It hadn't last night.

She removed her own shirt and took some time to fold it and set it neatly aside, giving her time to cool down. By the time she turned to face him, she was more composed. She was no innocent maiden and it wouldn't do to act like one. It took great force of will not to cover her body up, but she managed it.

He wasn't looking anyway. He moved to the bed and sat with his long, muscular legs crossed at the ankles. A white, ridged scar ran the entire length of his thigh. The wound must have hurt when it had been fresh. Finally, he lifted his gaze to hers. He did not look at her breasts or any other part of her. Only her face. He held out his hand. "Come here, Lady Oxley."

She took his hand and knelt on the bed beside him. It had been almost a year since she'd made love to a man. Lord Slade had not come to her in the last months of his life, preferring his mistress's company. He'd given up on getting Cat with child and it would seem he'd lost his taste for her too.

"Tell me what you like," she said. "Tell me how to please you."

"Do whatever pleases you," he said, still smiling as if he were listening to a polite conversation.

What pleased *her*? That wasn't what coupling was about. It was about the man's pleasure, so that he could plant his seed inside her. She would simply enjoy the intimacy of being close to him, holding him and being claimed by him.

A small frown lined his forehead and a kernel of panic punctured her chest. What was she doing wrong? She lay down, her hands by her sides, yet he didn't move to cover her with his body. Perhaps he preferred it the other way. She went to roll over, but he placed a hand on her shoulder.

"Cat." His thumb gently stroked her in slow circles. His gaze focused on it, but it was bland and not at all heated with desire. His member had deflated again too. Her nakedness didn't appeal to him. "Cat, did your husband never see to your pleasure?"

"I don't want to discuss him. You are my husband now."

He blew out a breath. "My apologies. I don't want to upset you."

"You're not upsetting me." She sat up and his gaze lowered to her chest. She placed a hand across her breasts and not for the first time wished they were larger so she could display them proudly. His gaze shifted away to the bed. He couldn't even look at her.

Tears stung her eyes. It was all falling apart. Her dream husband, her dream house and life…it was over before it had really begun.

But she wouldn't give up so easily. She *had* to secure him as soon as possible. A marriage wasn't solid until it was consummated. She would consummate it this night if she had to turn somersaults to do it.

She shuffled across the bed and extinguished one of the candles.

"Good idea," he muttered, putting out the others. The room was as dark as a moonless night. Even when her eyes adjusted, she could only make out his shape and not his features.

It would be easier for him to do his duty if he couldn't see her pathetic body. To her utter relief, he touched her. First her shoulder, as if he were searching for her in the dark, then down past the curve of her breast to her waist. His light fingers skimmed across her skin, sending a wave of tingles skittering in their wake.

"Silky," he said on a breath. "You have beautiful skin, Cat."

Oh yes, putting out the candles had been an excellent idea.

His hand traveled up her middle and cupped her breast. She expected him to sigh with disappointment and move on, but he didn't. He thrummed her nipple with his thumb, teasing it to a point. Heat throbbed in her veins, spreading to every inch of her body. Exquisite tension rose, tightened, curled. She wanted more of it, yet it drove her mad. She would surely lose her mind if he continued.

She moaned and was shocked at her wantonness. She moved away, suddenly ashamed. Stephen had never paid her breasts any attention, except for when he'd first seen them. *He* had sighed with disappointment. After that, he simply ignored them.

"Don't," Hughe said, voice thick. "Come here. I want to touch your nipples."

She kept out of his reach and covered her breasts again, even though he couldn't see her in the dark. "Why?"

"Why?" he echoed, sounding confused. "Why wouldn't I?"

Was he teasing her? Was this his way of pointing out her deficiencies? "Because they're small. Boyish, so I've been told."

He laughed softly and her heart sank further. Tears hovered close. "Cat," he murmured, "I've never seen a boy with such plump, ripe nipples before."

"I'm not talking about the nipples, I—"

He was suddenly right there, kissing her, swallowing her protest. But he ended it too soon. He took both her hands in one of his and gently drew them behind her back. And then her left nipple became wet. He was licking it! She tried to squirm away, but he didn't allow her to move, trapped as she was. His tongue circled her nipple, teasing it to a point. Then he drew it into his warm mouth and suckled. If his touch sent tingles washing through her, his mouth drove her to the edge of a precipice. She wouldn't have cared if she fell into it. She *wanted* to. Her mind filled with him, only thoughts of him, and her body was alive like it had never been before.

She arched into him, wanting him to keep going, to suckle the other nipple. She wanted to tell him that she liked it very much, but the words wouldn't form. Her head had turned to mush, yet her body was alert like never before. Every lick of his tongue brought her closer to the edge, and then he would retreat, giving her time to step back and recover, only to close his mouth over the nipple entirely and nip it with his teeth.

Maddening.

She was wet for him, throbbed for him. "Hughe," she whimpered. She wanted to tell him to take her, but she couldn't speak. He finally let her hands go, but instead of covering herself, she reached down to his member. Her fingers circled the smooth, ridged shaft, so thick and long.

He sucked air between his teeth and let it out on a groan. She smiled. This night was going to be wonderful after all.

Hughe cursed silently. This night was not going to plan at all. Cat was a siren and he was helplessly drawn to her. When she'd removed her shirt he thought his cock would explode. Her body was everything he'd imagined it to be. Better. Her narrow waist exaggerated the swell of her hips and rear, and her nipples...dear lord, her nipples were the color of ripe cherries and just as plump. He couldn't resist taking one in his mouth and tasting it. Her response swelled his cock even more.

He had hoped extinguishing the candles would help him maintain composure while he performed his husbandly duty. Surely if he couldn't see her eyes, he wouldn't lose himself in them. But he hadn't counted on her breathy reaction to his suckling, hadn't expected her to open herself to him, be so wet for him. Nor could he have known that simply touching her would make him harder than he'd ever been. She had the body of a nymph, and she was using it to bring him near release. And he'd not even entered her yet.

"Take me," she whispered. "Take me, husband." She guided his cock to her opening. She was hot and moist and he ached to enter her. Even more than that, he wanted to hear her cry his name in ecstasy. He wanted her to know what pure, deep pleasure felt like. He wanted to be the one to show her.

He wasn't supposed to want it, but he no longer cared how this night was *supposed* to play out. His plan to maintain control was already shattered. He might as well do everything he wanted to do and suffer the consequences tomorrow.

He did not enter her, even though it hurt like hell. He reached down between their bodies, snaking his rough hands over her smooth stomach to her curls. He touched one finger to her nub and she gasped. Her fingers dug through his hair and she drew his face to hers.

He kissed her. It was no less magical than when they'd kissed in London, but much sweeter, gentler. Her tongue darted out to meet his and together they deepened the kiss.

He pressed his thumb into her folds and she clasped his shoulders. Her fingers dug into his skin, pinning him. Her legs parted and he slipped his thumb all the way into her slickness. He rubbed the nub and her body arched higher, higher. Her breath quickened. Her thighs trembled. He could feel her tighten against him and feel the moment her release hit.

She broke the kiss and cried out in surprise. She throbbed around his fingers, against his knuckles, and threw her body back into the mattress. His arm was beneath her, cradling her.

"Did my little Cat like that?" he murmured, skimming his lips over her nipples. He breathed deeply, drawing in the scent of her slaked desire.

"Mmmmm," she murmured between her heavy breaths. "That was...I am...you are... Dear God."

He chuckled and nipped her nipple with his teeth. "A mere man."

Her slender hand wrapped around his cock and he almost burst. He had to get inside her *now*. He wanted to couple with her while she was still trembling from her release. He found her mouth in the darkness and kissed her thoroughly as he slipped his throbbing cock all the way in to the hilt.

They moaned together, and he tightened his hold on her, trapping her against his body. He would not allow even the smallest space to separate them. She was his wife now. All his.

He kept that thought with him as he rocked with her, drawing in and out, as slowly as possible. It was hell, but he managed to be gentle and not end too soon.

But his resolve fled when she wrapped her legs and arms around him and held him as tightly as he held her. It was a simple gesture and she probably wasn't aware she'd even done it, but it made his heart swell. His cock too. She wanted him and there was no place he'd rather be than inside his wife.

The tension coiled in his belly and shot to his groin. Everything tightened until he thought he'd fray like a rope pulled too hard. Then, finally, he crested the wave and the release slammed him. He spurted into her. He might have growled or moaned or shouted, but he couldn't be sure. He didn't care. All he cared about was staying inside his wife for as long as possible and holding her in his arms while he climbed down from the great heights she'd taken him to.

They lay together, side by side, still joined. She tucked her head beneath his chin and pressed her lips to his throat. Their arms and legs remained entwined so it was impossible to tell where each body began and ended. He closed his eyes and enjoyed the feel of her heart pounding against his ribs. Its beat slowed after a while and her breathing grew less ragged. She was asleep.

His wife. In his arms. Sated. And blissfully unaware that he was cursing himself. Now that his own thirst was slaked, he could think clearly again.

Hell and damnation. He'd just bedded the widow of the man he'd killed and he'd *liked* it. No, not liked. That didn't begin to explain the consuming passion, the sheer delight he'd felt in taking her, and the possessiveness he felt toward her now. He'd reveled in their love making, in Cat, and now he was going to pay the price in guilt.

Guilt for killing her husband. Guilt for not telling her his greatest secret.

* * *

FOR THE SECOND morning in a row, Cat woke up without Hughe beside her when he'd been there the night before. She touched the empty space. It was cold. Perhaps it meant nothing. Perhaps he simply liked sleeping in his own bed. He had enjoyed their coupling, she was quite certain of that.

But had he enjoyed it to the same level as Cat?

She was drunk on him. Her body felt loose and wonderful, womanly. There was no soreness, no shame, no regret. She had not known that a man could give a woman such pleasure with a few teasing licks and touches. Hughe had held her as she crashed into the abyss, as if she were the most precious thing he owned. He had cherished her, taken delight in her, shown wonder at her response.

So why wasn't he there when she'd woken?

Her maids helped her wash and dress, and then she went in search of her husband.

Some of the revelers were still in the great hall, holding their aching heads or still sleeping on the benches. She found Hughe crossing the courtyard with his four friends. They were an impressive sight, their riding capes billowing behind them, like avenging angels, or the four horsemen of the apocalypse.

Hughe greeted her with a smile and a chaste kiss on her forehead. "Dear wife," he said in that simpering tone she loathed. "Are you well?"

"Thank you, I am."

"What will you do today?"

She frowned at him, wishing he would dispense with the ridiculously formal conversation and just kiss her thoroughly. This was not the man who'd claimed her last night and held her tenderly in his arms as if he couldn't bear to let her go.

"I thought I might help Elizabeth settle into the gatehouse."

"An excellent notion! I believe she's there now, with Susanna and Lucy." He kissed the top of her head again. "I'll see you at dinner."

He went to walk off, but she caught his hand. He swallowed heavily and tilted his head to the side in question. "Hughe, will you come to me again tonight?" she asked, keeping her voice low.

His false smile slipped a little. He gave a barely noticeable nod. "I have to," he said simply. He slipped his hand from hers and left with his friends.

He *had* to? Well, of course he would want to be certain that his seed was planted in her. But that was a rather odd way of putting it after the passion of the previous night. There'd been no light in his eyes, no knowing smile on his lips. He'd been cool and distant, as if bedding her was simply another activity to tick off his list for the day.

It seemed she would have to seduce her husband all over again.

* * *

SHE MADE love to Hughe again that night. It was as beautiful and wonderful as their first time, yet once again he was gone in the morning and cool to her during the day. The following night, he came to her again and they coupled in a frenzy, standing up against the wall. The fourth night, he was slower, gentler, but no less hungry for her. He took delight in trailing his tongue over the curve of her back and buttocks and they made love while he cradled her from behind. They slept in the same position, but he was gone before dawn.

Every night for the next week, he came to her, drove her to the edge and held her tenderly as she rode the waves of passion and collapsed in his arms, sated. They made love with the candles blazing because he wanted to see her body, so different to that first night. She no longer felt too thin or plain beneath his hot gaze. He made her feel like the most beautiful woman in the world. Like she was the only woman he could ever desire.

Yet each time she thought she'd finally won him over, he was distant the following day. After two weeks, she'd had enough. She confronted him after he had been out all day with Edward Monk. His other friends had returned to their homes, but Edward and Elizabeth remained in the gatehouse.

Cat waited until the men parted at the stables, then intercepted Hughe as he crossed the courtyard. "We cannot go on like this," she said, hands on hips. She felt like a shrew, but so be it. He'd driven her to the point of sheer frustration.

"Like what, my dear?"

"Like…like strangers!"

He pouted in thought. "We are?"

"Yes! You love me at night and treat me like…like a sister during the day."

The light in his eyes dimmed, but only for a moment, and then it returned, brighter than before. "A sister! My dear, I rather think I wouldn't like a sister. Domineering creatures, so I've been told, always telling a fellow what he can and can't do. I already have one of those females in my life. No, I much prefer my little Cat wife." He tapped the end of her nose, just like an amiable brother would.

"Hughe," she said, softer, trying to turn the discussion into a more serious one. But she didn't continue. How to explain that she wanted things to be different between them? He saw that she had everything she needed. She had lovely clothes, sweet maids, a friend in Elizabeth Monk, and every comfort a woman could desire. He was cheerful, undemanding, and pleasured her at night. She was fortunate.

Yet something was lacking. She saw the way Edward looked at Elizabeth when he returned from a ride. He would kiss her thoroughly on the lips, as if they'd been parted a month. They stared into one another's eyes as if there was no one else in the world, as if they were enough for one another. Cat wanted that with Hughe. What's more, she knew she could give him that, if only he wanted it in return.

He gave her chaste kisses and friendly pats on the shoulder. He gave her gifts, but not himself. Well, only when he coupled with her. It was as if he lusted for her, yet didn't love her.

"Is it the secret?" she asked.

He laughed. "I have no secrets from you, Little Cat."

"I know you're keeping something from me. I heard you talking with your friends the night before our wedding. You said 'the other part of my life must remain separate.'"

His eyes narrowed ever so slightly. His lips twitched, the smile wavering. Then it returned harder than ever. He laughed again. "Dear wife, you must be mistaken. I do recall I was very drunk that night. Alas, I can't recall what I said to anyone. But I can assure you, I have no secrets from you."

Then why did he not quite meet her gaze as he said it? Why did the pulse in his throat throb? Those small signs that appeared only when he lied to her.

He rested his hands on her shoulders, the way one would to a friend. "You are my heart, dear one. You fill my soul and…other parts of me. La! That was almost poetic, except for that last bit. I have been working on my poetry. Perhaps you could read some and tell me what you think? After all, you and you alone are my inspiration."

He kissed her nose, tossed her a smile, and sauntered off.

She watched him go with her hands on her hips. She didn't trust him one bit. There must be a reason why he continued to behave coolly toward her, and she was determined to learn what it was.

CHAPTER 9

"We'll leave tomorrow," Hughe announced to Monk. "I see no alternative."

Monk glanced at Elizabeth, sitting next to him in Hughe's study. Hughe still found it strange, including his friend's wife in their work, but there was no way around it. Both she and Monk insisted on her involvement. This was the first assignment for the three of them. At least it wasn't an assassination; more of a rescue mission.

"Agreed," Monk said heavily with another longing glance at his wife. She frowned down at the hands folded in her lap, the picture of a demure female. Yet Elizabeth Monk was anything but demure.

"It will seem odd for us to return to Sutton Grange so soon after our last visit," Hughe said. "We need to think of a valid reason to give Lynden and others."

"I have a suggestion," Elizabeth said, looking up. "We can tell Jeffrey that I miss my friends and wanted to visit them."

"You're not coming," both Hughe and Monk said together.

"Why not? I'll be safely tucked away at Sutton Hall with my dull cousin, far from Larkham."

Hughe leaned over the desk. "Elizabeth, you don't need to

come. Stay here and settle into your new home. We won't be gone long and I'll take good care of him."

Monk snorted. "I don't need mothering."

Elizabeth lowered her head again and studied her fingers. "I want to be near my husband while I still can. One day, when we have children, that won't be possible, but for now, I'd rather not be parted."

Monk covered her hands with his own and she smiled up at him. He smiled back. "She's coming," he told Hughe.

Hughe recognized a losing battle and surrendered. At least she would be out of harm's way at Sutton Hall. "That story will account for you and Monk being there, but not me. No one will believe that I miss Cole and Orlando."

"You don't have to come," Monk said. "I can get Widow Renny and her sons out of Larkham on my own."

Hughe shook his head. "Their predicament is partly my mess in the first place, and I want to see them happily resettled." The rescue mission wasn't for someone in Sutton Grange, but the neighboring village of Larkham. Hughe had organized for Cole to assassinate Widow Renny's husband some months ago. The vicious man had raped young women in his village, but had not been brought to justice. Hughe's services had been engaged through his network and he'd sent Cole to kill the cur. Afterward, there'd been problems with Renny's friends. At the time, Hughe thought it had all been smoothed over and the villagers calmed, but he'd just received word from Cole that trouble brewed again. Cole and Orlando had kept an eye on the situation and had learned that the Larkham villagers had turned on the Renny boys, claiming they would one day be just like their father. Widow Renny worried for their lives and had begged Cole to help her and her sons escape.

Hughe had organized the assassination. It was up to him to help them, just like he'd helped Cat after killing her husband.

Cat. He hated leaving her so soon after their wedding. He hoped she would miss him; he knew he would miss her terribly.

Not only their wonderful nights together in her bed, but also their brief encounters during the day. They weren't nearly enough to fulfill him, but it was all he could allow himself. It was bad enough that he couldn't hide his affection during their lovemaking. He needed to be doubly sure to be cool during the day to make up for his weakness.

"Cat can come with us," Elizabeth said. "You can tell Jeffrey that you wanted him to meet your new wife. He'll be so delighted that you think so highly of him that he'll never question it. It will also solve the problem of Cat missing you too much."

"She won't miss me," Hughe said. "She has everything she needs here." He'd made sure of that.

"Everything except her husband."

He sat back heavily. Cat *needed* him? Perhaps in the evenings, to make an heir...

He thought back to the way she'd confronted him yesterday after his ride with Monk. She'd been upset with him for being cool toward her. She didn't know how it frustrated him. He wanted to be himself, yet that would mean telling her everything.

But he'd hardly call that need. Irritation, mayhap even anger. Both of those emotions were good. That was exactly what he was trying to fuel. But need? No. She was much too happy in herself for that.

She may not need him, but he was certain that she was growing attached to him, thanks to his inability to keep his desire in check. The truth was *he* needed her. He needed to lie with her, needed to feel her slender body against his, to find release with her. He doubted he could ever be with another woman again after being with Cat.

The thought startled him. He'd not considered taking another mistress ever since meeting her. Why would he, when he could have such perfection every night?

Except it was having her every night that was almost bringing about his downfall. The more he let her see the real Hughe during their lovemaking, the harder it was to be the foppish Hughe during the day.

The sooner he got an heir on her the better. Then he could stop visiting her at night. Making love to her was playing havoc with his resolve to keep his distance. And his secret.

* * *

"I LEAVE TOMORROW," Hughe informed his mother. "I'm taking Cat with me." He'd hoped to find them together, in his mother's chambers, but Cat wasn't there.

"Why?" the dowager asked, setting her sewing aside and fixing him with those emotionless eyes.

"There are people I wish her to meet."

"Can't they come here to meet her?"

"No."

The dowager dismissed her ladies with a flick of her fingers. Whenever she did that, Hughe knew he was in for a lecture, or a confrontation, or both. He sighed. He didn't have time for this. He had to see Cat.

Once the ladies were gone and the door closed, his mother caught his hand. Her boney fingers had a surprising amount of strength in them. "I hoped you would stay home now that you have a wife, but I see you're not only insistent on abandoning me, but having Catherine abandon me too."

"We're not abandoning you, Mother." Where did she get these foolish notions from?

"Then why are you leaving?"

"I told you—"

"I want the truth."

He bit his tongue and sat. "That is the truth."

"Don't lie to me. I know you keep secrets from me. A mother cannot expect to know everything that goes on in her son's life, but...but I had hoped to see a change in you. Indeed, I thought I had." She shook her head and smoothed her hands over her skirt. "I don't understand you, Hughe."

"I have no secrets from you, Mother. I simply like to travel."

"I believed that at first, years ago. Young men like to see the world. But then you grew older and there were so many rumors about your indescretions. I suspected you left here to visit them. But now...now you're taking your wife with you. I know some men are vulgar enough to keep their wife in one chamber while they pay court to their mistress in another, but I think I brought you up better than that."

"You didn't bring me up. The nursemaids and tutors did."

Her head snapped back. Her hands stilled. Hughe worried that he'd said too much, but surely she couldn't be surprised by his words. It was simple fact.

Before she could respond, he added, "I'm not going to see any mistresses. I don't have any now. There's only my wife."

"Do you love her?"

Her question startled him. What did love have to do with anything? He was simply taking Cat away with him. He thought about his friends, the way they doted on their wives, cherished everything about them. Even big, grim Cole was a puppy in Lucy's hands. Hughe wasn't like that. He liked Cat and found deep satisfaction in her body, but love was for simpler fools.

"I want to protect her," he said, carefully. "I don't want to hurt her. That's all you need to know."

"I see. Did she tell you that I told her about the will?"

He shot to his feet. "You did what?" he growled, jaw achingly tight.

"I told her how you changed the will before you married her. I thought she ought to know and I didn't think you would inform her."

"I didn't think *you* would."

"Why did you do it, Hughe?" She spoke quietly, idly, as if it weren't of any consequence. But he knew better. "She would have enough as your widow without a will. Why give her more?"

"I told you. I want to protect her. Her first husband left her with nothing. Worse, he left her reliant on a cruel man's good will. I don't want to do that to her. She is my responsibility."

She pressed her lips together in thought and sat like that for a moment, staring straight ahead. Then she nodded at him. "Send in my ladies. If I don't see you before you leave, have a safe journey."

Dismissed, Hughe left and went in search of Cat. His conversation with his mother had been strange, but most of his conversations with her were. Old age and infirmity were affecting her mind. He dismissed it when he finally found Cat in the apple orchard. The day was warm and sultry, the air thick with the promise of rain.

She glanced up when he arrived and smiled. She looked so content, sitting on the grass with her feet tucked up under her skirt. But as he drew closer, he saw shadows brewing in her eyes as surely as the storm brewing on the horizon. He'd put them there, and he hated himself for it. Hopefully, in time, the shadows would disappear.

"Good afternoon, dear Cat," he said, plopping down near her but not too close. "You look like a wood nymph sitting under the tree."

"I went for a walk, but it grew hot."

"You poor thing! Come inside where it's cooler."

"I will soon." She looked up at the sky. "It's going to rain."

He followed her gaze because looking at her worried him too much. "I hope tomorrow is fine."

"Do you have plans?"

"We're leaving in the morning for Sutton Hall."

"Oh." The flatness of her voice made him turn back to her. She plucked at the grass and did not meet his gaze. "How long will you be gone?"

"We," he corrected. "How long will *we* be gone?"

She stopped plucking. "We?"

"You're coming with me, Cat, and so are the Monks. We'll have a grand time! I can't wait for Lord Lynden to meet you. He'll adore you. He's a fool and a dullard, but serves splendid feasts."

She smiled. "Your other friends live near there too, don't they?"

"Aye, they do. They'll be pleased to see us all again."

"And I them."

He got to his feet. "Shall I set your maids to task with the packing?"

She began to rise and he held out his hand to assist her. She took it and stood. "No need. I'll return to the house." They walked side-by-side out of the orchard and were almost at the knot garden's hedge when Cat said, "I'm glad I'm coming with you. I wasn't prepared to farewell you just yet, even for a few days."

"You're too kind, my little Cat, but of course I couldn't leave you alone with my mother so soon after the last time. There's only so much one can endure of the old dragon!" He laughed and avoided looking at her. He couldn't bear to see the disappointment on her face. Perhaps he should have admitted that he would miss her too.

But that would have been foolish indeed.

"The storm draws closer," he said to steer the conversation into safer territory. "I hope it breaks tonight to clear the way tomorrow."

The storm did indeed break that night. Hughe made love to his wife with the shutters open and the rain splashing on the window panes. The thunder drowned out her cries of ecstasy as he brought her to release with his tongue, and the lightning lit up her pretty face, softened by pleasure. He entered her slowly and kept the rhythm steady. Sweat slicked his back and shoulders as he strained not to release too soon. He loved being inside her too much and prolonging the ending was sweet torture.

He left her bed once he was certain she was asleep and returned to his own rooms. He lay on top of the bed covers and linked his hands over his ribs, where it felt like a gaping hole had opened. He stared up at the canopy and wondered if he'd made the right decision to take Cat to a place where so many people knew the truth about him.

* * *

SUTTON HALL WAS a grand house with extensive lands, nestled within a pretty valley, a brief ride from the village of Sutton Grange, after which it was named. Cat didn't get to see much of the village, however, as the Oxley party traveled through without stopping. Hughe acknowledged some of the villagers with nods and waves as he passed. One man even commented that he was surprised to see him again so soon. It would seem her husband was no stranger to the area.

Lord Lynden, Elizabeth's cousin, greeted the Monks politely, if somewhat coolly. His reaction upon seeing Hughe, however, was vastly different. He embraced him then held him at arm's length to gaze upon him.

"My dear Oxley!" he cried. "I hear you were married during your absence. What ill luck!" He pulled a face. "I suppose it must happen to us all one day."

Hughe cleared his throat and pulled away. "Lord Lynden, may I present my wife, Lady Oxley." He drew Cat's hand to the crook of his arm and beamed at her. "Isn't she a little thing?"

Lord Lynden's eyes bulged and his face colored. He quickly bowed to hide it. "My apologies, Lady Oxley. I didn't realize you were coming too."

"That's quite all right, my lord. I hope it's no inconvenience."

"I'll have an extra room prepared, my lady."

"Near mine," Hughe said.

That brought more color to Lynden's face. "Of course."

The Monks went on ahead while Cat walked in slowly with Lynden and Hughe.

"You didn't invite me to your wedding," Lynden said, pouting. "I thought we were such good friends."

"We are, my dear fellow!" Hughe said with a hand on his heart.

"Intimates, I assure you. But the wedding was a small affair. Nobody of consequence was there, just some rag tag villagers and neighbors. It was no fun at all. I didn't want to bore you."

Lynden didn't seem to notice Hughe's lie, yet how could he not? Hughe's smile was a little too hard and his gaze didn't quite meet Lynden's. The signs were obvious. Lynden must be a fool indeed.

"Be sure to invite me to your next wedding," Lynden declared.

Hughe placed his hand over Cat's, still on his arm, and squeezed. "Of course, dear man. Of course!"

Cat pressed her lips together to suppress her smile.

The house steward showed Cat and Hughe to their chambers, which were indeed situated close to one another and shared a common sitting room. Once they were alone, Hughe sighed.

"Lynden is as dim as an unlit dungeon," he muttered. "I'm sorry you had to listen to his blathering."

"Why do you court his attentions if you don't like him? Surely he's not important enough that you need to."

Hughe eyed her for a heartbeat. "Because you never know who will be important one day. Besides, I like to visit my friends from time to time, and it's easier to stay with Lynden. Orlando and Cole don't have the right sort of house for an earl." He flashed a grin and she shook her head at him and smiled, even though she wasn't entirely sure if he told the truth or not. Sometimes, she thought he didn't care about the trappings of his station, and at others, he seemed to care deeply.

"Does my little Cat need to change?" he asked, stepping up to her. He unhooked the topmost fastening of her jerkin.

"I brought a maid for that," she murmured. His nearness made her feel a little light-headed. He had never made love to her during the day. Never even kissed her. "I hear her moving around in my bedchamber."

He pressed his lips to her throat above her ruff and trailed delicate kisses up to her ear and along her jawline. "Let me be your maid." His nimble fingers quickly worked to remove her jerkin. His hands dipped beneath and rested on her waist. He gently drew her against his hard body and she could feel how much he wanted her through his breeches.

She sighed against his mouth, relieved to see that he'd shed his foppish persona.

He drew away and frowned at her. "If you're tired from your journey, I'll leave you in peace."

"No. Don't leave me, Hughe. Take me. Here. Now." She would not let this opportunity to explore her husband in daylight disappear. They didn't have long, however. The sun was already sinking.

His grin turned wicked.

A knock sounded on the door. "Oxley!" It was Lynden. "Oxley, are you in there? Come and share my wine. I've purchased the best French stuff I could find."

Hughe closed his eyes and pressed his forehead against Cat's. He sighed heavily. "I'll kill him."

"That will set you back," she teased. "You'll have to start all over again, courting the new Lord Lynden."

Lynden knocked again. "Come out, Oxley!"

"Go," Cat said, breaking contact. "Enjoy his wine. I'll see you tonight, my lord." She gave him a little curtsy.

Hughe bowed elaborately. "I'll look forward to it." He straightened with a toss of his head. He tilted his chin and made his way to the door with a walk that was not his usual stride, but shorter and somehow lighter. Cat was forgotten.

* * *

CAT AND ELIZABETH visited Susanna and Lucy the following day, at the Holts' residence of Stoneleigh. The house was a large manor, although not on the scale of Sutton Hall. Susanna showed her around the orange grove inside a walled garden that protected the exotic fruit from the elements.

"You must try Susanna's succades," Lucy said. "They're delicious. She makes them herself from the peel."

Cat spent the morning with the ladies, eating succades and

sipping a sweet wine that had been stored in a cool room. She learned more about the women and their husbands, but what she didn't learn was how they knew Hughe. If the ladies could be believed, the men all simply met and became friends. Yet their different stations implied there must be more to it than that. Earls did not associate with carpenters' sons like Edward Monk, no matter how much they enjoyed one another's company.

"Edward and Hughe rode out this morning," Cat said idly. "The stable groom said they were going all the way to Larkham."

Lucy shuddered. "I loathe that village."

"Why?"

Susanna placed a hand over Lucy's and the two exchanged a brief yet meaningful glance. "You questioned the grooms?" Susanna asked. "Why not simply ask your husband?"

"I did." All three women went unnaturally quiet, and none met her gaze. The hairs on the back of Cat's neck rose. She'd not thought it odd that Hughe and Monk traveled to Larkham—until now. "He said he was simply going riding for the day. I thought he might come here to see your husband, or to your farm to see Cole, Lucy. It would seem I was mistaken."

Lucy gave a nervous little laugh. "They must have thought Larkham held more appeal today. It's some distance and perhaps they needed the ride."

"They were in the saddle all yesterday."

She shrugged. "You know what men are like."

"So what's wrong with Larkham?" Cat asked. "Why don't you like the village?"

Lucy reached for a succade. "It's very...dull." She popped the sweet into her mouth rendering her unable to speak further.

The baby gurgled in his cradle and Susanna went to pick him up. Everyone, including Cat, cooed over his tiny feet, his chubby cheeks, his adorable little ears. But all the time, her mind was on Hughe and what he could be doing in Larkham. And why were these three women keeping the secret from her? Cat liked them, and was quite sure they liked her in return.

So why weren't they telling her the truth?

* * *

CAT AND ELIZABETH rode into the village of Sutton Grange in the afternoon. Cat didn't need to purchase anything, but some of the shopkeepers were so sweet that she couldn't resist. Everyone was nice to her, and more than a few expressed surprise that Lord Oxley had found himself a wife when he seemed like a confirmed bachelor.

"Where is your fine husband today, my lady?" asked Ann Lane, the chandler's wife. Cat had purchased a pair of heavy iron candlesticks that would suit Hughe's study with their bold masculine lines. Ann wrapped them up in a cloth while Elizabeth went to speak to Ann's husband in his workshop out the back. She left the door open and the smell of tallow soon stank out the shop.

"He went to Larkham," Cat said.

Ann stopped wrapping. Her brow furrowed. "What does he want to go there for?"

Cat tried not to show her curiosity. She pretended to study a decorative lamp hanging from the ceiling. "I'm not sure. I think he had to meet someone." She knew nothing of the sort, but she seized upon the opportunity to learn more about Hughe's reason for going there. The more she thought about it, the more Cat didn't believe that he and Edward had simply gone for a ride.

"I didn't think they knew too many folk in Larkham," Ann went on. "Indeed, I thought they avoided it."

"They?"

"Lord Oxley, Mr. Monk and their friends. After the problems Mr. Coleclough endured with the Larkham louts, I expected they would avoid the village altogether."

"What trouble?"

"Why, when Mr. Coleclough killed that man—"

"Killed!"

"Aye. They didn't tell you?" She frowned at the doorway leading to the workshop. "I see."

"What happened, Mistress Lane? Why did Cole kill someone?"

"A man called Renny did some bad things there. Mr. Cole-clough heard about it, so they say, and took it upon himself to slit Renny's throat, since justice wasn't served. Only he was seen. Since no one knew the disgusting things Renny was up to, they wanted to spill Mr. Coleclough's blood. Nearly succeeded too, but it was all sorted in the end when the truth came out."

That explained why Lucy had looked fearful when Cat mentioned the village. "Was my husband involved in this disturbance?"

"He was here at the time, and it came out later that he and Coleclough are friends. I'm not sure how involved he was in the events," Ann said. "But he was there at the end when it got smoothed over."

How remarkable. Why had no one told her any of this? Were the Colecloughs ashamed that Cole was a murderer? But Ann Lane made it sound like he'd brought justice where there was none. Why would he shy away from a noble act? Why would Lucy keep it to herself?

"Why do you think Cole did it?" Cat asked.

Ann shrugged and handed the wrapped candlesticks to Cat. "I don't know, my lady. He's a big brute of a fellow. Mayhap he thought no one else could do it."

The sound of swishing fabric came from the doorway, but Cat saw nobody there. Had Elizabeth been listening in? If so, why?

"Did Cole know Renny beforehand, or the people he wronged?" Cat asked.

"He was new to the valley. Not a soul knew him here." She smiled, apparently oblivious to Cat's curiosity. "All of them are new to us here, but we couldn't imagine life without them now."

"All of who?"

"His lordship and his friends." Ann gave her an odd look, as if she was surprised Cat knew none of this. Cat's own surprise was growing too. "We'd never met any of them until last autumn, I think it was. First came Mr. Holt. And didn't the maidens swoon upon seeing him! But he only had eyes for Susanna. We met Lord Oxley at that time too, and some even think Mr. Coleclough was with him then, but I would have noticed a big fellow like that wandering about. Mr. Monk was working for Lord Lynden, up at the hall, but he and Lord Oxley became such good friends that his lordship asked him to be one of his retainers. So there you have it. Your husband and his men have made quite the impression on our little part of Hampshire. I only hope there's no more trouble in Larkham, although I've heard rumblings."

Cat's breath hitched. This was beginning to sound dangerous. "What sort of rumblings?"

"Some of those fools in Larkham who used to call themselves friends to Renny, until they learned what he did, are now blaming Renny's boys."

"For what?"

"For being like him."

"But…is there any evidence that they are?"

"Course not. But they're furious that Renny fooled them for so long, and they want to blame someone for something. They've got a notion that boys turn out just like their fathers." She shook her head and frowned. "If Lord Oxley has gone there today, mayhap he will see that it's resolved. I haven't been to Larkham myself in some time, but I hear it's an unpleasant place."

Cat cradled the heavy candlesticks closer to her body. Why would Hughe involve himself in a volatile situation in a village that was nowhere near Oxley House? Did he feel some sense of responsibility, because Cole was his friend? But it would seem this latest situation had nothing to do with Cole.

There was another reason, however. One that had niggled at the back of Cat's mind ever since Ann had mentioned Widow Renny and Hughe's frequent visits to the valley.

"Is Widow Renny an old woman or young?"

"Not old," Ann said as she packed candles into boxes. "But not young either. She's quite pretty, some would say, and gentle natured. A nice Larkham fellow wanted to wed her, but he died suddenly and she found herself alone again. Mind you, she's not short of coin, so I've been told. I don't know where it comes from. She must have a secret benefactor," she said with a laugh.

A secret benefactor who was also an earl? Cat swallowed heavily. Widow Renny was pretty, had money, and Hughe had gone to see her. The widow must be another one of his mistresses. Either he'd simply gone to see her because he wanted to, or because she was in some difficulty and he felt he needed to help. But his mistress she must be.

The lump in Cat's throat grew. She could feel the tears brewing, so she quickly thanked Ann. "I need a little fresh air."

"Aye, it does stink on occasion. We make most of our tallows in a workshop out of the village, but sometimes Mr. Lane brings them here when the smell is still strong."

Cat left the chandler's shop and waited by the horses until she regained her composure.

Elizabeth emerged soon after, drawing on her gloves. She had a look of grim satisfaction on her face. "Shall we return to the house?" she asked. "Or would you prefer to keep shopping?"

What Cat really wanted to do was ride out to Larkham and see Widow Renny for herself, and find out what she meant to Hughe. But she did not suggest it. "The house," she said.

Their grooms helped them to mount and they rode out of the village along the Sutton Hall road.

"Is everything all right?" Elizabeth asked after they'd gone some moments in silence. "You're very quiet."

"I'm hot," Cat said. The sun did indeed beat steadfastly down on Cat's head and a drop of sweat dripped down her back. But that wasn't why she was quiet, and for some reason, she wanted Elizabeth to know it. "Mistress Lane told me about Cole killing a man in Larkham. A terrible man, it would seem. Why has no one told me this?"

Elizabeth was a gentleman's daughter and in that moment, it

became obvious. She held her chin high, her shoulders square, and sported an air of authority, if not superiority. "We didn't wish to frighten you," she said. "It was Cole's request, not Hughe's," she added quickly.

Cat hadn't suggested that it was. More to the point, she didn't believe Elizabeth. "Why did Cole kill this man, Renny? Did he know him? Know the families he hurt?"

Elizabeth's shoulders slumped a little and her chin lowered. The self-assured air vanished completely. "I...I couldn't answer that."

"Why not? Because you don't know, or because you don't want me to know?" It was perhaps unfair to confront her so directly, but Cat had no other choice. Hughe was an expert at diverting conversation away from anything serious. Cat suspected if she were going to get any answers, she would have to ask people like Ann Lane and Elizabeth.

"Please don't ask me, Cat."

"Very well. I'll ask something else. Why is my husband giving Widow Renny money?"

Elizabeth swung around in the saddle. "How do you know?"

Cat's jaw hardened so much it ached. "I didn't."

Elizabeth's eyes fluttered closed. "I just told you, didn't I?"

Cat opened her mouth to ask her if Hughe was coupling with the Renny woman, but she shut it again. It wasn't fair on Elizabeth, and besides, the grooms were listening. She urged her horse forward, faster. She wanted to be alone with her misery in her chambers until she could confront Hughe. Perhaps she could use the little bit of knowledge she had to leverage more answers.

"Cat," Elizabeth said, drawing alongside her. "It's not what you think."

"Isn't it?" she said. Of course Elizabeth would take Hughe's side. He was her husband's employer and friend.

"Hughe cares for you very much."

"I know." Just like he cared for Widow Renny and countless other women he was intimate with.

Elizabeth gave a decisive nod. "Good. I'm glad that's settled. But if you have any doubts about anything, I urge you to speak to your husband. If you're unsatisfied with his answers, continue to question him. Do not give up, Cat."

"I won't. Not this time."

* * *

Hughe didn't return to Sutton Hall until after supper. He was hot, filthy and drained. His head was abuzz with plans, and he'd spent much of the journey back talking them over with Monk, ensuring they'd missed nothing. They stopped in the late afternoon at the stream near Stoneleigh and bathed in the cool running water. Then they went in search of their friend. They'd already told Cole of their plans when they stopped at Coleclough Farm earlier, and now they discussed it with Orlando. By the time they were finished, they were clean and dry and ready to push on to Sutton Hall.

As soon as Hughe left the Stoneleigh lands and crossed over to Lynden's estate, he shed all thoughts of Larkham and thought only of Cat. No matter how tired he was, he would visit her again tonight. He could take her while they both looked out the window across the valley. The moon was full and the view would be beautiful. Or perhaps he could bring her to release while she rode him. He liked that position.

He parted from Monk at the foot of the stairs and headed straight up to his chambers. Cat would probably be at supper or sitting with Elizabeth somewhere, but he should change out of his riding clothes before going to see her. How long would he have to sit with the others before it was acceptable to retreat with his wife to make love to her?

He opened the door to the sitting room he shared with Cat and was surprised to see her there. She sat in the embrasure, her feet tucked up beneath her, looking out upon the valley bathed in the eerie glow of dusk.

"My little Cat," he murmured. "I'm glad you're here." He tried to inject the lilt into his voice, but failed. It would seem the fop wasn't joining them tonight. He didn't care. He was going to make love to her and that meant being the real Hughe. Being anyone else didn't seem right.

But she didn't turn around. Something was wrong. His stomach lurched as if he were ill. "Cat?" He came up behind her and placed a hand on her shoulder. She trembled.

He sat down, trapping her skirt beneath his thigh, and cupped her face. She hadn't been crying, thank God, but something troubled her. The eyes she turned on him were filled with turmoil, hurt and something else he'd never seen in them before. Anger.

Dread filled him. What had she found out? Had Elizabeth told her? She'd promised she wouldn't and Hughe trusted her. So who had? How much did Cat know?

CHAPTER 10

*H*ughe stroked his thumb along Cat's cheek. The skin was soft and fine, but the muscles beneath were taut as bow strings. "Cat, what's wrong?"

"Where did you go today?" Her question was spoken calmly, casually, but the underlying steel could not be mistaken.

Hughe silently cursed. *What did she know?* "I told you. I went for a ride with Monk. We stopped at both Coleclough Farm and Stoneleigh. What did you do today?"

"I spoke to the grooms in the stables. According to one of them, you rode to Larkham."

Hell and damnation. "We did reach that far. It's not the most pleasant—"

"I haven't finished telling you about my day."

He cleared his throat. "Go on, my dear little Cat."

"Don't use that tone with me," she snapped. "Leave the fop out of this conversation. Leave him out of everything. I don't want to see him ever again."

He swallowed and lowered his hand to take hers, but she balled them into fists. His breath quickened. He couldn't think what to do next. He, a man who was never lost for words, couldn't think of a bloody thing to say.

"Elizabeth and I visited Susanna and Lucy at Stoneleigh this morning," she went on. "You'll be pleased to learn that none of them gave away your secrets, although I knew they were keeping something from me. By the way, I don't think it's fair to involve them in your lies. They're clearly uncomfortable. This afternoon, we went to the village. I bought some pretty lace to make into a collar and some herbs from the wise woman. Then I bought you a gift from the chandler. They're on your bed."

"I, uh, thank you." He wasn't deceived by her emotionless retelling of her day. He braced himself. "Anything else?"

"I learned that Cole killed someone in Larkham."

He waited. If that's all she'd learned, it might not be so bad. "A nasty fellow," he told her. "So I heard."

"I heard that too. It would seem Cole is to be applauded for ridding the world of such a man." She cocked her head to the side and frowned harder. "But what no one can tell me, is *why* he did it? Why did Cole take it upon himself to kill a stranger when he didn't know the man's victims? What's more, how did he learn of this Renny fellow in the first place?"

Hughe lifted one shoulder. "Perhaps one of the affected families told him. Or the man's wife may have mentioned it."

"Ah, yes, the widow. I hear she's pretty and quite well off. The problem is, nobody seems to know where her income comes from."

"Sometimes villagers take care of their own."

"Not this village. By all accounts, the Larkham people want to take out their anger on her sons. If that were so, why give their mother coin to support them?"

"Perhaps she has another source of income." He knew where this was heading. He was tumbling downhill, right into a bloody mess, and there was nothing he could do to stop it.

"Are *you* that source of income, Hughe?"

It was time for the truth. Or part of it at least. "I am." He held up his hands before she could ram him with accusations and more questions. "When I learned of her predicament, I decided to help.

My friend had just killed her husband. The villagers didn't want to support her. I felt a sense of duty toward her."

"How noble of you. Did you visit her today?"

Hughe hesitated, quickly weighing up how much more of the truth he could get away with. "I did. I wanted to see if she needed anything further."

"Well, why didn't you say so?" She smiled. There wasn't an ounce of happiness or relief in it. "We could have avoided these awkward questions."

"I didn't think you needed to know about the whole affair. It's unpleasant."

The smile vanished. "Don't lie, Hughe."

His heart ground to a halt in his chest and turned to a lump of heavy coal. "I'm not."

"You are. For one thing, you would have divulged where you were going today if everything you just said was the truth and there was nothing else to it. There would be no need to pretend to be out riding, yet that's what you led me to believe. And secondly, you play the fool when clearly you're not. Why?"

"It's just the way I am."

"Stop it," she hissed. She tried to get up, but he was still sitting on her skirt. She yanked it out from under him, tearing the hem. "Stop these lies, stop the foppish facade. I hate that fop. *Hate* him," she snarled, baring her teeth. Her chest rose and fell with her seething temper.

His sweet, gentle Cat had been replaced by a ferocious woman he didn't recognize. And he had no one but himself to blame.

"Cat, please." He had to keep on trying. Had to win her over again. He stood and reached for her, but she slapped his hand away. "I'm not lying," he tried.

"Don't. I know you are. I know the signs."

Signs? He had no signs. He gave nothing away. In fact, he was a bloody good liar. How could a woman who'd known him mere months not be fooled, when everyone else was? He didn't dare ask. She looked like a ferocious she-wolf.

Her nostrils flared. Tears welled in her eyes. "I know I cannot ask you to give her up."

He frowned. "Pardon?"

She placed her hand to her stomacher. Her breathing calmed a little, but her eyes were still filled with angry tears. "I know you had mistresses long before you wed me, and I know you'll continue to have them."

"No. You're wrong."

Her lower lip wobbled until she bit it so hard he worried she'd draw blood. "But I had hoped you would wait until you stopped sharing my bed before you ran back to one of them!" She spun around and ran to her bedchamber.

But Hughe ran faster. He caught her round the waist and held her against him, her back to his chest. She kicked out and struggled, but he wasn't letting her go. Not yet. Not when so much was at stake.

"Shhh, Cat. Calm yourself."

"I. Will. Not." She clawed at his hand and it stung worse than a thousand wasp stings. But he didn't let go. If he let her go now, he might not get her back.

"Listen," he said in a tone he hoped she knew to be serious. "Listen to me. Please. Let me explain."

She stopped fighting him, and went still in his arms. But he wasn't fooled. He didn't loosen his grip. She must be able to feel his heart hammering into her back. It beat furiously, as if it would break out of its cage.

"There are no others, Cat." He heard the desperation in his voice and didn't care. He had to make her understand. "You are the only woman. My only one. You always will be now, I promise you." He felt like he'd just sliced his chest down the center and exposed more of the real Hughe than he'd shown to any woman. If she didn't believe him when he opened himself to her like that, there was no hope of winning back her trust.

"How do I know you're telling the truth," she whispered, "when all you've fed me are lies?"

144

Not all, he wanted to tell her. But that would mean admitting that he had lied about some things. And no matter what happened, revealing those things would cause an even bigger mess. One he could never claw his way out of. As it stood now, he still had a chance to prove to her that she was the only woman for him.

"You have to believe me on this. Please, Cat. I can't give you up." Everything inside him felt tight, fragile. With one elbow to the ribs, he might shatter. He buried his face in her hair and breathed deeply. Her scent filled him, made his head dizzy like the strongest wine. He loosened his grip so she could turn around and face him.

But instead she pulled free and ran to her bedchamber. He did not chase her, but watched her go with a heavy heart.

She stood by the door and fixed her tearful gaze on him. "I know I cannot stop you from having them, but I need time to adjust and—"

"There are none, Cat. I can swear to that on every Bible."

After a very long moment, she inclined her head. "I'm glad to hear it."

He approached her slowly, carefully, so as not to alarm her. "Then will you come here and kiss me?"

She put her hand out to stop him drawing closer. "I'm tired tonight. I'm going to bed."

She shut the door and slid the bolt home. He stood there and stared at the solid wood and wondered where this strong-willed, jealous woman had come from. He thought the lady he'd married was demure and amiable. In truth, in the beginning, he thought he could keep her at Oxley House and his mistresses elsewhere, and have the best of both worlds. It was, after all, what all noblemen did, many with the blessing of their wives.

Now he knew that she would never give her blessing. He smiled, despite everything. He was glad of it; more glad than he could ever have imagined mere weeks ago. He didn't want a mistress; he wanted his clever, spirited wife. Now all he had to do was win her back. It would take time to earn her trust again, but he would not give up.

Just as long as she never found out about his *other* lie.

* * *

CAT DIDN'T WANT to be a jealous shrew of a wife. She hated ranting and raging at her husband, but she couldn't help it. Her emotions were spilling forth and she couldn't keep them in check.

For years she'd turned a blind eye to Stephen's indiscretions, but she couldn't do that with Hughe, even if she'd previously thought she could. Not once had she felt as bereft then as she did now. Her heart clenched in pain and she couldn't stop the cascading waterfall of tears.

Despite Hughe's assurances that he kept no mistresses, she didn't believe him. He was lying. She knew that as surely as she knew she loved him. He sounded so convincing, however, with his gentle yet insistent voice assuring her she was the only one. And then when he wrapped his powerful arms around her and held her as if he didn't want to let her go, she could almost believe that he loved her.

But then came the lies again and she knew it was all a game for him.

She must have fallen asleep because she woke up to the sounds of her maids moving around the chamber and sunlight peeking around the edges of the shutters. They eyed her with sympathy and kept eerily silent. For two chattering girls, that was quite a feat.

Cat was in no mood to speak to them. She was in no mood to speak to anyone. She kept to her bedchamber, not even venturing into the sitting room she shared with Hughe. He was the last person she wanted to encounter.

So when he knocked on her bedchamber door and asked to see her, she had one of her maids tell him she was unwell. Cat heard him ask if he could fetch the wise woman, but the maid said she just needed to rest for the day. He left with a promise that he would return later.

Elizabeth came to visit in the afternoon. Cat allowed her to enter. She hadn't cried all morning, perhaps because she'd used up all her tears the night before, so her eyes wouldn't be too swollen.

Nevertheless, Elizabeth knew Cat wasn't ill the moment she saw her. Elizabeth sat on the bed and drew her into an embrace. Cat's eyes banked with tears once more.

"If it makes you feel any better, Hughe is miserable too," Elizabeth said, drawing away but holding Cat by the shoulders.

It didn't make her feel better. It only served to confuse her. Perhaps he had been telling the truth. Then what was he hiding, if not his mistresses?

"Pass me the comb," Elizabeth said to one of the maids. The girl did as she was bid then left when Elizabeth dismissed them both. "I'm going to fix your hair."

"I don't want my hair fixed," Cat said.

"Then do it for me. I used to comb my sister's hair all the time, and I find the activity soothing."

Cat shifted down the bed to allow Elizabeth to settle behind her.

"You have lovely hair," Elizabeth said, running the comb through.

"It's a dull brown shade and dead straight." Not like Lady Crewe's glossy locks.

"It reminds me of wood worn smooth over time."

Wood? That was the best she could do? After hearing how plain she was, first from her parents and then Stephen, she knew she was no beauty. No amount of flattery could make her believe she was anything but ordinary.

Elizabeth stroked the comb through her hair then arranged it into a style. Cat allowed her to do it, mostly because Elizabeth had fallen blessedly silent. She didn't want to hear any more about how miserable Hughe was.

Well, perhaps a little bit.

"Has he gone back to Larkham?" Cat asked.

Elizabeth's hands stilled. Cat held her breath as she waited for an answer. "No."

"Is he still here?"

"He and Edward are out."

"Where have they gone?"

"I don't know."

Lies, lies and more lies. "Elizabeth, what are you all hiding from me?"

Elizabeth was saved from answering by one of the maids re-entering. "M'lady, a Lord Slade has arrived."

Cat spun around to face her, bumping Elizabeth's arm. "Slade! What's he doing here?"

The maid gave her a blank look. It would seem that was a question only Slade could answer.

"Is that your brother-in-law?" Elizabeth asked.

Cat nodded. It was very odd. Had Slade come all the way to see her? Whatever for? She'd not expected to see him ever again, and now this, at a time when she was feeling too fragile to face anyone.

Elizabeth closed her hand around Cat's arm and gave her an encouraging smile. "Shall we see him together?"

"It's kind of you to offer. Thank you."

Elizabeth helped her dress in a rust-colored gown with a fine lace ruff and heavily embroidered forepart. She was determined to look every bit the countess and show him how far she'd risen. He could not injure her now.

They found Slade with Lord Lynden in the summer parlor, making polite yet stilted conversation about crops and sheep. No doubt Lynden was enjoying telling his poorer guest how many head he kept, if his puffed chest was any indication. Hislop was nowhere in sight, thank goodness. Hopefully he hadn't even come.

"There you are," Slade said, rising. He bowed, but not deeply. "Dear sister-in-law."

"What are you doing here?" she asked. It may have been blunt but she was in no mood for idle chatter with Slade. He was quite possibly the last person she wanted to see.

Lynden shifted in his chair and looked embarrassed by her bald question, but Slade showed no signs of discomfort. "I wanted to see my sister-in-law again. I've missed you."

"Nonsense."

He cleared his throat. "Lord Oxley's people told me you came here together, so I decided to continue on. It's only another day's ride from Oxley House and I'd already come so far." His smile was as oily as his hair. Cat didn't trust it.

She knew she would not get a real answer from him while the others were nearby. She also suspected he was there because of his ridiculous claim that Hughe had killed Stephen.

Her spine tingled. She'd learned much about her husband since arriving at Sutton Hall, including that his friend Cole was a killer.

Cole.

The name scratched at the edge of her mind, but she couldn't place it.

Hislop strode into the room ahead of a scurrying Sutton Hall servant, who glanced anxiously at his master. Hislop stood in the center of the room, feet a little apart, hands on hips, looking every bit like *he* was the master.

"Who are you?" Lord Lynden asked, rising to his feet. Cat was impressed that he could put on such a haughty air in the face of Hislop's commanding stance.

"My man, Hislop," Slade said quickly.

Hislop's gaze swept over Lynden and Elizabeth with bored indifference. It stopped when it reached Cat and a sneer distorted his lips. "Lady Oxley," he said without bowing. "Always a pleasure to see you again. How Slade and I have missed you these last weeks." The slippery tone slithered across Cat's skin. She shivered and nodded a greeting.

Elizabeth closed her hand over Cat's. The gesture was a comfort. She was not alone now, she had nothing to fear from these men.

"There appears to have been a mistake," Hislop said to Lynden. "I've instructed your man to find me a room in the house. He seems to think there are none and has placed me in the stables with the grooms."

The manservant standing behind Hislop colored and bowed his head. Surely there'd been a mistake, as Hislop suggested. A house the size of Sutton Hall must have more guest chambers fit for a retainer. On the other hand, Cat liked the thought of Hislop sharing an empty stall with the spotty stable lads. She had to press her lips together hard to stop her smile from escaping.

"I, er, that is…" Lynden appealed to his man, but the servant merely pulled a face at Hislop's back. Clearly he didn't like the brute either, and thought the household would be safer with him outside.

"There are no more rooms in the house," Elizabeth cut in before her cousin could speak. "There are a number of guests at the moment and the only space is in the stables. Unless Lord Slade wishes to share with you." She arched her brow at Slade.

"No," Hislop snapped before Slade could answer. He narrowed his gaze at Elizabeth. "Who are you?"

"Elizabeth Monk, companion to Lady Oxley. Who are you?"

He turned to Cat without answering. "My, my, how you have risen. You have companions, no less! Where is your husband?"

"Out," Cat said. "I'm sure he'll be pleased to see you both, although somewhat confused as to why you came at all."

"I told you," Slade said with barely disguised irritation. "Weren't you listening?"

"I was, but I simply don't believe you. You were never interested in me before."

"On the contrary! You are family, even now. I have always been interested in your welfare. And besides, we have much to discuss. I hoped you would have some news for me." He might as well have winked at her, his intention was so obvious. It would seem he hadn't given up his quest to blame Hughe for Stephen's murder.

Cat may have her own fresh doubts about Hughe's honesty, but she would not share them with Slade. Whatever Hughe had done, he was still one hundred times the man that Slade was, and a thousand times better than Hislop.

Slade rose and approached Cat. He gave her one of his odd half-smiles that didn't reach his eyes and barely even reached the corners of his mouth. He held out his hand. "Care to walk with me, Cat?"

"Not now."

His fingers curled up. "When?"

"I don't know. I'm tired and—"

Determined footsteps approached quickly and Hughe appeared at the door, Edward Monk behind him. Between them they looked like two furious warriors seeking vengeance. Hughe's pale eyes coldly assessed Hislop and then Slade, finally settling on Cat. The rigidity left his jaw and his gaze warmed, but only a little. Rarely had she seen him look so menacing and it chilled her to the bone. Her husband was not a man to be trifled with.

"Slade," he said, flatly. "I hope you're not bothering my countess."

Slade held up his hands. A flicker of panic passed across his face and he looked to Hislop, perhaps for reassurance. Hislop remained where he was, his hands still on his hips, his eyes narrowed to pinpoints as he watched Hughe.

"Bothering her?" Slade said. "Not at all. We were about to go for a walk."

A muscle throbbed in Hughe's jaw and his fists closed at his sides. Slade eyed them warily while Hislop took a step forward. So did Edward, his fingers twitching near his sword. One quick move, one lunge, and the men would be brawling in the parlor.

"I'm not going anywhere," Cat said, rising. "My head aches. I'll be supping in my rooms tonight and don't wish to be disturbed."

Hughe watched her from beneath heavy lids. "Let me escort you to your chamber." It was not a suggestion, but a command that a wife could not refuse in front of others. It served her purposes well enough to have him with her anyway. She only wanted to diffuse the situation and get the men away from one another.

They passed by Edward, facing Hislop, his hand resting on his hip near his sword hilt in what appeared to be a casual pose, but Cat suspected was so that he could draw quickly if necessary. What had Hughe told him about the two?

"Are you all right?" Hughe asked as they climbed the stairs together. He didn't touch her, but she could sense the tension in him.

"Yes. He only just arrived."

"Do you know what he wants?"

"No." She thought about suggesting that Slade may not want anything, but she knew Hughe would see through the lie. It seemed better to keep to simple answers, and avoid Hughe altogether until Slade left.

They came to a stop in the small outer chamber that led to her bedchamber. They faced one another, but Cat couldn't meet his gaze. She knew he would see into her and know her thoughts.

He lifted his hand, but lowered it before touching her. He closed it into a fist, as if he didn't know what else to do with it. "What about...?" He cleared his throat and blew out a breath. Gone was the masculine bravado from the parlor. He seemed to be having difficulty speaking. "Have you thought about what I said last night?"

"You mean do I believe you no longer keep mistresses?"

He flinched and inclined his head in a nod.

"I have thought about it. It's all I've thought about until Slade arrived."

"And?" The word was barely a whisper.

She sucked in a deep breath and let it out slowly. "And I know you're lying about something, Hughe."

He blinked rapidly. His swallow was audible. The fop was nowhere to be seen, thank goodness, but gone too was the self-assuredness that Hughe always possessed in abundance. The absence of it shocked her to the core. He'd never shown shyness or doubt, even when his defenses were lowered during their love-making. His cockiness was very much a part of Hughe, something she hadn't realized until now when it was nowhere to be seen.

Dark shadows circled his eyes and extra lines tugged at his mouth. He looked exhausted. Resisting the urge to draw him into her arms and hold him was the hardest thing she'd ever done. She ached to cradle his head in her lap as he drifted off to sleep, and to lie with him until he woke up. But there would be no intimacy between them now.

He looked away, dragging his hand through his hair, already messed up from his day's ride, and down the back of his neck. "Bolt your doors tonight. Until I find out why they're here, don't trust them." His gaze flicked to hers then away. "Good night, Cat." He bowed stiffly and walked off.

Cat watched him go with a bruised heart. It would seem keeping his secrets to himself was more important to him than his wife.

* * *

"M'LADY," said one of Cat's maids when she awoke the next morning. "Your husband is outside."

"Oh?" She sat up in bed and rubbed her eyes. "Does he request an audience with me?"

"No, m'lady. He's asleep sitting up in a chair by the door. He's wearing the same clothes he wore yesterday. I think he's been there all night."

Cat blinked at the closed door leading to the outer chamber. Her heart sank. Hughe had been there all night to keep Slade and Hislop from her door? He would have slept terribly, and he was already exhausted.

She got up and threw a housecoat around her. She padded across the rush matting and opened the door. Hughe wasn't there. She looked at the maid and the maid frowned at the empty room.

"He was here a few moments ago, m'lady! God's truth, I saw him right there in that chair, his head tipped back against the wall."

"Perhaps you disturbed him and he woke."

The maids served her breakfast in the sitting room then dressed her. Still Hughe did not appear. Had he retreated to his bedchamber to sleep some more? Or had he left the house already to do whatever it was he and Edward did during the day?

She thought about trying to extract some answers from Elizabeth again, but knew she'd fail. Elizabeth was loyal to her husband and her husband was loyal to Hughe. That didn't stop Elizabeth from seeking Cat out, however.

"Shall we go for a walk in the gardens?" Elizabeth asked. "It's a lovely morning."

"As you wish."

They headed out to the terraced garden and strolled along the gravel path in the sunshine. The day promised to be another hot one. To Cat's surprise, and relief, Slade and Hislop were nowhere in sight.

"Did my husband ask you to stay close to me today?" Cat asked.

Elizabeth plucked a pink rose petal from a bush beside the path. "He's worried about you, with those men here." She touched Cat's hand. "He told me that they've been cruel to you in the past."

"Sometimes I wonder if that's why Hughe married me. Because he was worried about leaving me with them." She gave a hollow laugh. "But that's silly. Of course, he married me because he had to. The pressure from the dowager must have been enormous."

"True. That's why he married. As to why he married *you...do* you know?" She smelled the rose petal, without taking her gaze off Cat.

"I confess that I don't. I'm undemanding, I suppose, agreeable. Someone he could live with and who would put up with his mother and not throw her out at the first opportunity if he...died. He professes not to care for her, but he does. Very much. She's all he had in the world for a long time, and he's taken good care of her since her health declined. Her companions told me all that he's done to make her life easier since his father passed and he inherited the title. It's not insignificant."

"He's like that," Elizabeth said quietly. "He takes great care of the things he loves, even though he's not always aware that he loves them."

Cat stopped and stared at her. Was Elizabeth trying to tell her that Hughe loved her?

"Cat! There you are!" a grating male voice interrupted.

She looked up to see Slade approaching from the house. Hislop was nowhere to be seen. Good. Cat could manage her brother-in-law when he was on his own.

"May I speak to you?" he said, breathing heavily from the exertion of catching up to them.

"Of course." She waited, but he glanced at Elizabeth. "Elizabeth, if you wouldn't mind," Cat said. "I need to speak to Slade alone."

Poor Elizabeth looked caught. Hughe had given her one order, and now Cat gave her another. But Cat would not be put off. She'd gotten over her shock at Slade's arrival and now it was time to get rid of him. The only way to do that was to talk to him, tell him she thought his idea regarding Hughe was mad, and order him to leave. She outranked him now. She could do this.

"I'll be all right," she assured Elizabeth. "Perhaps go and find Mr. Hislop and see that he has everything he needs."

Elizabeth must have understood that Hislop was the real threat and that finding him would ensure she could keep both Hughe and Cat happy. She nodded and left, although she didn't look too pleased about it.

"What do you want, Slade?" she asked. Forget preamble and niceties; she wanted this discussion to be over. She wanted him gone from her life forever. "Why are you really at Sutton Hall?"

"Walk with me."

"No. We remain here and you answer my questions."

"My, my. Your rise has gone to your head. Do you forget where you came from? Hmmm? You were nothing before my brother married you."

"And I will always be grateful to him for thinking me worthy of becoming his baroness. I will not, however, be grateful for the situation he left me in upon his death."

"His *untimely* death." He plucked the head of a rose off the bush and pressed it to his nose. When Elizabeth had taken in the scent of the petal, it had been the act of a lady admiring a lovely flower. Slade made the same action seem sordid, like the unnecessary destruction of something pure and sweet.

"Is that what you want to discuss with me?" Cat asked.

He threw the flower away. "You know it is."

"Do I?"

"Don't play games with me, Cat. We've known each other a long time. It's true that I want to seek vengeance for Stephen's murder."

"You didn't when he died. Indeed, you were quite certain it was an accident then. You refused to believe me when I suggested something sinister was afoot."

"That was before I spoke to the witness, Wright. Ever since then, anger has boiled inside me. I want answers and I want the murderer uncovered for the cur he is. My brother had his faults, but he didn't deserve to have his life cut short."

"We agree on that."

"Do we? I wondered…"

She frowned. "Wondered what?"

"Whether you were too enamored of your new life as the countess of Oxley to care about Stephen."

"Of course I care. I also think he was murdered, but not by Oxley. Why would he do it?"

"Assassination, of course. A cuckolded husband employed him to kill Stephen."

Cat scoffed and walked off, away from the house. "That's absurd. He's no assassin."

His footsteps came up behind her, very close. "Isn't he?" He grabbed her arm and jerked her to a stop. His long fingers pressed into her skin, cutting off the blood flow. "I've been gathering proof ever since arriving. Proof that he's not merely an earl. He's something altogether more dangerous."

"What proof?" Even as she said it, she knew what his answers would be. The same as hers. Hughe was involved in something outside the law at Larkham. A man had been murdered there by Hughe's good friend Cole.

Cole.

The memory of that name crashed into her. It was the name Wright had overheard one of her husband's killers call the other. A big brute of a man, he'd claimed, and dark. Like Cole. His accomplice had been tall too, but not as broad, his hair blond.

Hughe.

Oh God. Oh God. Everything began to click into place, like the pieces of a puzzle. Hughe was a killer, an assassin, and so were his group of friends. Hughe did not only associate with murderers, he was one. And he'd killed Cat's first husband.

Then he'd married Cat out of guilt.

CHAPTER 11

Cat's stomach and heart dropped like stones. Hughe had killed Stephen, a man who did not deserve to die, in cold blood. For money. The gentleman who'd made love to her with such tenderness every night since their wedding was living a lie. Everything about him was false. He had no honor, no conscience, no heart. The only emotion he was capable of feeling was guilt toward his victim's widow, but he probably assumed marrying her absolved him.

How convenient for him. He gained an agreeable, necessary wife and rid himself of remorse.

The ground tilted beneath her feet. She put her hand out for balance and Slade caught it. His fingers tightened around hers and she could not pull away.

"You know it was him, don't you?" His slick voice held an edge of triumph in it. "Tell me what you know, Cat."

Her suspicions were based on a little knowledge of the events in Larkham and at Slade Hall, and a lot on instinct and guesses. But she knew—*she knew*—it was the truth. It all made sense. The lies, the unusual friends, the strange manner in which Stephen died. But most of all, it explained why he'd married Cat, a plain, dull, nobody.

"There's nothing to tell," she heard herself say. Her voice sounded weak, pathetic.

Slade's fingers tightened, crushing hers. "Tell me," he growled between clenched teeth.

"Why? What do you hope to achieve? Justice?"

"Of course. What else?"

She swallowed past the lump in her throat. Would he do it? Would he dare take his evidence to the authorities? Cat couldn't be sure. Slade was a slippery eel, driven by greed. He would try to get whatever he could out of the knowledge before he turned Hughe in.

"He is my husband. I won't do anything to risk his life. I'm sorry, Slade, but you must do what you think is right and I must do what my conscience tells me."

"You foolish girl!" He twisted her fingers hard.

White-hot pain shot through her hand and ripped up her arm. "Let me go! You're hurting me!"

He bared his teeth and growled low in his chest. He glared at her with those black eyes and she glared right back. She would not give in to him. He could break every bone in her hand, but she would not aid him in his scheme to blackmail Hughe.

With a grunt of frustration, he let her go. She placed her throbbing hand behind her back and tried to keep her face schooled. She would not show pain and weakness around this man ever again.

"You silly creature." Spittle flew from his wet lips and landed on the grass between them. "You're loyal to the man who murdered your husband!"

"Hughe is my husband now." She turned and walked away as regally as she could. Slade did not follow her, and when she looked back, he was gone.

* * *

HUGHE RETURNED LATE in the afternoon to find Slade and Hislop had been gone most of the day. He sank onto a bale of hay in the stables with relief and buried his hands in his hair. Common sense told him that they wouldn't dare harm Cat in daylight, but niggling doubt had eaten at him ever since riding out that morning. He'd ordered Elizabeth to remain with her at all times, but what could a single female do when faced with two armed men? He should not have left.

Yet he had to, for Widow Renny and her boys. Monk didn't know the farmers who had agreed to shelter the family and they wouldn't trust anyone but Hughe. He needed to be there. They'd ridden across half the country—or so it felt—to set in motion the plan for Widow Renny's flight, yet Hughe's mind had only been half on the task. Slade's arrival at Sutton Hall had taken him by surprise, and Hughe hated surprises.

He'd been sick with worry all day and now he felt sick with relief. He had to find Cat and see how she fared. He had to find her, talk to her, and win back her good favor. Spending another night outside her bedchamber instead of in it was not his idea of a well-spent evening.

Monk's dusty boots came into Hughe's vision. "You need some sleep," he said.

He needed to see his wife. "As do you." He lowered his hands and stood. "Come, Monk. Let's go and see what our wives got up to today." He slapped his friend on the shoulder and walked off. The grooms eyed him as if he were a stranger. Perhaps he was to them; ordinarily he played the fop, but he'd forgotten to maintain the pretense. He was forgetting more and more of late and had dropped the façade entirely in Cat's company.

They strode across the courtyard shrouded in the house's shadow and entered through one of the back doors to avoid a grand entrance. Today he felt anything but grand. Maids stopped and stared at him before curtseying and quickly hurrying on their way to and from the kitchen. Monk chuckled and accused him of scaring the girls.

"They'll think you're spying on them," he said.

"If they think that of me, they probably think the same of you," Hughe said.

"They're used to me entering this way." Monk sighed. "Sometimes I feel like I never leave this place."

"As soon as this is over, we're returning to Oxley House. I don't want our wives here any more than necessary."

"*Your* wife, you mean. You don't want her finding out about you. My wife is quite happy to be near her friends, and she already knows my faults. She won't learn anything new from Cole or Orlando."

Hughe's pace slowed. Monk was right. Hughe didn't want Cat here, where she could learn the truth about him. Bringing her had been a mistake. He prided himself on not making very many in his life, but allowing her to accompany him to Sutton Grange had been a monumental one.

He was already paying the price.

"I need to speak to Elizabeth before I see Cat," Hughe said.

"Aye, I know. Make it quick. I want her to myself."

They found Elizabeth with Cat, however. Monk had to lure her out of Cat's sitting room while Hughe remained out of sight. The three of them slipped into a small empty chamber on the other side of the landing.

"Did you discover anything about Slade and Hislop's reason for visiting?" Hughe asked Elizabeth.

She shook her head. "Slade spoke to her alone this morning—"

"He did *what*?"

Elizabeth flinched at his harsh tone. Monk gave Hughe a murderous glare and slipped his arm around her waist. "Watch your tongue," he said. "She's not Cat's keeper."

"Cat ordered me to leave her side and go in search of Hislop," Elizabeth said. "I made sure he didn't go anywhere near her. He was preparing their horses the entire time."

Hughe let out a long breath. "Where did they ride out to?"

"I don't know and the grooms don't know either. They've been gone all day."

"Did you find out from Cat what Slade wanted?"

"No. She wouldn't tell me, even though I asked directly. But she was...different after their conversation."

"Different how? Upset?" His mouth became dry. "Did he hurt her?"

"I don't think so. She wasn't upset, more troubled, thoughtful. Whatever he said to her, it got her thinking. She's been very quiet all day."

Hughe slumped against the wall and dragged his hands over his face. When he looked up, Elizabeth and Monk were staring at him with varying degrees of sympathy. He must look a wretched sight to elicit compassion from Monk. "Thank you, Elizabeth. You've been a good friend to her."

"And a good spy for you?"

He tried to smile, but couldn't manage it. "I'm sorry you had to do this. It's not what I wanted."

Her face softened and she nodded. "I know. Did you have success today?"

"Aye," Monk said. "The plan is all set. Tomorrow night we ride out to Larkham to get Mistress Renny and the boys."

"In disguise?"

"Aye. We'll leave the horses somewhere nearby and don beggars' clothing."

"You're not going," Hughe told him.

Monk frowned. "Why not?"

"Disguises are not one of your talents."

"I beg to differ. I'm an excellent actor."

Elizabeth huffed. "Hughe's right. It's best if you stay here and meet them at the first stop tomorrow night with fresh horses, supplies and more disguises."

Hughe gave her a genuine smile. "I knew there was a reason I brought you."

Monk didn't look pleased about missing out on the initial action, but he didn't argue. Elizabeth was right. He had a necessary role to play. If he didn't do it, Elizabeth would take it upon herself to deliver the change of horses and clothing, and Hughe knew Monk didn't want that.

"I have to go to my wife now," Hughe said, pushing off from the wall. He went to move past Monk, but his friend stopped him with a hand to his shoulder.

"You look exhausted," Monk said. "Get some sleep tonight or your wits might fail you tomorrow."

Hughe nodded, even though he had no intention of sleeping in his own bed. It was either Cat's bed or the chair outside her door. He hoped it wasn't the latter; he'd snatched only an hour or two of sleep the night before.

He found Cat still in her sitting room, her maids with her. She did not dismiss them, nor did she look up at him. Her head remained bent over her sewing.

"Leave us," he ordered her maids.

The girls scurried out, yet still Cat didn't look up. She set her sewing aside, however.

He knelt before her and took her hands. She sucked air between her teeth and snatched her hand away. He frowned.

"Are you hurt?" he asked.

She shook her head.

"Cat, let me look." He went to take her hand, but she tucked it behind her back.

"It's nothing. I bumped it as I passed through a doorway."

He saw no choice but to believe her, so did not persist. "How was your day?"

"Pleasant enough."

"Has Slade been near you?"

"Elizabeth just told you that he has, so why are you asking me?"

Heat prickled his skin and made the small ruff at this throat feel tight. "I, uh…"

"It's not fair to ask her to watch me," she went on. "I am not an invalid in need of monitoring, like your mother." She lifted her face a little, perhaps to see his reaction.

He should have known she would discover that he paid his

mother's companions extremely well to be with her constantly. At least Cat seemed to understand that it was for the dowager's own good.

"Cat—"

"Don't pay people to be my friend, Hughe. Ever."

"I'm not. I am paying the Monks, but not to be your friend. Elizabeth genuinely likes you, as do Susanna and Lucy. I'm not paying *them*." There, she couldn't argue with that.

"Then why are they keeping secrets from me? To protect their husbands? To protect you?"

He shifted to alleviate his aching thigh. His old injury hurt on occasion, but more so after riding all day. "No one is keeping secrets."

"Stop it," she hissed.

"I have no mistresses, Cat. I don't know how many times I can say it or in how many different ways." He touched her chin to force her to look at him, but she jerked her head away. No. She had to look at him or he couldn't get his message across. He caught her chin between his thumb and forefinger. "Look at me." The plea turned his voice harsh.

Her gaze met his, defiant, fierce, angry. And yet there were shadows in them too that worried him more.

"I don't want any other woman but you, Cat. I think only of you, all day and night. You fill my head, my dreams. There's no room for anyone else and I don't want there to be."

Her eyelids shuttered, breaking the connection. But he forged ahead.

"I want to lie with you tonight, Cat. All night. I want to sleep until dawn with you in my arms." God help him, he did and he would, if she allowed it. If he had to lower some of his barriers to get her to believe him, make love to him again, then he would lower them. He had dispensed with the fop already, and now it was time to end his conviction never to spend an entire night with her.

All that mattered was getting her to believe him and trust him again.

"If you speak the truth, then tell me one thing," she said. "What is between you and Widow Renny?"

He let go of her chin and rose. He rubbed his thigh. "Nothing. Cole killed her husband so I want to see how she fares now that I'm back here. She is not my mistress, Cat."

"How many men has Cole killed?"

The question rocked him. He sat heavily on one of the chairs and tried to collect his wits. If he weren't so tired, would this be easier? "Is that what Slade said to you today? That Cole has killed many men?"

"Answer my question," she snapped.

What had happened to her? She used to be sweet and demure. He recalled the delighted look on her face when he asked her to marry him, and the wonder in her eyes upon first seeing Oxley House. And then there was the breathy way she said his name when he made love to her. There'd been no sign of her temper until recently. He felt like he hardly knew her. One day she was basking in being Lady Oxley, and the next she was being willful and questioning everything. How had he lost control of his marriage so quickly?

How could he wrestle it back without losing her forever?

"Cole is a good man," he said carefully. "Whatever Slade has told you is a lie."

"And what if it wasn't Slade who told me, but something I worked out for myself? Are you suggesting that everyone has lied to me and only you speak the truth?"

"Perhaps you've simply jumped to the wrong conclusions. Perhaps Slade has put ideas into your head. He's angry at me for taking away his sport—you—and he wants to make you hate me too, as revenge."

She got to her feet. Her sewing slid from her lap onto the floor. "I am not a child! Do not talk to me like one. Slade has only confirmed what I already suspected."

His insides knotted. He was going to be sick. "He's told you that I have kept my mistresses?" he asked quietly.

Her body trembled. Her face crumpled and tears fell. He wanted to wipe them away, but knew she wouldn't let him near. Not now. Oh God, what had happened? How had he lost her after coming to realize he couldn't live without her?

She sobbed. Her tears flowed unabated and dripped off her chin. She edged closer to the bedchamber door, shaking her head over and over, as if she didn't want to believe something.

What did she know?

"You…" she spat between wracking sobs. "You killed Stephen."

Fuck, fuck, fuck! How was he going to talk his way out of this? He'd never been short of words or ideas. Never felt backed into a corner he couldn't escape from. Never felt so sick to his stomach with fear. He was losing her, losing something more precious than jewels and coins and land. He was losing his little Cat.

No, he'd already lost her.

But he couldn't let her go without a fight. If only he could think of *something* to say to calm her.

"Cat." He stood and approached her carefully. He held his arms out wide so she could see that he wouldn't hurt her.

She shoved him in the chest, hard, then cried out in pain. She cradled her hand and sobbed anew.

His heart ground to a halt. "You're injured. Let me look."

She turned and fled into her bedchamber. Before he could reach the door, she'd slammed the bolt home.

He tried the knob. "Cat! Please, let me see your hand."

No answer.

"Cat, I want to speak to you. I need to…" His labored breathing made it impossible to continue. His heart felt like it was going to explode into a thousand pieces yet it continued to throw itself against his ribcage without a care.

He pressed his forehead to the door and closed his eyes. How could he ever win her back when she knew the truth? He couldn't deny it anymore. He couldn't pretend that Slade was lying. She was too clever for that. She was hurt, scared, alone, and it was all his fault.

"I'll tell you everything, Cat. I'll give you all the answers you seek. Just come out here now and let me see to your hand."

"Tell me through the door."

"But your hand! At least let the wise woman look at it."

"After you talk."

He was losing this battle too. She was slipping through his fingers like water and he couldn't grasp her. "Very well." He sat heavily on the floor and leaned back against the door. He glanced at the door opposite to make sure it was closed. No one must hear this except Cat. "You're right. I killed your husband. Actually, Cole did it, but I ordered it. We're assassins, Cat. People commission us to take lives and I was commissioned to end Stephen's. But I can assure you, we only assassinate the deserving," he added quickly. It was important she understood that part. "Murderers, rapists, vile people who've escaped justice one way or another."

He waited, but no sound came from the other side.

"Cat? Did you hear me?"

"Stephen was none of those things. You should have checked before you took the money from an anonymous coward." Vile hatred dripped from her tongue. If she believed Stephen innocent, then it wasn't surprising that she thought ill of Hughe.

"He murdered a man." He didn't tell her that the man Stephen murdered was the husband of the woman he supposedly raped. Hughe had found that accusation more difficult to prove, since the woman in question hadn't spoken of the incident to anyone except her husband.

"He didn't kill anyone. Your facts are wrong."

"I checked them thoroughly, Cat. I know, beyond doubt, that he killed a man named Crabb."

She fell silent.

"I can assure you, I would never take a commission without being positive of my target's guilt, and certain that he wouldn't face justice the usual way. I know we haven't known one another long, but I would hope that you know that about me. I am not an indiscriminate killer, Cat."

Again, silence. He waited, his heart pounding in his throat. Perhaps he should try and break the door down. Then finally he heard a soft cry.

He turned and pressed his palm to the door. The wood felt warm, smooth. "Cat, my sweet. Open the door. Let me in."

Her cry turned to a sob. "Stephen wouldn't do that! He was a fool, but no killer! You ended an innocent man's life for a few *coins*. You sicken me, Hughe. I'd rather be married to a poor fool like Stephen than you, with all your wealth and deceit. I hate you. *I hate you!*"

Her words punched him in the gut and robbed him of breath. He gasped for air, but his throat was too tight, his chest too. He could hear her crying on the other side of the door, but there was nothing he could do about it. Nothing to make it better. Only worse.

Nevertheless, he must continue and tell her everything. She deserved to know the truth. Whether she believe him or not remained to be seen, but he *had* to try and make her see that he was no villain. Having her shun him was one thing, but having her hate him was worse than any injury he'd ever incurred.

"He was seen by no less than three men," he persisted.

"Then why didn't they go to the authorities and let them arrest him?"

"Because they were paid not to. They were poor men, peasants. They were given more money than they receive in a year of hard work."

Her gasp came through loud and clear before she fell silent once more.

"I paid them more to talk and they did, but they feared for their lives and wouldn't go to the authorities." It was time to tell her the rest too. If he were to convince her he needed to tell her the full story. "When I dug further, I discovered that your husband had... taken advantage of Mistress Crabb, against her will."

"No! He would never do that."

"The woman's husband found out and confronted him, bit

Stephen killed him. One night, when Stephen got drunk, he boasted about it to his retainers in an inn. The innkeeper overheard him."

Still she didn't speak, but he hoped she was listening.

"I know it's a lot to take in, but you must believe me when I tell you that he wasn't the man you thought he was."

"Neither are you." She spoke so quietly he almost missed it.

"No," he murmured. "Neither am I." His heart had finally calmed somewhat, only to reveal a hollowed out cavity in his chest instead. He waited, hoping she would unbolt the door, but she didn't. "Can I come in to check your hand?" he asked.

"No," she croaked. She was crying again.

"Can I send for the wise woman?"

"Yes."

He heaved himself to his feet with great effort. His thigh ached, his head felt heavy and his heart bruised. He found one of her maids and asked her to send for Widow Dawson from the village. Then he settled himself back on the floor by Cat's door and waited. But it was no use. He couldn't think straight. Could only recall the echo of her words:

I hate you.

* * *

WIDOW DAWSON ASSURED Cat that her hand wasn't broken, only bruised. It would heal perfectly, but she must use it sparingly. Fortunately, it was her left.

The wise woman applied a comfrey-scented balm to the swollen skin then bound the hand. She worked quickly and spoke in a heavy country accent to her young daughter who stood nearby. The girl, Bel, was apparently learning her mother's trade, only she didn't appear to be listening. She stared wide-eyed at Cat the entire time. Or rather, stared at Cat's clothing and jewels.

"There," Widow Dawson said, tying up the end of the bandage.

"Be careful with it, m'lady. Don't go doin' whatever it was that did this again."

"I hit it on a door," Cat said.

"So you told me, m'lady."

Cat didn't have to look her in the eye to know Widow Dawson didn't believe her. She hoped the wise woman wouldn't share her suspicions with Hughe.

"Is there anything else I can do for you, m'lady?"

"That's all, thank you."

The wise woman's gentle, knowing eyes narrowed to slits. "I have remedies for the heart—"

"My heart is well."

"Is it? Only the swelling of yer eyes tells a different story."

"Tears of pain." Cat indicated her hand.

"Hmmm." Widow Dawson pressed the stopper into the jar of balm and returned it to her basket. "Bel, pass me the cloth."

The girl didn't answer. Her attention was focused on the fabric of Cat's skirt. She rubbed the smooth silk between her thumb and forefinger. She'd probably not seen anything so fine.

"Bel! Listen to me, girl, and stop yer gawping."

Bel colored and dipped her head, but needed to be told again to fetch the cloth.

"She's not usually so addle-brained," Widow Dawson said with a smile. "Can't keep her quiet most days. Talks about this and that all day long. S'pose I'll be hearin' about the lovely Lady Oxley now."

"Mama!" Bel whispered with an embarrassed glance at Cat.

"If there's anything you need, m'lady, be sure to have them fetch me."

"Thank you." Cat watched the little girl as she efficiently packed away her mother's things. "Just a moment," Cat said, crossing to her sewing basket. She pulled out a ribbon of green velvet that she'd intended to halve and use as garters. "Would you like this, Bel?" she asked, holding the ribbon out to the girl.

Bel's mouth fell open. She went to reach for the ribbon, but her mother stayed her hand.

"His lordship has already paid me, m'lady."

"This is a gift," Cat said. "For your daughter."

Bel looked to her mother with a heart-rending plea in her eyes. Widow Dawson nodded and smiled at Cat.

"Thank you, m'lady," Bel said, kissing Cat's hand. "Thank you, thank you." She held the ribbon to her cheek and rubbed it against her skin.

"Put it in the basket, child," Widow Dawson said. "Don't get it dirty now."

The girl did as she was told, only to cast longing glances at the basket. Cat couldn't help smiling, despite her mood.

"There now," Widow Dawson said. "It's nice to see you smile, m'lady. You've got pretty eyes when they light up."

Cat walked with them to the door and Bel opened it. Hughe rose from a chair in the outer chamber. A frown scored his forehead and weariness settled into the lines around his eyes and mouth. He swallowed and his gaze connected briefly with Cat's before turning to the wise woman.

"How is her hand?" he asked.

"Nothing broken," Widow Dawson said. "Just some bruising. Her ladyship is to be careful with it, m'lord."

"I'll see that she's taken care of," Hughe said with a tentative smile at Cat.

Her heart took a dive. It had been lurching here and there in her chest ever since Hughe's declaration through the closed door. She'd managed to put aside his accusations about Stephen while Widow Dawson and Bel were with her, but now they came rushing back with a vengeance. On the one hand, she believed Hughe. He sounded so convincing and his evidence seemed reasonable. Yet he had lied to her all along. Why should she believe him on this? Particularly when Stephen had not been cruel to her. He wouldn't kill a man or force a woman. It was absurd!

"And who will take care of *you*, m'lord?" Widow Dawson asked. At Hughe's frown, she added, "You look in need of a good night's rest. I can make up a sleeping draft."

"You worry too much." He gently tugged Bel's braid. "Be good to your mama."

"Aye, m'lord." Bel gave an awkward curtsey then giggled.

She left with her mother, but Hughe didn't walk them out. He turned to Cat and opened his mouth to say something. She shut her bedchamber door before he could speak. He did not knock or call out to her. Whether he remained in the outer chamber, she couldn't say. She would ask her maids when they returned. Or perhaps it was better not to know.

A few moments later, she heard two male voices raised in anger, one Hughe's, the other Slade's. Cat pressed her ear to the door.

"Get out," Hughe growled. "Stay away from her. In fact, leave Sutton Hall. Today."

"My lord Oxley! I am wounded. Cat is my sister-in-law. I only wish to see how she is. They told me the wise woman was here. Something to do with Cat's hand?"

"You won't be seeing her or speaking to her again. Get. Out." The dark thread of fury changed Hughe's voice to one Cat didn't recognize. She shivered. For the first time since learning of his work, she could well believe he was a killer.

"My lord," Slade said. He didn't sound like a threatened man or a worried one. He sounded smug. Cat hated him. No matter what Hughe told her, she would not divulge a word of it to Slade.

She returned to the bed and sat on the mattress. She picked up one of the cushions and cradled it against her chest. It would seem there wasn't a single person in her life that she could trust anymore. She was truly alone, more so than she'd ever been.

* * *

HUGHE SETTLED the pallet across the doorway to Cat's bedchamber. Her maids had gone in to her some time earlier, eyeing him curiously. No doubt they thought it unusual for an earl to be watching over his wife. Lynden had also come to voice his concern. Unmanly, he'd called it. As if someone like Lynden knew what manliness was. Hughe had told him so too, although he regretted that now. He'd still been seething after Slade's visit. The prick wasn't going anywhere near Cat. Not while there was breath left in Hughe's body.

He knew Cat hadn't simply hit her hand against a wall or door. According to Widow Dawson, whom he'd spoken to away from Cat's apartments, the bruising was not confined to one spot. It looked as if her hand had been enclosed and crushed.

Slade must have done it. Not Hislop; Elizabeth had assured Hughe that the brute had gone nowhere near Cat that morning. But Slade had. He'd done that to her.

What did the cur have over her? Why was she protecting him? Because of some sense of duty to her brother-in-law? Or because she feared what Hughe would do to him?

She knew he was a killer now, and he suspected she didn't quite believe his motives were altogether pure. She hated him for what he'd done to her first husband, and perhaps even feared him too.

Christ. Hughe pulled his knees up and rested his elbows on them. He buried his head in his hands and fought against the wave of sorrow threatening to undo him. He'd lost his wife. There was a chance, albeit a slim one, that he could win her back, in time, but the task seemed monumental, considering the amount of lies he had to untangle. Lies of his own creation. Yet he was determined to try every day for as long as he lived. He might manage it too, if she didn't leave him entirely.

The thought brought a fresh wave of nausea. She wouldn't leave him. Would she?

He finally drifted off to sleep sometime late into the night, only to be plagued by dreams of Cat's first husband professing his innocence. Then Cat appeared, naked and enticing on the bed. She beckoned him with her finger and arched her back, offering herself to him. But Hislop descended from nowhere and whisked her away. Hughe reached for her, but she shook her head and said:

I'd rather be married to a poor fool like Stephen than a heartless wretch like you.

The two of them disappeared, replaced by a bulky, shadowy figure with its right arm raised. Moonlight glinted off a blade grasped in the man's hand. The stink of sweat and horse filled the chamber. Hughe snapped fully awake, but did not move. He was not dreaming.

Someone had come to kill him.

CHAPTER 12

$\mathcal{T}$he man approached carefully, his footsteps surprisingly light for a big fellow. Yet there was the smallest crunching of the rush matting under his boots. It must have been that sound which woke Hughe.

He waited without moving, his eyes opened barely a slit, until the fellow was alongside him. Then he grabbed the man's legs and tripped him over before he had a chance to plunge the blade. The intruder fell backward, arms flailing. Hughe jumped to his feet, snatched the knife then caught him by the jerkin. The thump of his landing would have woken Cat and he couldn't allow that.

He dragged the fellow out to the landing and shut the door. In the faint moonlight filtering through the window, Hughe could just make out his face. Sweat glistened on his bald head and above his top lip. He was grimy, his chin covered in stubble. Hughe recognized him as a Larkham man, Upfield. The same fellow who'd organized a mob of villagers to kill Cole, and had recently turned on the Renny boys.

What in God's name was he doing *here*? Hughe flexed his fingers around the knife handle. Upfield must have come to kill him. How had he known of Hughe's involvement in the saga? He'd visited the village wearing a disguise on all occasions but one.

"Who sent you?" Hughe hissed.

The fellow's lips peeled back from his teeth. "I'm here to make sure you stay out of Larkham affairs. We take care of our own."

"I've seen the way you take care of people. But what makes you think *I* am involved in anything to do with Larkham?"

"You were seen at the Renny place."

"And?"

"And we know you're goin' to help them little turds escape. I'm here to make sure you don't."

"Those boys are innocent."

"They're their father's sons. Who cares what you think?"

Hughe twisted his fist in the man's jerkin. "Cocky, aren't you, considering I've got your blade."

Upfield merely chuckled. Hughe felt rather than saw him twist and reach into his boot. He deflected the second blade when it was mere inches from his head. Upfield was strong, but Hughe was stronger and faster. He grasped Upfield's arm, wrenched it behind his back, then sliced through his throat with the man's own knife. Death was swift, but it made a mess of the floor.

He hefted Upfield over his shoulders and carried him to Monk's door. He whistled softly and a moment later, Monk emerged, yawning.

"What in God's— Bloody hell." Monk shut the door on his sleeping wife. He squinted at the face of the man draped across Hughe's shoulders. "Is that Upfield?"

"He tried to kill me."

Monk swore. "The world is well rid of him."

That's what Hughe had thought after assassinating Cat's first husband. Now he wasn't so sure. Pure, primal instinct had driven him to cut Upfield's throat. But now, as his pulse slowed, he wondered if it were the only choice he could have made.

"Want me to dispose of the body?" Monk asked.

"Would you? I've got to clean up before the servants wake." He helped Monk to position the body over his shoulders then slapped him on the back. "Good man."

Monk shook his head. "This does not bode well for our rescue. Who else knows of your involvement?"

"I don't know. I didn't get a chance to ask him. He shouldn't have known of our plans."

"He may have forced Widow Renny to tell him."

"In which case, she's in danger. Upfield may have come here alone, but he would have told others of his movements. Once his friends learn of his death, they'll want vengeance, but not upon me. I'm too difficult to bring down. She's not."

Monk nodded. "I'll hide the body well so that it's not found for a few days. She'll be gone by then."

"Aye, she will be. We'll act today instead of tonight. It'll be more difficult during daylight, but we must do it before a Larkham mob forms. And believe me, it will form."

"Even if Upfield's not found?"

"Even then. I'd wager as soon as they realize he's missing."

Monk hefted the body higher as it began to slip. "Want me to come with you to Larkham?"

"Keep to the plan. I'll leave for Larkham as soon as dawn breaks and you go on to the first farm as we discussed. Arrive early to be sure no one sees us coming."

"Aye."

"Be careful, Monk."

"You too, Hughe."

SLADE AND HISLOP sank further into the shadows along the brewery wall as Oxley's man passed them carrying Upfield's dead body. The stench of blood and death followed him as he hefted his cargo off into the darkness.

Once Monk was out of sight, Slade thumped the brick wall. Everyone was failing him. Cat wouldn't spy on Oxley, even after he told her that her second husband killed her first. All he wanted was for her to confront Oxley and learn for certain whether the earl was the assassin. That way Slade could silence him before Oxley discovered he'd been manipulated. Without her, Slade had only a few pieces of information to slot together, none of them definitive. They'd even gone to Larkham that day to find out if Oxley's visits to the village were suspicious, only to leave none the wiser, albeit with another plan set in motion.

And now that plan had backfired too. Upfield was dead, unable to report back. He was supposed to sneak up on Oxley as he slept and question him at knife-point over his involvement with the Renny family. Slade didn't care about the Larkham matter, except where it could help prove Oxley was an assassin. Upfield, however, cared deeply.

On the other hand, perhaps Upfield's death *did* prove something after all. Oxley would have followed the law and had the local Justice of the Peace look into an attack by an intruder if he were innocent, but he'd chosen to avoid the official process. In his opinion, that was the action of a guilty man with something to hide. Slade's spirits lifted. All was not yet lost.

"I was right," Hislop whispered. "Oxley's the assassin." It seemed he'd come to the same conclusion.

"*You?*" Slade studied his man in the dim light. He was a ferocious beast with his scarred face and soulless eyes. It hadn't always been so. When they'd first met, Hislop had bowed and scraped along with everybody else. He'd called Slade 'sir' and whispered things in his ear that encouraged Slade to aspire to be more than the second son to an older, more stupid brother. Sometimes Slade wondered if Stephen would still be alive if it weren't for those whispers.

The change in Hislop had happened so slowly that Slade had hardly noticed. Somewhere, sometime, he had stopped whispering and started ordering. Before Slade knew it, he'd given Hislop his best horse, allowed his dogs to sit at his feet, and given him the finest cuts of meat at dinner. Hislop took it all without thanks.

"Aye," Hislop said. "It was my suggestion to send Upfield there to find out if Oxley were up to something in Larkham. Seems Oxley knew it. Killed him to keep him quiet, I'd wager."

"And why would you wager on that?" Slade asked. It was time to wrestle back some of the things he'd given to Hislop.

"It's what I would do if a fat prick like Upfield threatened me and my trade. If I had a good income, I wouldn't let anyone get in the way." The weak dawn glow cast shadows over Hislop's face and turned his grin into a grotesque warping of lips. "Don't pretend you wouldn't do it either, Slade. You would. You *have*. You killed your own brother to get what he had."

Slade bristled. "I'm no killer."

Hislop chuckled, low, guttural. "You may not have shot the arrow, but you handed it to the man who did."

"The assassin's to blame, not me. Oxley. I simply pointed out some facts to him through a few letters."

"If you truly believe that, then why are you going to all this trouble to discover the assassin's identity before he realizes who wrote those letters *and* paid him?"

Slade swallowed. A breeze brushed the ends of Hislop's hair against his handsome cheek. Slade had liked that face once. Liked the power in the jaw, the ethereal golden eyes, and even the scars. Now...now he couldn't remember why he'd thought Hislop handsome. There was nothing admirable in his sharp features, his thin lips and soulless eyes.

"You've poked the beast and now he'll come for you." Hislop nodded in the direction Monk had walked with the body. "You see what Oxley does to his enemies."

"You're his enemy too."

"Aye, but I can say that you ordered me to speak to Upfield and paid him to attack Oxley."

"You think he'll believe that? You think anyone believes I have sway over you?"

It may have been still quite dark, but Slade saw the flicker of uncertainty in Hislop's eyes as he glanced away. He was just as worried about Oxley as Slade was.

"Why are you doing this?" Slade asked. "Why have you gotten involved with me and my scheme?"

Hislop patted Slade's cheek the way he used to do in the early days. "Because through you, I get what I want."

"And that is?"

"Respect."

Slade knew Hislop had come from nothing, but he'd not thought being the second in command at Slade Hall would be so important to him. How quaint peasant folk could be. "If I fall, you fall with me." Better that he remind Hislop of that before he decided he wanted to climb even further.

"I know that, fool," Hislop snarled. "That's why I'm behind you every step of the way. Hiding Upfield's body points to Oxley's guilt, in my opinion. Now we must act before he realizes you commissioned him to kill your brother."

Slade nodded. "I'll go prepare. There isn't much time."

Hislop caught Slade's shoulders. He dug his fingers into the joints until pain rippled down Slade's arms and his fingers tingled on the brink of numbness. "This is our last chance. Fail at this and Oxley *will* know it was you."

And I will make sure he knew you were behind me every step of the way.

* * *

HUGHE WATCHED Monk ride off just after dawn produced enough light to see by. It was not his usual horse, but one of Lynden's. With so much riding of late, the grooms recommended Charger and Zeus be rested if another long day in the saddle was planned.

While the grooms prepared his horse, Hughe checked Charger over from hoof to nose. The gelding didn't seem himself. His head hung lower and he seemed to favor one leg. He ran his hand over Charger's muscular withers and was about to inspect the hoof once more when a maid approached. He glanced at her then straightened. She was one of Cat's girls. What was she doing in the stables?

"Is Lady Oxley well?" he asked.

"Aye, my lord. She slept well." The girl offered him a cup. "She wishes you to drink this before your journey."

"She knows I'm leaving?"

The girl nodded. "The day will be hot and she asked the kitchen staff to prepare this brew. There are herbs in it to keep you alert." She extended the cup further.

He took it and smiled. As peace offerings went, it was an unusual one. It was better than silence, however. Hopefully the wine was only the first step. Hopefully it meant she was ready to receive him again.

"Tell her ladyship that I will thank her for the wine when I return. I regret that it won't be until later today, but I would like to see her before she retires for the night."

He drank half the contents and placed the cup down on the floor in the corner. The girl left, only to have Slade take her place. Good. Hughe needed to threaten the cur again before he left.

"Is your horse lame?" Slade asked, eyeing Charger.

"He's in need of rest."

"You ought not exercise him so much."

"And you ought not meddle in affairs that don't concern you." Why was the man at Sutton Hall? At any other time, Hughe would have found the answer, but he'd been so preoccupied with the Larkham problem, and Cat's ire, that he'd let the prick do whatever he wanted.

That would change after today. Tonight, he would confront Slade, with the point of his blade if he had to.

He stepped up to Slade. "Stay away from my wife," he said, voice low. "Do not go near her. If I find that you have, I will ruin you and then kill you."

Slade's swallow was audible. "I have no wish to harm her." He frowned. "Oxley, you look unwell. Is everything all right?"

Hughe rubbed his temple where the devil had set up a workshop in his head. Blood pounded behind his eyes, between his ears. "Stay away from my wife," he told Slade.

"As I just informed you, your wife has nothing to fear from me. She is my sister-in-law, my family. And anyway, it's not me she fears." The smile he gave Hughe was twisted, cruel.

Hughe backed up against Charger. What did he mean? Cat feared him?

Slade might as well have punched him in the stomach. Cat was afraid of Hughe, the one person who would never hurt her. The thought made his belly clench, his head hurt. He should go and speak to her, tell her...

What?

Christ, he couldn't think. His head... And now his stomach, too. It felt like someone had tied his insides together and was pulling the knot tighter, tighter. He looked around for somewhere to sit. To gather his wits and shake off the pain.

Slade's face came into view. "You do look ill. How strange. A moment ago, you seemed perfectly well."

Pain tore through Hughe's insides. He doubled over and vomited in the corner of the stall.

Slade came up to him and held out the cup. "Drink this."

The wine. The wine from Cat. No.

No!

He fought down the next wave of nausea, but the effort nearly did him in. He dropped to one knee and placed a hand against the wall for balance. Standing was an impossibility. Thinking too, almost.

There was one thing he did know. The wine was poisoned.

"Cat," he said on a groan as his stomach tied itself into knots again. Christ, everything hurt. His gut, his head, his skin. But most of all, his heart.

Cat, why?

CHAPTER 13

"I've seen this before," Slade was saying. He was behind Hughe, or beside him. He couldn't be sure anymore. He didn't care. "A fast illness, aching head, vomiting, tiredness. You do feel tired, my lord?"

Hughe turned to him, but Slade was staring into the cup.

"Cat gave you this, didn't she?" Slade blinked at Hughe. Then he laughed, a low chuckle. "Well, well. It would seem I underestimated her. We both did. She's not the timid little creature she portrays. I suppose we should both have seen this coming."

Hughe wanted to tear Slade's tongue out, punch him in the face, stop him talking. Yet he was only confirming what Hughe already feared.

"All she wanted was a little freedom," Slade went on. "Did you know that? Freedom from husbands and marriage. The freedom to do as she pleased."

"Why?" Hughe could barely manage a whisper. His mouth was dry, his tongue thick. His insides were on fire, burning a hole in his gut.

"I won't pretend that I've been the best brother-in-law to her. I know she wanted to be free of me too. That's why she married you. That and your money. Ah well, it would seem she's about to become a very rich widow."

The money. The will. How did Slade know he'd left everything to Cat? Why had she told *him*?

He didn't get a chance to think it through. His stomach clenched once more and he threw up again. He closed his eyes. They were too heavy to keep open.

He heard footsteps. Shouts. Hands grasping him, faces appearing. Worried eyes. "My lord!" More shouts with very real fear threaded through.

"Fetch help." That was Slade. He hadn't been so eager to assist a moment ago. The cur leaned closer to Hughe and whispered, "Don't worry. I won't let her hang for this. I'll protect her."

"Not...Cat." Yet even as Hughe said it, doubt washed over him, as debilitating as the nausea. She wouldn't poison him. Would she?

"She told me this morning how much she hates and fears you after learning that you killed Stephen. I had not expected her to go to such extremes to see you punished, but I suppose I should have. Poison is a woman's weapon, and she is a fierce woman when angered."

The footsteps seemed to get further away, not closer. It felt like dozens of hands touched him, cradled him, lifted him, but not the pair of hands he wanted to feel. Not Cat.

Cat who hated him now. Hated him enough to kill him.

* * *

FRANTIC MAIDS WOKE Cat a little after dawn, their faces long. Hughe was gravely ill, they said. But that was absurd; he couldn't be. She'd only seen him the night before and he'd looked perfectly all right then. Indeed, he'd looked perfect. Her questions only led to shrugs and, in the case of the younger maid, tears.

Cat's heart dropped to her toes.

They tried to dress her, but she waved them off and ran out of the bedchamber, through the shared sitting room and into his adjoining chamber. Some servants surrounded the large bed, but she hardly saw their faces. She only had eyes for the person lying there.

Oh God, oh God.

Hughe lay on top of the covers, fully clothed in riding garb. The blue of his veins was stark against the marble white skin. Dark circles bruised his closed eyes. His breathing came in shallow, shuddering gasps. This could not be her strong, commanding, healthy husband. This man hovered on the edge of death, but her Hughe was a fighter. He would not be overcome so quickly by sickness.

She stared down at his prone form. Someone placed a house-coat around her shoulders and she folded the edges closed over her chest. Her aching, painful chest. Her throat constricted, and tears streamed down her face, dripping onto the bedcover.

No. No, no, no. This couldn't be happening, she couldn't lose him. She had only known him a few months and yet she couldn't imagine a life without him in it. She should hate him. She should want him to rot for what he'd done. But she couldn't. He was a deeply flawed man, but she loved him anyway.

And he was going to die without knowing it. It didn't matter that he didn't love her back, she just wanted him to know she was wholly his. There would never be another love for her on this scale.

She sat on the edge of the bed and pressed her lips to his cool forehead. "Hughe," she whispered. "My husband, my lover, my life."

A small furrow dented his brow and he turned his face toward her as if he were following the sound of her voice. His lips parted but no words came out.

She stroked his hair and pressed her cheek to his. Perhaps she could warm him a little, give him some of her life. Perhaps he wouldn't die if she could show him that she loved him.

"The wise woman?" she asked the maid.

"Widow Dawson has been fetched, m'lady. Shall I wake Mistress Monk?"

What could Elizabeth do? Cat shook her head and did not take her gaze from Hughe. What if she wasn't watching when he breathed his last? What if he tried to speak and she didn't hear it?

Her heart caved in. Her face crumpled as the tears streamed, unabated. "What happened to you?" she whispered.

She was dimly aware of her maids hovering at the doorway, too far away to hear. The grooms seemed to have disappeared altogether.

Hughe stirred and murmured something. She tilted her head to hear him better.

"Hughe?"

He opened his eyes. The pupils were huge, unseeing. "Cat." The word was a mere breath.

"Yes." She clasped his hand, but there was no reaction. "Hughe? Say something."

"Sorry."

"Don't," she murmured against his cheek. "Don't speak of it. It no longer matters. Just fight this. Get well. Come back to me."

The muscles in his face rippled with pain. He folded his hands over his stomach and curled into a ball. He rolled onto his side toward her. "Why?" he said on a groan.

She stroked his forehead as the spasm eased and he stretched his body out again. His hands remained on his stomach.

"Why, Cat?"

"Shhh." She kissed the frown between his brows. "Rest now, husband. The wise woman will be here soon."

"I have to…go." He tried to push himself up, but Cat circled her arms around him and gently laid him down again. He did not fight her and relaxed into her embrace.

"You can't go anywhere," she told him. "Whatever it is you need to do will have to wait."

He turned his head from side to side as if trying to dislodge a nightmare. "Sorry," he murmured. "So sorry, Mary. Forgive me."

Mary? Cat's heart stilled. Even now, her jealousy reared. "Who is Mary?"

"Mary...Renny."

He must mean Widow Renny from Larkham. He thought of her now, as he lay dying?

She swallowed, but the lump in her throat was too huge. It felt like something clawed at her heart, tearing it into shreds.

But now was not the time for jealousy. She had to think of Hughe. Only Hughe, and somehow making him well again. She would do anything to return him to his old self. She would even settle for the fop and long absences, as long as he came to her bed whenever he wanted to make a child. She would take a few moments with him, if that was all she could have.

"Hughe, this is Cat." Her voice sounded full of tears. She fought through them and forged on. She had to know the answer. Had to know what to do next. She couldn't make him well, but she might be able to make him happier. Somehow that mattered very much. "Can you hear me?"

"Cat?" His eyes opened a little wider and focused on her. But just for a moment and then he closed them again, as if it hurt too much to do otherwise. He lifted a hand and let it fall on top of hers. She stroked her thumb along his knuckles and once more felt her tears falling.

"Hughe, tell me. Do you love her?"

His face softened. The corners of his mouth lifted. "Aye."

Cat lowered her head and silently sobbed. At least she knew for certain now. He'd been such a good liar, so very good, that she'd believed him when he'd told her he'd given up his mistresses. But now that she knew, she could grieve for him even if he lived. And then she could move forward with her own life, separate from him yet still married. Or so she told herself.

But first, she had to help him live. Even now, knowing that he loved another, she would do anything to bring him back to health. Even if it meant surrounding him with his loved ones.

She swiped at her tears and drew in a deep breath. "Do you...do you want me to fetch her?"

"Cat?"

"I'm here. Shall I fetch Widow Renny?"

"Get her...her boys..."

She breathed. Breathed again. "If they're what you need, then I will."

He reached for her and she caught his clammy hand in her own. She bent and kissed his forehead. His skin was a little warmer now, thank God. Hopefully the wise woman could do something, but Cat wouldn't be at Sutton Hall to greet her.

She stood just as Lynden burst in. He wore an open jerkin over his shirt and no breeches, revealing lumpy knees. "Why wasn't I told immediately?" He stopped short of the bed and stared at Hughe. "God's blood. What happened?"

"He's taken ill," Cat said. "The wise woman is on her way."

Lynden nodded numbly, and lowered himself into a nearby chair.

"Watch over him until he wakes."

He didn't ask her why she didn't do it herself. He seemed not to see or hear her at all. His stricken gaze remained on Hughe.

Cat left the bedchamber, her maids in tow. "I'm going for a long ride," she told them. "Inform the grooms to prepare a horse. One of them is to come with me."

The younger girl rushed off. The older one hesitated. "But your hand, m'lady. You cannot ride."

Cat stared down at her bandaged hand. She'd forgotten about it. It throbbed a little, but the pain was insignificant compared to the ache in her heart. "I have to," she said.

"Where are you going?"

"Larkham."

The girl wrinkled her nose. "Why?"

"To bring someone here. Someone his lordship wishes to see before..." Cat shook off the thought. He was strong. He would fight this illness, especially once he had his loved one by his side.

"Can anyone else go in your stead? Mistress Monk?"

Cat shook her head. "I can't sit here and be idle while he... I have to do this. There's no need to wake Mistress Monk or her husband yet." It was still very early. The sun was a faint golden ball hanging low in the sky behind a bank of clouds.

She had no idea how long it took to ride to Larkham, but the sooner she left the better. She only hoped she could bring back Widow Renny before it was too late. She hoped too that she possessed enough strength of character to keep her jealousy suppressed.

* * *

ELIZABETH AWOKE IN AN EMPTY BED. That wasn't any cause for alarm. Edward often rose early of late and rode out with Hughe to set the wheels in motion for the rescue. But this time, she had a feeling something was wrong. For one thing, he was supposed to remain at Sutton Hall for most of the day and ride out tonight. For another, the hastily scrawled note on the table by the window simply said he'd gone out. Why so little information? Didn't he know that would only make her worry?

She threw open the shutters and spotted a cart driving toward the house at a fast clip. The occupants held onto the sides, but that didn't stop them being thrown from side to side in the back as the driver pulled up to the front door. Servants shouted and rushed to help the woman down. She ran into the house, a basket clasped to her chest, a girl at her heels. It was Widow Dawson and Bel.

Elizabeth dressed quickly, her heart in her throat. Who was ill? It had to be someone important or the wise woman wouldn't be in such a hurry and would not have entered through the front. Cat? Surely her hand couldn't be the cause of such commotion.

She stopped the first maid she came to, a young girl with tears in her eyes. "What's happened?"

"Lord Oxley." The girl's face crumpled. "He's dying."

Elizabeth covered her cry with her hand. It shook. "How? Why?"

The girl merely shrugged.

"Is Mr. Monk with him?"

"No, mistress. He's gone out riding. Left very early before all this."

Elizabeth rushed on to the Oxley apartments, but was stopped by Jeffrey at the closed door. He stood like a sentinel, his arms crossed over his sky blue jerkin.

"Widow Dawson wants no visitors," he said in that self-important, pompous prig of a way he had.

"But I must go in!" How to tell him Hughe was her husband's closest friend? That she needed to assess the situation for herself and decide what to do next? If Hughe couldn't make it to Larkham, she had to find Edward and have him head to the village instead. Ill or not, Hughe would want the rescue to continue. At least they had time on their side, as long as Edward returned in the next few hours.

Behind Jeffrey stood two of his servants, blocking the entrance. Did he think she was going to break the door down?

"How bad is he?" she asked.

Jeffrey rubbed his forehead and looked rather pale and sweaty himself. If it were the plague, they were all in grave danger.

"The maid said he's dying," Elizabeth went on. "Jeffrey." She grabbed his arms and shook him. "How bad is he?"

He wrenched himself free and screwed his face up in distaste. "Don't touch me. How do I know you don't have it too?"

"I'm perfectly well."

"As was he, only last night." He sighed dramatically. "Today he looks terrible. White as snow and weak. He hardly knows where he is or what he says. He rambles on about spare horses and a woman named Mary. Lady Oxley too, and I'm sure I heard Slade mentioned."

"Is Cat with him?"

The door opened before he had a chance to answer and Bel emerged. She looked more serious than Elizabeth had ever seen her. "My mama says to tell you he's very sick but he might live. She's given him a purgative and will stay with him until it works." She bit her lower lip and hesitated.

"What is it, Bel?" Elizabeth asked, resting her hands on the girl's shoulders. "You must tell us, no matter how bad it is."

Bel's remarkably steady gaze met Elizabeth's. "Mama says he's been poisoned."

"Poisoned!" Jeffrey cried.

The servants shifted uneasily and glanced at one another. Elizabeth sank back against the wall, the air knocked out of her. Someone had poisoned Hughe.

Oh God. If he died, Edward would be devastated. Orlando and Cole too. Hughe was their friend, their colleague, their leader, even though two of them no longer worked for him. He was the life blood of the Assassins Guild. If he died…

No. She couldn't think like that. Widow Dawson said he might live.

She pinched the bridge of her nose and squeezed her eyes shut. She had to think everything through carefully. The poisoner had to be found. The rescue had to go ahead. Hughe would not want his plan to be abandoned now and Elizabeth couldn't let that happen to the poor Renny woman. Edward was probably checking on things for the evening's rescue, so that left only her. She couldn't do it alone, particularly the part where Hughe was supposed to go to Larkham. She needed Cole and Orlando. They were far more experienced than she, and they would want to know about Hughe anyway.

She rushed off and sent a maid to tell the stables to ready a fast horse for her as she dressed for riding. Her mind kept returning to Hughe. She couldn't imagine the magnificent, handsome man lying helpless in bed. He was always so full of life, so strong in body and mind. It wasn't right. Whoever had poisoned him would pay dearly, his friends would see to it. At least Cat was with him. Wasn't she?

There was no time to find out, but of course she must be. Widow Dawson would allow his wife in, and Cat would want to be there, doing whatever she could to heal her beloved.

Elizabeth drew on her gloves as she raced out of the house and headed for the stables. She ordered one of the grooms to go on to Coleclough Farm to inform Cole and Lucy, while she mounted a horse and rode for Stoneleigh, the nearer of the two farms.

She prayed for Hughe the entire way.

* * *

LARKHAM WAS everything Cat thought it would be. Nobody in Sutton Grange seemed to like their neighboring village and she could see why. The houses and shops weren't old but they were poorly kept, their stoops dirty. Mud and the excrement of horses, pigs and God knew what else piled up in the streets. The gut-churning stink of a tannery hung in the air.

At first she thought nobody was about except a few stray hens and children, but she rounded a bend and saw what must have been the entire village gathered outside one of the inns. They spilled onto the street and over the other side to the green.

Cat couldn't hear what their meeting was about, and she didn't care. She had very little time. She wanted to get back to Hughe as soon as possible. It was already late in the morning. She and the stable lad, Warren, had been riding for hours and her hand throbbed beneath the bandage.

She caught sight of a woman standing in the doorway of a shop, a small child at her feet. Her gaze was intent on the mob further along, who were now focused on a fellow standing on a crate. "Can you help me?" Cat asked.

The woman looked up with weary eyes that quickly filled with surprise as she took in the horses and Cat herself. Cat wasn't an opulent dresser, but the quality of her clothing couldn't be disguised in a poor place like Larkham. The woman seemed unsure whether to curtsey or bow or call out to someone to come and view the spectacle.

"Ma'am?" the woman asked, scooping up the child as he began to toddle toward the horse.

"I'm looking for Widow Renny's house."

She frowned. Her mouth flattened. Her gaze flicked to the mob. "You should go, ma'am. Leave the village. Don't bother with the Rennys."

"Lady Oxley has asked you for directions," Warren bit off. For a spotty, skinny lad, he sounded quite authoritarian.

"I was only warnin' her," the woman said, hoisting the wriggling child higher on her hip.

"I will leave as soon as I see Mistress Renny," Cat said. "I have something to tell her." She opened her purse and tossed the woman a coin. The woman caught it, inspected it, then dropped it down her bodice.

She gave directions to a house two streets away. "Be quick. Real quick."

Cat thanked her and veered off in the direction the woman indicated, Warren behind her. A single angry shout erupted from the main street, followed by an answering one from the villagers. She glanced back. To the mob's left, almost obscured, was a horse with what appeared to be a dead body strapped to the saddle.

Cat spurred her horse onward. She planned on being 'real quick'. Larkham wasn't a place she wanted to spend more time in than necessary.

Widow Renny lived in a neat, small two-story house set amid a row of similar houses. However, where the other homes looked to be in need of repair, like the shops, hers was in good condition. She was not as poorly off as her neighbors then.

Thanks to Hughe. Her lover.

Cat's heart lurched. The prospect of facing the woman her husband loved filled her with black, vile jealousy. She forged on. Hughe needed to see Mary Renny and Cat would deliver her to him.

She handed her reins to Warren and knocked on the door. No answer. She knocked again and called out. Perhaps she was in the village with the mob. Cat wished she'd checked there first.

"Want me to go round the back?" Warren asked.

"Not yet. Mistress Renny! I'm Lady Oxley," she shouted through the door. "I have something very important to tell you."

Another shout rose from the main street. The mob were good and roused for whatever sport they were about to undertake. Cat needed to get this over with and get out before they became volatile. Men with a lot of ale in their bellies did not always care who or what stood in their way when they were riled up.

A boy's face appeared at the window. His round eyes fixed on Cat. His mouth fell open. His face was replaced by a woman's. She seemed pretty, but Cat hardly got to take in her features before she too disappeared.

The bolt slid back on the door and two hands pulled Cat inside. The door slammed at her back and the bolt slid home.

Cat got her first proper look at Hughe's lover. She was indeed pretty, with lovely dark hair and big eyes. But she was older than Cat expected, those wide eyes tired as if she hadn't slept properly in days. She looked thoroughly worn out.

"Mistress Renny? I'm Lady Oxley. I've come to take you to my... to Lord Oxley's sickbed."

The Renny woman gasped. "Sick? Dear God, no." She pressed her hand to her chest and her knees buckled.

A young man caught her from behind. He was tall and thin, and when he straightened, Cat realized he wasn't a man at all, but a boy of about fifteen or so. Another, younger boy stood nearby. Mistress Renny's sons.

Cat swallowed. Hard. Would Hughe want to see them too? Did he treat them like his own?

"Why did he send you here?" the taller boy barked as he helped his mother to a chair. "Where's Monk?"

Cat blinked at him. "I don't know. Does it matter?"

"Of course it bloody matters."

"Peter!" his mother scolded. "You're speaking to the countess of Oxley!"

Peter muttered an apology then approached the door. He pressed his ear to it and listened. "They'll be here soon."

"Who?" Cat studied each of the faces. All were filled with anxiety on a scale that Cat had never seen before. As if they feared for their lives.

A roar went up in the distance, just as a cold lump of dread settled in her chest.

"Christ," the older boy, Peter said. "They're coming. We have to get out of here." He grabbed his mother's arm and jerked her to her feet. She trembled violently and gathered her younger son to her breast. He began to cry.

Then Cat heard shouts of "Murderers!" and "Hang the devil's spawn!" from along the street. She stared at Widow Renny and her two sons and felt sick to her bones. The mob was after *them*. She was trapped too, and she'd left Warren outside, defenseless.

"So what does Lord Oxley need us to do, my lady?" Peter asked. "What's the plan?"

CHAPTER 14

*H*ughe's insides no longer felt like they were being squeezed by an invisible claw. Perhaps he didn't have any insides left. He'd thrown up enough times that it was possible.

He greedily drank the sweet liquid Widow Dawson gave him and asked for more. He was damned thirsty.

"It'll help restore your strength," she said, taking the cup from him when he finished. Her friendly eyes smiled at him. "How do you feel now?"

"Like I've been kicked in the head." And the heart. A fresh wave of nausea swamped him, but he had enough sense to realize it wasn't from the poison.

He closed his eyes and tried to shut out the image of Cat. But it was impossible. She would haunt him forever.

"My wife..." he began. "Is she here?" Did she want to see him?

"Lady Oxley was here early this mornin'," Widow Dawson said, folding a clean cloth on her lap.

"Did you speak to her?"

Widow Dawson shook her head. "She left before I arrived."

Hughe sank further into the pillows. Pain pierced his ribs, sharper than any blade, more debilitating than the poison that weakened him. He bunched the bed linen in his fists and rode it out. The stabbing stopped, but a duller yet equally painful pounding took its place.

Cat was gone. She thought he would have her arrested. She thought that poorly of him.

Yet *he* was thinking poorly of *her*, wasn't he? He'd assumed she'd poisoned him without thorough investigation. He'd already condemned her. Just like he'd condemned Stephen, and with just as little evidence.

He had evidence.

Evidence he now doubted.

He licked dry, cracked lips. "Is Elizabeth Monk here?" She might know where Cat had gone. Perhaps she'd even sent someone to bring her back. She was a clever woman and knew how much Hughe cared for his wife. She would know he would want her back, no matter what she'd done.

Christ. What a bloody mess. He just wanted to talk to his wife, hold her and have her run her hands through his hair. Her touch would alleviate his headache.

"No," Widow Dawson said. "She went to get—"

The door crashed back and Cole and Orlando barreled inside. Elizabeth trailed after them and Lynden brought up the rear, wringing his hands.

"Bloody hell!" Orlando said, his worried gaze sweeping over Hughe.

"You're awake." Cole grunted and stopped at the foot of the bed. "You look like death."

"Shut it, Cole," Orlando snapped. He let out a ragged breath and passed a hand over his eyes. "Christ."

Elizabeth sat on the bed and smiled crookedly down at Hughe. "You had me so worried."

"And me!" said Lord Lynden, sitting on the other side. He flapped a fan in front of his face then turned it on Hughe.

Hughe shoved it away. "Did you fetch them?" he asked Elizabeth.

She nodded. Her eyes filled with tears. "I thought you were... I thought they would want to know. And with Edward not here...I hope I did the right thing."

He patted her hand. "You did. But as you can all see, I'm not dying."

Cole grunted again. For anyone who didn't know him, he seemed unaffected, but Hughe knew better. The man's mouth was pinched, his fists locked at his sides. His bleak, black gaze connected with Hughe's.

"I'm all right," Hughe said again to reassure them. "Widow Dawson tells me I'll recover fully."

"Who did this?" Orlando asked. The hand that gripped the bed post turned white. "Who bloody did this, Hughe?"

"I don't know." If they thought for a moment that Cat was guilty, they'd not spare her life.

Lynden cleared his throat. "A cup was found in the stables near where you collapsed, Oxley. Some of the poisoned wine was left in it so I had it thrown out. It smelled innocent enough to me."

"Some poisons are odorless," Elizabeth told him.

"Who gave it to you?" Orlando pressed.

Hughe shook his head. If he could speak to Cat before they got to her, perhaps he could sort this out. Perhaps there was some mistake and she hadn't meant to poison him with a cup of wine she'd asked her maid to give to him.

Fuck.

"You two need to ride to Larkham," he said to divert everyone's attention. "Recent events have necessitated the plan be put into place early. Today and not tonight."

"What plan?" Lynden asked, blinking at him.

"Come, my lord," Widow Dawson said, rising. "We should leave Lord Oxley alone with his friends."

Lynden hesitated until Cole shifted a step closer. The big man didn't look menacing, but he had a dark look about him that not even a fool like Lynden would trifle with. Lynden rose and followed Widow Dawson and Bel, but stopped in the doorway.

"Elizabeth? You ought to leave the men alone to discuss their affairs too."

The glare she gave him could have cut through ice. His face blanched and he left.

Cole came around to the side of the bed. "The poisoner—"

"Forget that, for now," Hughe said. "This is more important."

Cole crossed his arms. "So say you."

"And I am still your leader." He swung his legs out of the bed. Dizziness filled his head and his volatile stomach rose. He felt as pathetic as a babe, his limbs as heavy as if he had sacks of grain strapped to them. His skin was tight, hot, and achy. He clenched his teeth and steadied his breathing, determined not to show weakness in front of anyone. Not even his friends. "Upfield was here early this morning. He's dead now."

Cole dropped his arms to his sides. Orlando blew out a breath.

"Edward?" Elizabeth whispered, her lips trembling.

"Gone to the first farm to keep an eye on things there. He buried the body before he left so it wouldn't be found, but we decided to get the Rennys out today instead of tonight, just in case."

She pressed a hand to her heart and lowered her head, but not before Hughe saw the tears in her eyes.

"If the body is hidden then we still have time," Orlando said. "Cole and I will ride to Larkham now and get the Rennys out."

"In disguise," Hughe said.

"Bloody hell," Cole muttered. "I hate dressing up."

A knock on the door was followed by Slade bursting in. He took in the group surrounding the bed, and must have noticed that Cat wasn't there. He alone knew the truth of the poisoning. Hughe had to keep him quiet for Cat's sake.

"You're alive!" Slade declared. Hislop appeared behind him, his eyes narrowing to slits. His jaw hardened as he stared at Hughe.

"Sorry to disappoint you," Hughe said.

"I, uh, not at all. Your death would have been a tragedy."

Then why did Hislop look as if Hughe's *recovery* was the

tragedy? Hughe got a very strange feeling in his gut, and it had nothing to do with the remnants of the poison.

"We came for Lord Lynden," Slade said. "But we see he's not here. Do you know where I can find him? I have important and rather disturbing news that requires his attention."

"What is it?" Hughe's question came out in a rush, but he couldn't stop it. Couldn't hide his fear. Cat...what if she...

"This concerns Lord Lynden—"

"Tell me!"

Slade cleared his throat. "A body was found buried in his woods."

A chill crept up Hughe's spine. "Whose body?"

"He was identified by one of the laborers as being a Larkham man named Upfield. Ah," Slade said. "I see by your reaction that you know him. I am sorry, my lord. I hope you weren't close."

Something was wrong. Monk wouldn't have buried the body where it could be found within hours. He was more competent than that. How had Slade and Hislop found it? And why did both of them seem too pleased with themselves? Hughe felt like he was running behind the pack and he was too slow to catch up.

"We had word sent to Larkham," Slade said.

"What!" Orlando bellowed. "You should have come here first. Lynden is the Justice of the Peace for this region."

Hughe lowered his head and shut his eyes. Christ. Word would reach Larkham faster than Cole and Orlando. It wouldn't be long before an angry mob was banging on Widow Renny's door, looking for someone to blame. It didn't matter that she and her sons were nowhere near Sutton Hall or Upfield at the time of his death. The villagers were already on the brink of being unreasonable. This would send them over the edge.

Slade held up his hands. "My apologies! I thought I did the right thing. I thought his family should know. They may be out looking for him."

"He was a long way from home," Hislop mused. "Very strange that he turned up dead here. Don't you think, my lord?"

Hughe didn't like his supercilious tone.

"You haven't asked how he died," Slade said to Hughe. "It was a cut clean across the throat. Not poison." He frowned. "How odd that you would be poisoned on the very morning that Upfield died. Do you think we have one villain or two?"

Hughe would not let them pin that on Cat too. He wouldn't let them accuse her of anything. Fortunately, it didn't seem as if Slade was about to. Perhaps he didn't want to see her arrested any more than Hughe did. "Get out of my sight," he growled.

Slade bowed. "As you wish." He backed away. Hislop did not bow, but he too left.

Hughe hauled himself off the bed and fought back the dizziness until he felt stable.

"Where are you going?" Elizabeth asked, also rising.

"Larkham."

A maid entered carrying a tray with a bowl of soup and some bread. She laid it down on the table near the window, apparently oblivious to the tension in the bedchamber.

"You're not going anywhere," Cole growled. "Orlando and I can do this without you. We're still capable."

"You no longer work for me," Hughe reminded him.

"This isn't work," Orlando said. "Rest, Hughe. Cole and I can go to Larkham on your behalf. We'll get there before anything happens to the Rennys. Don't worry."

Hughe hardly heard the end of his speech. He was staring at the maid. She stared back at him, her eyes as big as her face.

"Is something wrong?" he asked her.

"You talk of danger in Larkham?"

"Why?"

She swallowed. "Lady Oxley rode there this morning."

Hughe sat on the bed again. All the breath left his body. He tried to suck in air but it was no good. Fear had gripped him and wasn't letting go. Cat was in Larkham. He had to get her out.

"I don't understand," Orlando said. "Why would she go to Larkham?"

"It doesn't matter why," Hughe growled. "Getting her out safely is all that matters now."

"We'll leave immediately. Come, Cole."

Hughe gripped the bedpost to steady himself. "I'm coming."

"You can't," Cole said. "You're too weak. You can hardly stand."

"I don't need to stand. Tell the grooms to saddle a horse for me. Now!" he shouted when no one moved.

Elizabeth and the maid raced from the room. Cole and Orlando exchanged worried glances. If they tried to stop him, he'd kill them.

"If it was either of your wives," he said, "would you lie down while someone else fetched her?" Neither met his gaze. "I didn't think so." He stripped off his shirt and threw it on the bed. His limbs felt stiff, the muscles achy. He tried not to show weakness as he dressed in front of his men. It would seem he was going to have an escort the entire way.

WARREN HAD DISAPPEARED. Cat looked out the window and searched up and down the street, but there was no sign of him or the horses. Only the mob making their way toward Widow Renny's house like a tidal wave. The men at the front brandished clubs and sticks, or slapped their fists into open hands. Dogs barked and danced at their feet, excited by the cries of "Murderers!" and "Swine!"

Behind her, Widow Renny sobbed. "Where is Lord Oxley?" she cried.

Dying in his bed. Alone.

Cat closed the shutters and turned to the three frightened people who were dependent on her husband for help. They seemed to trust Hughe, and him alone. Except he wasn't there.

"I'll speak to them," Cat said.

The eldest son snorted. "And say what? What can a mere

woman do? We need Lord Oxley. Or Mr. Monk. They'll know what to do."

Red flashed before her eyes. Her husband lay dying, not knowing that she loved him. She was confused, terrified, and she no longer had a horse on which to escape. Warren had fled, as any sensible lad would upon seeing that mob. She didn't blame him. But she could blame this youth for not seeing that Cat was his family's only chance.

"You have me," she told him. "I may not look much, but I am all you've got. So I suggest you help your mother and brother out the back way. Run. I don't care where. Just run as fast as you can. I'll do what I can here to delay them."

"Forgive him, my lady," Widow Renny said, with a glare at her son. "Worry makes his tongue loose."

"My apologies," the youth muttered. "Come, Mother."

"But m'lady!" Widow Renny said. "They may not care who you are."

Outside, a roar went up. They were almost at the house.

"Don't worry about me," Cat said. "I've faced down angry mobs before."

The back door burst open, sending Cat's heart into her throat. Widow Renny screamed. Her sons stood in front of her to protect her.

It was only Warren. The Sutton Hall lad stood in the doorway, breathing heavily, his frantic eyes darting between the four faces.

"My apologies," he said with an awkward bow at Cat. "I would have knocked, but didn't think it would be heard over the din."

Cat could have kissed him. "Go!" she shouted at the Rennys. "Warren, take them away. Use both horses."

"M'lady! I can't leave you!"

"You can and you will. If you don't, I'll see that you're dismissed from your position."

The poor lad gurgled his protest, but didn't give voice to it.

"I'll be all right, Warren," she said, softer. "Go now. There's no time for more delays."

The Renny boys pushed past him to the rear of the house. Widow Renny went to follow, but paused and looked back at Cat. "M'lady, if...when you make it away from here, meet us at the Drewitt Farm, first exit off the Sutton Grange road. The barn is our meeting place if we got separated."

Cat nodded.

The back door closed on them just as fists and clubs pounded on the front. She stood a little back from it and waited. The longer she waited, the more time Warren had to get them away.

Yet the mob would not wait. The door splintered and the hinges popped. Men squeezed through the gap, clubs in hand, murder in their eyes. Their shouts died on their lips when they spotted Cat.

She lifted her chin in the way she'd seen the dowager countess do and fixed the men at the front with a glare she hoped showed none of the fear she felt. "Enough! Go home! Leave the Rennys in peace."

More men came through the door, bumping into their leaders. Outside, the shouts became louder, demanding to be let in. "Who are you?" one of the men asked.

"Lady Oxley. Some of you may know my husband, Lord Oxley."

"Is he here?"

"What does his lordship want with the Rennys?" called out another man.

"Aye," said one of the leaders. "Why is Lord Oxley getting involved in Larkham affairs?"

"Lord Oxley is concerned about justice," she said. "He wishes you all to go home and leave the Rennys in peace. Let the authorities decide what to do with them."

"Bah!" said the big man in the front. "They've escaped justice long enough. It's time to see the witch and her sons pay for their crimes."

"What crimes?"

"Just this morning they murdered one of our own."

Murdered? Surely that timid looking woman wasn't a murderess. It wasn't making sense. None of it was.

"Step aside, yer ladyship," the big man growled. The fellow beside him slammed his club into his fist. "You wouldn't want to get hurt now, would you?"

"Don't you dare come in," she said, squaring her shoulders. "I am Lady Oxley and *you* are trespassing. Go home."

The men at the front hesitated. A few of them exchanged uncertain glances. Cat could taste victory. The Oxley name was a powerful one, her husband known as an important man in the realm. It would only take a few more commands and another reminder of who she was to see them on their way.

Except the others at the rear of the mob hadn't heard her. They didn't even know she was there. Frustrated at getting nowhere, they surged forward, pushing the men ahead of them through the door like grains of sand through an hourglass. The big one tumbled headlong into Cat, shoving her backward. She tripped over the chair on which Widow Renny had sat moments earlier and put her hands out to stop herself falling completely.

Pain ripped through her injured hand, but there was no time to nurse it. The mob flowed through the doorway. Clubs and fists bashed into the walls, knocked over furniture and pulled down hangings. Cat tried to scramble to her feet to get out of the way, but she stood on the hem of her skirt and stumbled.

Somebody caught her and set her on her feet. It was the big fellow, one of the leaders from the front of the mob. "Get out while you still can, m'lady," he said gravely. "This is no place for the likes of you."

He let her go and joined his fellow villagers in searching the house. She needed to get away before they discovered the Rennys had escaped.

She pushed her way through them toward the front door. It was slow progress. Two steps forward, one step back as she was jostled between the stinking, seething mass of bodies. She almost fell over a dog that raced past her and received elbows in her ribs more times than she cared to count.

But she finally made it into the fresh air. Her hand throbbed. Her hair had come out of its arrangement and tumbled over her shoulders. The mob still surrounded the front of the house. Shutters were thrown open and faces appeared at upper windows, searching the street below.

An angry cry rose from somewhere inside. "They're not here!"

She had to get away. They may yet turn on her out of frustration.

She ran down the street, back the way she'd come, onto the main road that led out of the village. Mud flicked up on her skirt and her hair streamed out behind her. So much for the dignified Lady Oxley.

"M'lady!" called a female voice.

Cat turned to see the woman who'd given her directions to the Renny house. She still stood in her shop doorway, the child once more playing at her feet. She nodded at a horse and cart tied to a bollard at the edge of the village green.

"I'll tell the owner Lord Oxley will pay 'im for his troubles, shall I?" she said with an encouraging smile.

It had been some years since Cat had driven a cart, yet she saw no other choice. There were no other horses about and this one wasn't saddled for riding.

"Thank you," she said. She untied the horse and climbed onto the driver's seat. *Please be swift yet compliant.*

She urged the horse on with a flick of the reins and sped out of Larkham with a "Good riddance." A few stragglers from the mob had already returned and watched her leave, but did not try to follow.

It was only a matter of time before they made their way to Sutton Hall to accuse her of aiding the flight of a murderous family, but it would be up to Lynden to diffuse the situation then. Cat wanted nothing more to do with the Larkham mob. All that mattered now was getting the Rennys to Hughe's bedside. Let

Lynden determine who had been murdered and why. If one or more of the Rennys were guilty, she would face the consequences of her actions then.

She turned the cart onto the first track leading off from the road and headed for the barn she spotted in the distance. Warren emerged as she pulled to a stop, almost crying with relief at the sight of her. He grasped the reins and breathed deeply. "Thank God you're all right, m'lady. Thank God."

Peter appeared at the barn door. He glanced back along the track then emerged fully when he saw she was alone. "Come out!" he called over his shoulder.

His mother and brother followed, blinking in the daylight, clasping one another in terror. Warren returned inside and fetched the two horses.

"I'll drive," Peter said.

"Can you ride?" Cat asked him.

His face lit up. "Aye, my lady."

"Then ride my horse."

"M'lady," Warren warned, eyeing Peter. "Are you sure?" No doubt he didn't trust one of the expensive animals to a village lad.

"It'll be all right, Warren. Assist Mistress Renny."

Warren helped the widow up to the driver's seat beside Cat as her youngest son climbed into the back of the cart.

"Hold on," Cat told the boy. "We're going to be fast."

He grinned and clutched the cart's side with both hands. "Good," he said.

Peter steered Cat's horse in a different direction from the one she'd come. "I know another way out. Follow me."

Cat urged the horse forward, but the animal didn't seem to need much encouragement to follow the other horses. Peter took them along a rough, barely visible track through meadows. Grass reached past the horses' fetlocks and bees danced between wildflowers. The sun beat down on her back and the sky stretched endlessly blue into the distance. The serene scene was at odds with the fear burrowing into her.

Cat became aware of her hand throbbing again. It felt swollen to twice its size, but she dared not let go of the reins to remove the bandage and check.

"Thank you, m'lady," said Widow Renny beside her, sniffing. The woman's cheeks were damp.

Cat's heart softened a little, but not enough to conquer the beat of jealousy that had started afresh now that the immediate danger had passed. "Don't thank me yet," she said. "You're not safe until we reach Hughe."

"Who is Hughe?"

Cat swung round to face her. "Lord Oxley, of course."

"Oh, aye. Your husband. I didn't know his first name." She smiled through her tears. "Hughe's a nice name."

"He never told you?"

"No, m'lady."

Cat bit her lip until she tasted blood. She hated to think what this woman did call him in their intimate moments.

"Is he waiting at the first secure farm?" Mistress Renny asked.

"What farm?"

"Where we're to change horses and clothing. I assume Mr. Monk is there already."

Monk? Cat shook her head. The conversation was getting away from her. "Hughe is ill," she said. "I'm taking you to him at Sutton Hall. He asked to see you."

"Me!" Her fingers touched her throat. "But...why would he want to see me at the big house? Why not just send Mr. Monk for us so we could continue with the arrangements as planned?"

"What arrangements?"

"The escape." She nodded back in the direction of Larkham. "M'lady, do you mean to say you know nothing about it?"

"No."

"Then why were you in Larkham at all?"

"I told you! To fetch you and take you to my husband's sickbed. He wants to see you." Cat drew in a deep breath and let it out slowly. This was all becoming too much. The woman wasn't talking any sense. "We're going around in circles, Mistress Renny."

"My lady, I am very sorry that Lord Oxley is ill. I hope he recovers. But I don't think it's wise that you take us to him at Sutton Hall. Now that they've seen you, it's the first place that mob will come looking for us."

"Lord Lynden will sort them out."

Widow Renny snorted. "That fool?"

Cat had had enough. She was too tired to speak to this woman and her heart too sore. "Hughe is dying," she snapped. "He needs to see you. I have come all the way to fetch you and ended up saving your life. I've set aside my heart's desire and…" She swallowed a sob. "And I'm pleading with you to be by his side in case he breathes his last. He needs his loved ones around him now."

Thick silence greeted her speech. Cat turned to see Widow Renny staring at her.

"You think we're lovers?" she whispered, with a glance back at her son sitting behind them. "Me and Lord Oxley?"

"I… Yes. He told me so."

"No! No, my lady. Why would he say such a thing? It's not true."

Cat blinked at her. Was she lying? Did she think Cat would refuse to drive anymore if she admitted they were lovers? "If it's not true then what is your association with Hughe?"

"He's rescuing us. He and Mr. Monk."

"Why would he do that if he doesn't love you?"

"Because he thinks it's his fault that we're in this situation."

Cat studied the road ahead, even though the horse seemed content in following behind the others and wasn't in need of direction. "I think you'd better tell me everything, Mistress Renny. Starting with why Hughe feels responsible for your current predicament."

Widow Renny told Cat how Hughe was a leader of a group of assassins, which she already knew, and how his man Cole had assassinated Mr. Renny for terrible crimes. The victims had been too scared to accuse him directly, since he was too important in the village, so they'd gone to Hughe, albeit in a roundabout way since they didn't know *who* the leader of the infamous Assassins Guild was, not even after Renny's death.

It seemed Widow Renny was one of the few people who knew that Hughe was the leader, and indeed had only learned the truth in the last two days.

"Lately, the villagers had been looking to lay the blame for my husband's crimes on my sons," she went on. "Once Lord Oxley heard about the danger from Mr. Coleclough, he took it upon himself to get us out of Larkham and set us on a path to a new life. He had papers made for us, new names, money, even a small house in Kent prepared for us." She spoke wistfully, as if she couldn't wait to start afresh. "He's a good man, your husband. I owe him much yet he refuses any kind of payment and he seems embarrassed when I thank him."

"Because he thinks he's to blame," Cat whispered. "He took your husband's life and left you in a dangerous situation." The similarity to her own story was stark. "Mistress Renny, are you quite sure of your late husband's guilt?"

"Aye," she said quietly. "There's no doubt. I have the scars to prove it."

"I'm sorry," Cat murmured. "I thought…" She shook her head. She couldn't say it now.

"I know what you thought," the other woman said gently. "And it's a natural reaction when given only half the tale. I'm surprised Lord Oxley didn't tell you everything."

Cat wasn't at all surprised. Hughe had tried to keep the truth about his work from her for a long time. It was only when she'd accused him of killing Stephen that he had outright admitted it.

And now he was dying, not knowing that she forgave him and loved him regardless.

Tears pooled in her eyes and clogged her throat. Widow Renny wrapped her fingers gently around Cat's arm. "Is there anything else you wish to ask me? Anything? I'll gladly answer it."

Cat sniffed and wiped the corners of her eyes with the back of her good hand. "So…you and he…aren't…?"

"No, my lady. According to Mr. Monk, Lord Oxley is in love with his wife."

"Oh," Cat whispered. "He is?"

"Aye. Only he's not very good at showing it yet," she said gently. "But he'll learn, in time."

Time. It was the one thing they didn't have enough of. Cat's tears dripped down her cheeks but she no longer cared. "I wish he'd told me."

"He should have, true. Here's the thing, my lady. Only yesterday as I was talking to one of my boys and Lord Oxley overheard, he told me I ought to be careful telling them about their father."

"About the crimes he committed you mean?"

"Aye. Lord Oxley thought I should keep the truth from them, but I said loved ones should always tell the truth to one another. They should trust and speak honestly all the time. Secrets only cause problems."

"And what did his lordship say to that?"

"He said he believed that secrets protect loved ones from unnecessary hurt."

Cat *humphed.*

"He might be the kindest, most important person I've ever met, but your husband is a fool."

Cat laughed through her tears. And then she sobered. If he believed what he'd said, he must love Cat very much indeed because he'd lied endlessly.

They rejoined the main Sutton Grange road again. All was quiet behind them. Ahead, however, the pounding of hooves had them slowing down. Widow Renny's hand clasped Cat's arm tighter.

"It can't be them," Cat said, as much to reassure herself as the frightened woman. "Not from that direction."

They rounded the bend and were met by three riders. Orlando and Cole flanked Hughe in the middle. Cat gasped and almost leapt off the cart. He was as white as the moon, his face slick with sweat. He slumped in the saddle, but straightened upon seeing them.

"Cat!" His eyes fluttered closed. "Cat," he said, softer.

She did not go to him like she craved. The glare from Cole kept her pinned to the driver's seat. "You're safe," the big man said.

"Are you all right?" Orlando asked, coming up alongside the cart. He glanced from Widow Renny to Cat then back up the road past them. "How bad was it?"

"Bad," said the boy behind them. "We almost died! But Lady Oxley saved us."

Hughe opened his eyes again and stared straight at Cat. He'd looked relieved upon first seeing her, but not anymore. Now he seemed sad and...wary?

"You're better?" she asked him.

He inclined his head in a nod without once taking his pale, penetrating gaze off her. It was as if he were assessing her, trying to see beyond her words and expressions into her soul. He could do it too, with those ice-cold eyes of his. Despite his unhealthy pallor and the way he leaned heavily on the pommel, he still had a powerful presence and a commanding air. She gulped. Why didn't he come to her? If he loved her as Widow Renny said, why did he not show it? Was this part of his ruse, his disguise?

Her fingers tightened around the reins, only to remind her of her sore hand. She sucked air between her teeth and cradled her bandaged hand in her lap.

Hughe's gaze flared to life. "It hurts," he said simply.

"Sometimes."

"You shouldn't have gone anywhere with your hand like that," Cole barked at her. "Why did you go to Larkham anyway?"

"Shut it, Cole," Orlando snapped. "You're not helping."

"I'm not here to help, I'm here for answers when no one else seems to be asking the questions."

Cat had liked Cole at first. Now, she wasn't so sure. He was so big, his eyes fathomless in their darkness. He could snap Cat in two if he chose. She sidled closer to Widow Renny and swallowed hard.

"You can berate me all you want later, Cole," Cat said. "For now, the Rennys must be taken to safety. Or have you forgotten that is why Hughe is here at all?" She didn't feel bold, yet her voice gave away none of her anxiety, thank goodness. Even Cole looked surprised, if not impressed. "The mob may be on their way." Even as she said it, she heard the distant rumble of wheels and a cry.

They all heard it.

"Orlando, take the reins from Cat," Hughe ordered, squaring his shoulders. It was as if he'd shrugged off the illness and decided he needed to take command of the situation. "You and Cole are to lead the Rennys to the farm where Monk will meet you. Cat, are you all right to ride?"

"Yes, but—"

"Good. Take Orlando's horse and go with Warren to the Hall. Warren, gather as many of the male servants and laborers as you can and bring them back here. Now!"

Orlando dismounted and passed the reins to Cat. She did not mount, but watched as the Rennys, Cole and Orlando left. Warren waited to assist Cat into the saddle. She shook her head.

"I'm not going anywhere," she said. "Warren, do as his lordship commands and get help."

Warren bit his lip. The poor lad. She'd put him in an impossible situation again.

"I came through fine last time," she reminded him.

"Last time?" Hughe echoed. "Blast it, Cat! Go! Now! It's too dangerous for you here."

"If it's too dangerous for me then it's too dangerous for you. You're my husband. I'm staying."

"God damn you, wife!" he bellowed in a voice that held no evidence of his recent illness. "Why didn't you tell me when we wed that you were a stubborn wench?" There was no malice in it and ordinarily she would have smiled, but the wheels and hooves thundered closer.

Hughe cocked his head, listening, Cat apparently forgotten.

"Go," she told Warren. "Get assistance."

She mounted on her own after he left and arranged her skirts and underskirts so that she sat as modestly as she could in a saddle not designed for riding aside. Hughe watched her from beneath half lowered lids, but offered no assistance. Nor did he speak to her. He was not acting like a man in love. Widow Renny was obviously wrong.

Yet why did he look at her like that? Like *she* had betrayed *him*?

She hated this silence. Even now, with an unknown number of angry men descending on them, she just wanted her husband to look at her like he used to. Like he cared for her, desired her. "Did Widow Dawson know what caused the illness?" she asked.

His gaze searched her face and a deep line formed between his brows. "Poison."

"Poison!" The horse shifted at her shriek. She tried to control it while Hughe reached for the reins. "Dear God. Do you know how it was administered? Was it deliberate?"

His nostrils flared. He did not take that stark, assessing gaze off her. "In a cup of wine. It was deliberate."

Her stomach rolled. "Who would do such a thing?" But even as she said it, she guessed. Slade must have, out of revenge for Stephen's death.

Hughe pulled her horse closer to his. Their knees brushed against one another. "Do you fear me, Cat?"

Fear him? What an odd question at an odd time. "No. Never. Not even when I thought you killed Stephen for no reason." It wasn't until she said it that she realized it was true. He must be right about Stephen's guilt. Hughe was thorough and a good man. There was no way he'd kill an innocent man. "I only ever loved you, Hughe," she murmured. "Always. Right from the start."

Hughe's fingers sprang apart. He let go of her reins and their horses parted. He seemed to no longer be in control of his. It wandered off to the side of the road to nibble at the grass. He leaned forward over the pommel, drawing in great gasps of air as if he couldn't breathe.

"Hughe?" she cried, directing her horse over to him. "Hughe, you must return to Sutton Hall. You're ill."

He lifted his face and pinned her with those pale blue eyes that could be hard as diamonds one moment and soft as snow the next. His mouth twisted as he fought with his emotions. "Did you...?" he whispered. "Did you poison me?"

The world reeled. She felt herself sway in the saddle. She gripped the reins, the mane, anything to keep herself upright. She shook her head over and over. "No. Hughe, no." She wasn't sure if he heard her. Her voice was so weak and the approaching mob so loud.

And then the Larkham men were upon them, pulling their horses to a stop. Some spilled out of the backs of carts, clubs and knives in hand. There was about twenty, and at their helm was a man who made Cat's blood run cold.

Hislop.

CHAPTER 15

"You," Hughe growled at Hislop. "What has any of this got to do with you?"

Hughe positioned his horse between Cat and the mob, but one man could do little to protect her if they decided to strike. One very sick man. Hughe still looked pale and feverish, but at least he sat straighter in the saddle. Poison, he'd said. And he'd thought she administered it. All Cat wanted to do was plead with him and assure him she was innocent.

But first she had to disperse the crowd and make Hislop pay for what he and Slade had done to Hughe.

Hislop gave them a benign smile. "I'm assisting these good people to see the truth," he said. "They're deeply upset that their kinsman was murdered. They want to bring the people who did it to justice."

"Aye," said a man at his side, holding a club. "The Renny family is evil, the children born of sorcery and witchcraft. They do the devil's work."

"Nonsense," Cat said.

"Cat," Hughe hissed at her. "Quiet."

She ignored him. "Widow Renny and her sons want to live in peace, just like you do."

"They're not like us," said the thick-set man she recognized from the house. "They don't come to the village fair, or join in with dances, and they don't speak to their neighbors."

Perhaps because their neighbors wanted to kill them. But Cat didn't say that. The men believed the Rennys were evil and reason couldn't sway them.

"Go home," Hughe told the mob. "The Rennys will not be returning to Larkham. You got what you wanted. You've run them out of the village."

Murmurs and mumbles rippled through the group. They'd come all this way, only to be thwarted from achieving vengeance. Yet the wiser ones saw the truth in what Hughe said. They'd won. The Rennys were gone. Cat's heart lifted as she watched the anger disappear from their faces and their fists uncurl. She moved her horse alongside Hughe's, presenting a united barrier with her husband. Yet they were anything but united. She dared a glance at him, but he only had eyes for Hislop.

"And who assisted them?" Hislop cried. "*You*, Lord and Lady Oxley." He turned to the mob now beginning to disperse. "*They* do the devil's work!"

"Be careful, Hislop." Hughe's fingers danced along his sword hilt. Some of the color had returned to his face, either from anger or from the sun. His eyes, however, remained as cold as ever.

Hislop's top lip curled. "The Larkham folk only want to see justice served. They want to see the heads of evil removed from their bodies. It's only fair and right. Isn't it, men?"

"Aye," muttered some.

"The Rennys should answer to God!" cried one.

"Aye," echoed others, louder.

"They ought to pay for their sins and the sins of their father!" Hislop shouted.

The sickening "Ayes," and calls for blood, turned Cat cold.

"Why are you listening to him?" she asked them. But she realized it was the wrong question. She fixed her glare on Hislop. "What could you possibly gain from this?"

His only answer was a vicious smile that the mob didn't see. "I want to see these folk achieve justice. They work hard and yet have nothing to show for it. While you, my lord and lady, *you* get away with murder."

Gasps from the mob were followed by an unnatural silence. They shuffled forward, their gazes intent on Hughe as they waited for him to deny or confirm the accusation. A man could not accuse an earl of murder without proof and expect to live.

But Hughe didn't respond. Cat worried that he was gravely ill again, but he sat high in the saddle, his back straight.

If Hughe wouldn't defend himself, then she must do it for him. "How dare you," she said to Hislop. "How dare you speak to Lord Oxley as if he were a common criminal!"

"He is." Hislop's smile sent a shiver rippling down Cat's spine. "I saw his man bury Upfield."

"God's blood," someone from the mob muttered. "Are you sure?"

"Aye. Saw it with my own eyes. Lord Slade did too. I'd wager his lordship is to blame." He nodded at Hughe. "His man does what his master tells him to. Nothing more, nothing less."

"No," Cat whispered, shaking her head. "No. That cannot be." Monk buried the Larkham man that had started all of this? Surely Hislop lied. If so, why wasn't Hughe saying as much? Why did he sit there and listen to Hislop rousing the mob?

The men surged forward again, clubs and fists raised, angry scowls on their faces. They did not attack Hughe, however. They still had enough respect for authority to hang back. But for how long?

"You'd best run back to Sutton Hall, my lady," Hislop said, feigning interest in her welfare. "This doesn't concern you."

"It concerns me very much," she growled.

"Go," Hughe said to her.

"I'm not leaving you."

"Go!"

Her horse's head jerked up and down at the barked order. Cat turned him around and walked him a short distance away, but did not leave entirely.

"This is madness," Hughe said to the mob. "Hislop here is a dangerous man. Don't listen to him or you'll find yourselves in deep trouble."

"How?" the big man shouted. "Who will stop us?"

"Me."

The same man grunted a laugh and slapped his club into his palm. Hislop grinned too. He knew his plan was working. A little more nudging and the mob would attack Hughe, angry that he'd killed their friend and almost gotten away with it. But why was Hislop daring such a bold move? He risked his own life by accusing Hughe of killing Upfield. Was it to protect Slade? By accusing Hughe, Slade could justify poisoning him and effectively get away with attempted murder. Did Hislop care for Slade that much?

Or was his cart hitched to Slade so securely that he knew if Slade fell, so did he?

Cat watched the scene with a sickening heart. Hughe sat on his horse in front of dozens of angry men, a lone figure on the edge of a violent, stormy sea.

"Hand yourself over to Lord Lynden," one of the mob men said. "The JP will see justice served."

Hislop snorted and rounded on the fellow. "Justice? Lord Lynden and Oxley are thick! He would not arrest his friend. He'll twist the truth so that it makes Slade appear guilty when I know he is not."

"Isn't he?" Hughe said so quietly that Cat could hardly hear him.

"You know he's not. You killed his brother, I believe."

More gasps, but not from Cat this time. She knew what Hughe had done and accepted it.

"Vile," one of the mob said in shocked wonder. "Are you the devil himself?"

"Get him!" Hislop cried. "Before he turns his evil on us!"

The mob surged, brandishing clubs and fists. Hughe's horse

reared as he drew his sword. The mob cleared away from the punching hooves and circled around.

Cat did not scream. Doing so would only distract Hughe. She fought back a wave of terror and prayed hard.

But there were so many men coming at him from all directions. Hughe slashed out with his sword. His face was a picture of concentration, albeit deathly pale. He focused on Hislop.

Hislop merely grinned again. "Get him! Kill the devil's man! We cannot let him escape so he can commit more vile crimes!"

"Enough!" Cat shouted at him, at all of them.

"Cat," Hughe said, turning to her. "I told you to leave!"

She ignored him. To the mob she said, "Go home now and no harm will come to anyone. Continue with this madness and someone will be hurt."

"Aye!" the big Larkham man cried. "Oxley! Oxley will be brought to justice!"

A battle cry more bloodthirsty than any pagan warrior's erupted from the mob. Cat's heart clenched and her gut rolled. Hughe sat like a magnificent king atop his horse, slashing on both sides, keeping the men back. For now. But there were so many. He would soon tire, ill as he was from Slade's poison.

Just then Cole rode past her, straight into the mob. Some of the men skittered away, others fell, and one was trampled beneath hooves. He fought alongside his lord, cutting a swathe through the rabble, sending them back, back.

Hislop, safely to one side, slid his gaze to Cat. Then he charged.

"No!" Hughe shouted.

He tried to fight his way free, but the crowd was too thick around him. Cole was equally trapped. Cat's gaze momentarily connected with Hughe's and the fear she saw in him bolstered her. He would not be so afraid if he didn't care for her.

She jerked the horse out of the way as Hislop's sword descended. The blade whipped past her ear. Hislop growled in frustration and pulled his horse to a stop a little past her.

"The pack!" Cole shouted at her. "There's a blade in the front of the pack!"

She reached into the pack strapped to the saddle beneath her skirts and felt around for the knife. Her hand circled the handle and pulled it out. She swapped it to her good hand and clutched the reins with her sore one. Pain flared, but she blocked it from her mind and concentrated on Hislop, turning once more to charge again.

A knife against a sword. A man against a woman. Her chances were slim at best.

"I'll kill you, Hislop!" Hughe roared.

But Cat didn't look to him. Watching the mob swamp him would only distract her and she needed all of her wits now.

Hislop came at her, charging his horse at speed. She readied herself and focused on the hooves pounding in the dirt as he drew closer. Closer. Hislop raised his sword. He bared his teeth in a grin. And struck at her head.

She slid off the horse on the other side and once more his blade met nothing but air. He let out a growl of anger as she ducked under her horse's head and, before Hislop had gotten too far, threw the knife at his back. It struck him true between his shoulders.

"Witch!" he screamed. He desperately scrabbled at his bloodied clothing, but he couldn't gain purchase on the blade.

Cat had to finish him, yet she had no more weapons. She searched the ground for a stone large enough to strike him with, but not so heavy that she couldn't throw it. She found none.

"Cat!" Hughe called.

She glanced up just as he threw his sword to her. She caught the hilt and received a small, reassuring smile in return. Just as a man from the mob smashed a club into Hughe's middle.

Cat swallowed her cry and her fear and forced herself to turn back to Hislop. He'd given up on removing the knife from his back. She had only moments before he regained enough sense to charge at her again. This time, she was not on horseback, and her

C.J. ARCHER

weapon was one she'd never used before. She possessed none of the skills of an able swordsman.

But she possessed fortitude and a desperate need to help the man she loved. She would not fail.

She raised Hughe's blade above her head with both hands and ran at Hislop. He turned and saw her just as she drove the sword into his soft flesh. Eyes wide with shock and pain, he tumbled from his horse and fell face down on the ground. Lifeless.

Cat lifted the sword again and turned to the melee, but there was no need to join Hughe and Cole. Hughe sat on Cole's horse behind his friend. Several bodies lay around them and the living had backed away to their carts, their clubs lowered. They easily outnumbered Hughe and Cole, but must have realized they couldn't win. Either that or the fight had left them after Hislop's demise.

Hughe blinked big eyes back at Cat, as if he couldn't believe he was gazing upon her, alive and unharmed. Exhaustion pinched his face tight, but relief quickly overrode it. He suddenly drew in great gasps of air as, if he'd stopped breathing some time ago and only now remembered it was vital to survival.

"Go home!" Cat told the mob since no one else spoke. "This cruel man filled your heads with lies and led you to believe the most sickening things about Lord Oxley. They're not true. I can assure you, his lordship and his men are innocent. They did not kill Upfield."

"What about the Rennys?" one of the men asked.

"They're gone and better left alone now," Hughe told them. "No good can come of pursuing them. Indeed, if you return home peacefully, none of you will be punished."

That seemed to be enough for them. They gathered up their dead and injured, and turned toward Larkham. They left Hislop where he was and did not spare him a second glance.

Cat dropped Hughe's sword in the dirt and covered her face with her hands. Her body shook all over and her tears wouldn't cease. She'd killed a man. Taken a life. And yet she was safe. Hughe was safe. It was all too much.

Strong arms circled her and pulled her against a solid chest. Hughe. She knew the shape and touch of his body without needing to see. He rested his chin on her head and cradled her as if she were a kitten. He gently stroked her hair and whispered her name over and over. "My little Cat. My brave, strong wife. I am in awe of you."

Finally, after what seemed forever, her tears abated. She did not pull away from him, however. She liked being exactly there.

"He deserved to die," he murmured.

She shook her head. He'd got it all wrong. She wasn't crying over Hislop. The cur did deserve to die. She was crying because Hughe had thought she poisoned him, because she'd thought he loved another, and because they'd made a mess of what could have turned out to be their last few days together.

She cupped his face in her good hand and stroked his cheek. His color still had not completely returned, but his eyes danced with warmth and life.

"I'm sorry," she whispered.

"Shhh. It is I that am sorry, Cat. I don't know what I was thinking. I know in my heart you wouldn't hurt me, but I refused to listen to it." He pressed his forehead to hers. "Your maid said you gave her the wine to give to me, but it must have been a trick."

"Slade," Cat said. "He must have given it to her and told her it came from me. The poor girl will feel terrible when she finds out."

"You didn't tell him about the will, did you?"

"No. Why?"

He sighed. "He must have guessed I would change it to favor you, and used the knowledge to convince me of your guilt. I was too sick and confused from the poison to think clearly. Ah, Cat. I should have told you the truth from the beginning and none of this would have happened."

"And I should have trusted that you did what was right." She swallowed. "If you found evidence that Stephen had committed those crimes then I believe you."

He winced and dragged his hand over his face. "On that score, we perhaps differ."

She pulled away and blinked at him. "What do you mean?"

"It means I fear I may have killed an innocent man." He looked pale again and he swayed a little. He suddenly let her go and squatted on the ground. He buried his head in his hands. Cat looked to his friend. Cole stood near Hislop's lifeless body and gave her a grim look in return, as if he had expected this to happen.

She crouched before Hughe and clasped his face. She kissed his forehead and made him look her in the eye. "Don't blame yourself, Hughe."

"You said it yourself. He was a good man. I was tricked into believing otherwise, but it doesn't make it right. I should have checked the facts."

"You did."

"I should have kept checking." He squeezed his eyes shut. "Christ, I killed an innocent. How many others?"

"Don't," she said. "It's not your fault."

"How can it not be my fault? I gave the orders. I organized everything. Hell." He wiped his mouth with the back of his hand. "I can't do this anymore."

She shook her head. How to make him see? Did she even *want* him to see that he did important work? He would be gone from her for weeks at a time, putting his own life at risk. Yet she loved him and could not bear to see him shattered like this.

"You can," she said. "You have to. Think of the people like the Rennys, who would be in grave danger if not for you."

"I exposed them to that danger in the first place."

"You *saved* them. You saved the Larkham people, and countless others, who will never know you saved them. Your work is important." She stood and held out her hand. "Come, Hughe. We must speak to Slade. He is behind all of this. He poisoned you. He wanted me to spy on you. I believe he paid you to kill Stephen so he could inherit. It's likely he encouraged Stephen to murder that man because he knew you would require irrefutable proof of a crime before carrying out the assassination."

It made sense. The more she talked, the more likely it seemed that Slade had set Stephen up to murder Crabb. She doubted whether Stephen had raped Mrs. Crabb, but the cuckolded husband perhaps believed he did, thanks to Slade.

He took her hand and stood. "Hislop is involved too." He nodded at the body still lying in the dirt. "He saw Slade as a weak man he could control, someone who could help him rise. It wouldn't surprise me if Hislop encouraged Slade all along, even suggesting he hire me to do his dirty work and keep his own hands clean."

It lifted her to see Hughe fight for what he believed in, against cruelty and injustice. As dangerous as his work was, she had to stand by him now, when he needed her most.

He clasped her hand in his own and looked to Cole as he strapped Hislop's body to his horse. "I told you to go with Orlando and see the Rennys to safety," he growled.

"Shut it," Cole said with the hint of humor in his voice. "I don't work for you anymore. If I want to come and save your hide, I will. Orlando didn't need me."

Hughe swallowed heavily. Then he held out his hand and Cole clasped his arm. The glance they exchanged was filled with a respect and depth that Cat had never seen before.

"You look like death," Cole said. "You must get back to the house."

Hughe did indeed still look ill, his color as pale as his eyes.

They mounted and set off.

"Think I better have a bath before I return home," Cole said as he rode at the front. "Lucy will scold me if she sees all this blood."

Cat smiled at the ridiculous image of little Lucy berating her big brute of a husband.

They rode back to Sutton Hall. Cole took all the horses around to the stables, while Cat and Hughe made their way to the house.

Hughe held his wife's small hand in his own as they crossed the courtyard and thanked God for the hundredth time that she was alive and unharmed. He'd been so sick with fear and the remains of the poison and could hardly think straight. If he had been thinking, he would have made sure she left the scene with the mob immediately and not been there as a target for Hislop to attack.

But his brave little Cat was back in his arms where she belonged. He didn't care how sick he was, he was going to worship her and love her for the rest of his days.

Love. Well. It seemed he loved his wife. Tonight, he was going to show her just how much.

"My lord!" cried Lynden, running across the courtyard to them. His soft shoes hardly made a sound on the stones. "My lord Oxley! I've been so worried about you." He grasped Hughe in an embrace that drew Hughe away from Cat.

He heard her chuckling and he smiled. He set Lynden at arm's length and spied Elizabeth approaching, her face drawn.

"You're back," she said to Hughe, hands on hips. "You should not have gone. Look at you! You're so pale and— Whose blood is that?"

"I'll explain later."

"Is everyone safe? Cat?"

"I'm fine," Cat said.

"Where's Slade?" Hughe asked, scanning the long gallery walkway above.

Elizabeth glanced past his shoulder. "He's right there. Why?"

Even as she said it, he heard Cat gasp. Hughe turned, his gut churning again. What he saw made him want to throw up.

Slade had his arm around Cat's waist and a knife at her throat. He dragged her away. Her feet scrabbled for purchase and her hands clawed at his sleeve, but it was no use. Slade was too strong.

"No! NO!" Hughe roared. *Give her back to me. Give back my Cat.*

"I'll kill her," Slade snarled. He swung around as Cole entered the courtyard from the direction of the stables. "Get over there with the others."

Cole did as he was told, his face grave. Slade continued to back away with Cat.

"What's this?" Lynden asked. "I don't understand. Lord Slade, what's going on?"

"Shut it, fool. This doesn't concern you."

Lynden fisted his hands on his hips. "It does indeed! This is my house! The Oxleys are my guests. Unhand Lady Oxley this instant!"

A line of blood appeared at Cat's throat near the blade. She winced. "Quiet," Hughe snapped at Lynden. If he had to shut the fool up himself, he'd do it with his fist.

"Forget this," Slade told them, his eyes darting between them. "Forget all of this and let me go."

"Let you go?" Lynden snorted. "I think not."

Cole's hand flashed out and grabbed Hughe's wrist before he could punch Lynden into silence. "It won't help."

Cole was right. Hughe's first priority was getting Cat away. Sweat beaded across Slade's forehead and his eyes shifted back and forth. He looked like a trapped animal.

Hughe took a slow, careful step forward. Slade didn't respond so he took another.

"Stay back!" Slade shouted. "If I die, I take her with me."

"You harm my wife and I will gut you, slowly and painfully." Hughe's stomach rolled again. He swallowed bile.

Cat remained stoic, but he saw pain ripple across her face as Slade pressed the knife harder against her throat. Christ. He had to get her away. Slade was capable of anything.

He took another step, so slowly and so small that it would hardly have been noticeable. He did that several times until Slade shouted at him to stop once more.

"Let me go!" he screamed, his voice high. Stringy black hair fell across his wild eyes. "It wasn't me! It was Hislop! It was all his idea. *He* told Crabb that Stephen had forced himself upon Mistress

Crabb. Then it was *he* who whispered in my brother's ear, urging him to murder Crabb before Crabb murdered him. Then he helped cover it up. Hislop wanted me to inherit, see. He told me I was the better baron and he was right! I am. Stephen was *useless*. Cat knows, don't you? Tell them."

He glanced down at her and Hughe took the brief moment to step forward again. But not far enough. He was still five or so feet away.

Cat closed her eyes, and Hughe knew it was so he couldn't see the pain in them. She didn't want him to know that the blade bit into her soft skin, but he could see it from the blood trickling down her throat and staining her ruff.

Hughe had to act now.

"Diversion," he whispered to Cole, right behind him.

Without a word of acknowledgement, his friend called out, "Warren! Careful, lad!"

Slade turned around in the direction of the stables. And Hughe wasted not a moment. He drew his knife from his boot and lunged. Slade turned back after seeing no one behind him, but by then it was too late; Hughe had sunk the blade into Slade's side and grabbed the hand that clutched the knife, staying it.

Cat slipped down and away, out of danger. Hughe gripped both of Slade's arms and forced him to his knees onto the stones. It wasn't difficult. The man's life drifted away as the blood drained from his side and his body finally crumpled in a heap. Dead.

Hughe fell to one knee, partly out of exhaustion, but mostly from relief. A pair of light, supple arms circled his shoulders and he was drawn against Cat's breast. He closed his eyes and held her against him. She was alive, safe, and she was all his.

He held her as she cried, and continued to hold her as Slade's body was removed and his blood washed away. He didn't want to let her go. Couldn't.

"Hughe," she finally murmured. "Hughe, you should be in bed. You're unwell."

He parted from her, just enough so he could look her in the

eyes. "I am well as long as I have you with me, Cat." He stroked his thumbs over her face, wiping away her tears, and gently down to the wound at her throat. It didn't look too deep. "You are my heart, my soul, my *whole*. I love you, my sweet little Cat. I love you forever and always."

Her lip wobbled and she began to cry all over again. "I love you too, Hughe."

She kissed him. Thoroughly. Completely. He felt like he was drowning in her and he didn't care. This was what happiness was, a wholeness that filled him up to bursting. It was desire in its rawest form, but it was more than that. It was wanting to be with another so much that it hurt to be apart. It was not being able to imagine your life without them in it. It was a kind of madness, and yet brought peace too, and a certainty that the world was balanced, right.

"I will protect you always, but only with the truth," he murmured against her lips. "And the truth is that I will never let you go, Cat. You and I will be together in this life and the next."

EPILOGUE

*C*at leaned back against the solid wall of her husband's chest and gazed upon the Hampshire countryside as the setting sun bathed it in the golden tones of late summer. It wasn't Oxley countryside, but she felt a sense of rightness nevertheless. Perhaps it was because so much had happened to them in the valley, or it might have been because their good friends sat with them on the Sutton Hall garden seats, equally contemplative. Or perhaps it was simply because Cat felt safe, enveloped as she was in her husband's powerful arms. She knew without needing to hear him say it, that those arms, this man, would never let her go.

Baby George gurgled in his father's lap, transfixed by his own fist waving in front of his face. Cole placed his hand over his wife's belly and she smiled up at him. She had announced a few days earlier that she suspected she was carrying.

"How do you feel, Hughe?" Susanna asked.

"Better," came the rumbling answer at Cat's back. "Widow Dawson thinks the poison has left my system entirely."

"Finally," Cat said on a breath. Hughe had been sent back to bed for a week by the wise woman after Slade's death. A week was a long time for an active man. He was up and giving orders again by the second day, until Cat scolded him. To keep him quiet, she sat him down and together they made plans for the future.

"So, what's next?" Cole asked, twirling a lock of his wife's hair around his massive finger. "Do you have your next target?"

"Not yet," Hughe said.

Monk kissed his wife's cheek. "I wish to stay home awhile, to settle into Oxley Gatehouse."

"Not forever," Elizabeth said. "Cat and I cannot constantly have you two under our feet."

Cat rather liked the idea of having her husband near, but she knew he'd grow mad with boredom after a few weeks.

Hughe chuckled and kissed her temple. "I cannot promise a less dramatic life than the one we've lead thus far, but I do promise to be more careful."

Cat knew he was talking about thoroughly checking on the person who commissioned him, not just the target, but she didn't say so. Hughe still felt horrid that he'd been duped into assassinating Stephen by Slade. He had told her that he also regretted not making sure she received the money he'd left for her. She reminded him that it didn't matter. If anything had been different, they may never have met and she regretted none of it; she had even come to terms with his marrying her out of guilt. No matter what his original motives had been, she knew he now loved her as deeply as she loved him.

"You would wither on the vine if you had less drama in your life," Orlando teased Hughe.

"And drive us all mad," Cole said, his eyes twinkling.

"It's all right for the two of you," Monk said over the rim of his cup of wine. "We have to live near him. Elizabeth and I won't have a moment's peace."

"I protest!" Hughe said with a hint of his foppish disguise. "I would not bother you and your lovely wife. I have my own wife to bother." He squeezed her waist. "Luckily she adores me. She even puts up with my vying for the prime position in front of her looking glass!"

Orlando groaned. "Cat, you have our permission to thump him if he begins to think himself too high."

"Or too pretty," Cole added.

Cat giggled. "My husband's right. I do adore him too much. However, I have it on good authority that the dowager countess will scold him and remind him frequently of an earl's duty."

He groaned and rested his forehead against the back of her head. "I have plans to build Mother a new house. I'm sure she'll like that."

"Will it be at the edge of the estate?" Orlando asked with a wicked grin.

"With no easy access to the main house?" Cole said.

"I can help you dig a moat around it," Monk offered. "And a drawbridge that just happens not to open with ease."

Elizabeth nudged her husband's arm. "You're all wicked. I happen to like the dowager."

"So do I," Cat said. "She's got a strong spirit."

"And a sharp tongue," Hughe added. But there was no malice in it, Cat was glad to see.

She turned and kissed him. "Never fear, dear husband. I have the perfect solution to dowager dragons."

"And what is that, my love?" he said.

A warm breeze stroked her cheek and teased her hair. She placed her hands over his, resting on her belly. "Presenting her with a grandchild."

Around them, others gasped. But Hughe stared at her, his eyes huge. How could she have ever thought them cold? There was so much love and wonder in them, so much depth of feeling, that it was overwhelming.

"Truly?" he whispered.

She nodded through her tears of happiness. "It's early, but I think so."

He swooped down and kissed her hard, possessively, but it soon turned achingly tender. When they finally parted, Elizabeth, sitting to Cat's left, caught her hand.

"That makes three of us with child," she said softly. "You, Lucy and me."

"You too!"

"Little play mates for George," Orlando said, stroking his son's cheek.

Monk grinned at them all like a simpleton. "We are lucky men." Elizabeth rested the back of her head against her husband's chest and smiled.

"Aye," Hughe murmured without taking his gaze off Cat. She felt as if she were glowing as bright as a beacon. "Four assassins—five if you include Rafe Fletcher—and all of us brought to our knees by love. They'll write ballads and plays about us."

"Forget ballads," Cat said. "I'll settle for a long and happy life instead."

Hughe's arms tightened around her. "As will I, my love. As will I."

Thank you for reading. Turn the page for a list of books by C.J. Archer.

ALSO BY C.J. ARCHER

SERIES WITH 2 OR MORE BOOKS

After The Rift

Glass and Steele

The Ministry of Curiosities Series

The Emily Chambers Spirit Medium Trilogy

The 1st Freak House Trilogy

The 2nd Freak House Trilogy

The 3rd Freak House Trilogy

The Assassins Guild Series

Lord Hawkesbury's Players Series

The Witchblade Chronicles

SINGLE TITLES NOT IN A SERIES

Courting His Countess

Surrender

Redemption

The Mercenary's Price

A MESSAGE FROM THE AUTHOR

I hope you enjoyed reading this book as much as I enjoyed writing it. As an independent author, getting the word out about my book is vital to its success, so if you liked this book please consider telling your friends and writing a review at the store where you purchased it. If you would like to be contacted when I release a new book, subscribe to my newsletter at http://cjarcher.com/contact-cj/newsletter/. You will only be contacted when I have a new book out.

ABOUT THE AUTHOR

C.J. Archer has loved history and books for as long as she can remember and feels fortunate that she found a way to combine the two. She spent her early childhood in the dramatic beauty of outback Queensland, Australia, but now lives in suburban Melbourne with her husband, two children and a mischievous black & white cat named Coco.

Subscribe to C.J.'s newsletter through her website to be notified when she releases a new book, as well as get access to exclusive content and subscriber-only giveaways. Her website also contains up to date details on all her books: http://cjarcher.com She loves to hear from readers. You can contact her through email cj@cjarcher.com or follow her on social media to get the latest updates on her books.

facebook.com/CJArcherAuthorPage

twitter.com/cj_archer

instagram.com/authorcjarcher

pinterest.com/cjarcher

bookbub.com/authors/c-j-archer